Deadly Stalker
Jessica West

Joyful Books Press

Deadly Stalker

Printed in the United States of America

First Printing, 2024

ISBN- 978-1-7349363-8-4

Special Thanks:

God- Thank You for this blessed life that You've given me. I marvel at Your goodness and love. Thank You for giving me these stories to tell.

Robert- You always believe in me, even when I don't believe in myself. I love you.

Abby, Jojo, Samuel, Matthew, Timothy, Gideon, Enoch, and Judah- I love y'all. I'm so thankful God allowed me to be your mom.

Mom- Thanks for your support, and for being my biggest fan. I love you.

Teresa Kirkpatrick- Your faithfulness in reading my first draft weekly is so helpful.

Isaiah 43:2

"When thou passest through the waters, I will be with thee; and through the rivers, they shall not overflow thee: when thou walkest through the fire, thou shalt not be burned; neither shall the flame kindle upon thee."

Deadly Stalker, Jessica West

Chapter One

"Pretty flowers, Ms. Smith," a student called over her shoulders as she yanked her book bag off the peg and raced into the hall.

Kayla stared at the bouquet of white roses. When was the last time anyone had sent her flowers? She stuffed a folder of papers into her bag, hoping to grade them later, when her mind could focus. Her pulse quickened as she stared at the harmless roses. To a bystander, the roses looked like a thoughtful gift, but to her, the contents of the vase sent goosebumps crawling over her arms.

Get a grip, Kayla. Nothing nefarious is happening. One of your students sent flowers. End of the story. Except she had been a teacher for a year, and the only thing her sixth-grade students sent her was a hard time. At twenty-three, and a recent college graduate, Kayla didn't have her pick of schools. She had a lot to prove and the McMinn County Schools were the only school system willing to take a risk on her non-experienced-self. The old sixth-grade English teacher retired suddenly, putting the school in a bind. Thus, why they hired her. Moving to East Tennessee after attending NC State was a big decision, but she didn't regret being closer to family.

The roaring bell knocked her out of her thoughts as an attractive man in his late-twenties sauntered into the classroom. "Secret admirer?"

"What?" Kayla shook her head, causing her bangs to fall over her eyes. "No." Why was he in her room again? The man never gave up.

"I thought you didn't date? Someone thinks otherwise." He leaned against her desk, staring at her with a predatory stare. Something about Thomas Holmes made her uncomfortable. He had worked for the public school system as a substitute math teacher for three years before transferring to Athens City Middle School full time.

"A sweet gesture from a parent." Kayla's fingers trembled as she stuffed the rest of the papers in her bag. She wanted to get far away from Thomas and school for a few days. Good thing it was past three o'clock on a Friday and the last day until spring break was over.

"Not buying it." He trailed his fingers over the white envelope as Kayla snatched the card from his grip. "Who's my competition?"

"Please, Thomas, I'm not in the mood." Why didn't he take no for an answer?

"How about dinner at my place?" Thomas Holmes asked, his tan face illuminated by a bright smile. His brown eyes twinkled with anticipation. Kayla couldn't deny that he was attractive, but his persistence was overwhelming. She knew she couldn't date, not after that unforgettable night five years ago. The memory still haunted her, a constant reminder of her past weakness.

"No," Kayla replied firmly, her wavy blond hair swaying as she tossed it to the side. She adjusted her strap on her shoulder, feeling the weight of it. All she wanted was to retreat to the comfort of her home and indulge in a relaxing bubble bath, hoping to wash away the tension that had built up. But first, she had to dismiss Thomas so she could finally escape.

"You're no fun." He touched the top of her arm as warnings flared up her body.

"It's been a stressful day. I just want to drown my sorrows in a carton of mint chocolate chip ice cream while watching horrible reality television."

"Bobby White, again?" He pounded his fist in his open palm. "Someone needs to teach that kid a lesson."

"I'll settle on teaching him how to diagram a sentence." Kayla gripped the card between her sweaty fingers. If not for the phone calls and eerie feeling of being watched, she'd assume the flowers were an innocent gesture, but nothing was that simple.

"Read the card already." He snatched the envelope out of her fingers, smirking at her astonished look. "Soon, my sweet Care Bear, we'll meet, and no one will separate us again." His voice trailed off at the words.

"Give me the card." Her pulse quickened as the words attacked her common sense. She was tired of this silly mind game. Who was stalking her? No, not stalking, sending unwanted extra attention. Maybe it was Thomas, but his forward ways would never hide behind a mystery admirer.

"Kind of creepy, if you want my opinion." He ran his fingers through his tad-bit-too-long brown hair. "Need me to follow you home? I have a black belt in karate."

"Generous offer, but Sarah and Rachel should be home by now." Kayla glanced at the wall clock as the second hand quickened around the clock.

"Oh, yes, your infamous sisters that I have yet to meet." He flashed her his million-dollar smile. The kind that caused half the female teachers at Athens Middle School to swoon over his charm. Not her. She dealt with too many good-looking-I-always-get-what-I want types to last a lifetime.

"I can be a true Southern gentleman. Let me escort you to your car." He slid her bag off her shoulders, clenching the strap between his large fingers.

"You're too persistent," Kayla huffed in exasperation. "Go pick on another female teacher." She grabbed her bag from his fingers, frowning.

"Fine, but you won't get rid of me that easily." He saluted, then stepped into the hall. His shoes echoing down the tiled-hall.

"Finally." Kayla tossed the roses into the trashcan, flipping off the lights.

She stepped into the empty, darkened hall as the silence sent a wave of panic coursing through her body. Heavy footsteps sounded down the long corridor of the first floor of the school. Thomas? No, his footsteps had a musical swag to them. Besides, he probably slipped out after her rejection.

"Hello?" Her voice bounced off the lockers.

Silence.

Why did Kayla insist on parking in the farthest lot from her classroom? Probably because she was at the bottom of the totem pole and Principal Langley had designated the suitable spots for his favorite staff. Which she would never be.

A low-pitched growl reverberated through the dimly lit hall, echoing ominously as the heavy footsteps drew nearer. *Stop being paranoid,* she chastised herself, her heart pounding in her chest. The faint scent of fear hung in the air, mingling with the faint aroma of musty books.

In her haste, her feet tangled together, causing her to stumble and crash onto the cold, unforgiving floor. Agonizing pain shot through her legs, intensifying the panic that surged within her. Frantically, she gathered her scattered papers, the crisp sound of rustling documents filling the tense silence.

Suddenly, a gloved hand clamped tightly over her mouth, stifling her desperate cries. Panic flooded her senses, suffocating her in its grip. No! Kayla pleaded silently, her muffled screams falling on deaf ears. The metallic tang of fear coated her tongue, her mind racing with a primal instinct to survive.

A deep, foreboding voice whispered into her ear, its chilling words causing goosebumps to erupt across her flesh. "Soon, Care Bear, we'll be together." The air turned heavy with an unsettling aura, thick with menace. Trembling, she felt a surge of adrenaline coursing through her veins, heightening her senses.

In a desperate bid for escape, Kayla's hand instinctively reached for a fallen pencil, its familiar weight giving her a sense of fleeting empowerment. With a swift, determined motion, she drove it into her assailant's shoulder, eliciting a startled grunt of pain. Without daring to look back, she sprinted towards the exit, her heart pounding in her ears.

Outside, the cool evening air washed over her, offering a momentary respite from the suffocating fear that had consumed her. She hurriedly made her way to her small Dodge Journey, her trembling hands fumbling with the keys. One glance at her flattened tire made her think things she shouldn't. She jumped into her car, locking the door behind her.

She punched in a number on her phone as she looked around for her assailant.

"What's up, Kayla?" The deep voice sounded over the phone.

"Someone attacked me at school, and my tire's flat." Her voice rose an octave as her fear tried to choke her.

"Where are you?"

"In the parking lot. Locked in my car." She checked her mirrors out of nervous habit.

"Stay put. My partner, Zach Rivers and I will be there soon."

"Zach Rivers?" It couldn't be. The universe wasn't that small.

"Yeah, we've worked together for two years."

He'd been in the same town as her for two years? Kayla leaned over as the phone slipped from her fingers. *I'm gonna be sick.*

"Kayla?" Ignoring his call, she opened the door and puked into the parking lot.

****

"You know I can't do that." Zach ran his fingers through his hair, noting that he needed a haircut soon.

"Do I?" Paul stopped his SUV at a stoplight, frowning. "What is with you and women?"

"Man, get off my tail about dating. I'm not interested." That was only partly true. His stupid mistake five years ago hindered any future relationships. Besides, the only woman he wanted to see probably used his picture for target practice. If she hadn't burned them years ago. She had every reason to. Back then, his emotions, not his logic, guided his actions.

"Belle has some really pretty friends." Paul stepped on the gas, sending the SUV cruising down the only main road in town.

"No offense, but I'm not interested." Same conversation. Different lecturer. How could he tell anyone

11

about his past mistakes without feeling like an idiot? He made that impulsive decision before he became a Christian and it followed him, haunting him every chance it could. No one knew this shameful secret. And no one ever would. He'd carry it to his lonely grave. Hopefully, as an old man. At the tender age of twenty-four, he had already experienced the horrors of death more intimately than most his age. It was during his first year as a detective in West Virginia, under the watchful eye of his father, the police chief, that he witnessed a disastrous standoff. The echoes of piercing screams and the deafening gunshot continued to haunt his nightmares, leaving an indelible mark on his soul. Watching his partner die almost caused him to walk away from law enforcement. One reason he moved to East Tennessee. Two years in a growing rural town almost healed his tormented mind. Rekindling his Christian walk and his relationship with God aided in his healing. But lately, he went through the motions of going to church, but his heart wasn't anywhere near it. He was drifting, and didn't know how to stop it.

"At least come to Mary's sixth birthday party tomorrow. Free food. You know how Mrs. Smith can cook." Paul pulled his vehicle into an empty parking lot behind the only middle school in town.

"Fine. If it'll get you off my back." Zach let out an agitated sigh, opening his door and scanning the parking lot. "Why are we here?"

"Female, possible stalker, slashed tires, attacked. You know the drill." Paul rambled the words in a monotone voice; no hint of emotions.

"Looks deserted. You sure it wasn't a prank call?" Zach knew the teens in this up-in-coming town were looking for some excitement besides hanging out at the library. A prank call wasn't uncommon, especially at a middle school.

"No. Belle's cousin made the report." Paul touched the top of his gun as he pointed to a lone car in the farthest parking space in the lot. "A pretty girl causes men to act like vultures. Not uncommon."

"Maybe, but slashing her tires seems extreme." Zach let the comforting feel of his metallic gun pulse through his fingers. He'd never let a routine call end in a shootout again, at least not with a dead partner.

"Crazed, obsessed, infatuated fits the MO of a stalker. Starts out small, but progresses quickly."

"How's it going teaching Criminal Profiling 101 at the local college?" He would have loved a professor like his partner, sharp, knowledgeable, and with a personality.

"I'm only filling in until the actual professor gets back from maternity leave." Paul stopped walking mid-stride and turned to Zach. "Next week is spring break. I'm taking my kids to Disney World. Getting an early start and leaving after the party tomorrow. Will you be okay?"

A smirk spread across Zach's creamy-white face. "I think I can handle the Coffer feud and any other petty crimes this town has."

Paul patted his partner on the back. "I hoped you'd say that. I already bought the tickets."

"Let's get this over with. I have a few of the guys coming over to watch baseball." At one time, he envisioned being married with a couple of kids at twenty-four. But life had a way of punching on the disappointment.

Paul tapped on the car window, motioning his cousin to open the door. With a quick hug, he pulled out his notepad, ready to jot down her statement.

"I didn't see the person's face. Could have been anyone." Kayla rested her head on the steering wheel, having no energy to climb out of the car. She related the incident to the detective.

"Any male teachers a little too friendly? Extra attention, flirtatious, showing up at odd places?" Paul glanced around the parking lot, then back at Kayla. The steering wheel concealed her face and voice.

"You just described half the single men in town." Kayla's voice rose an octave. "It's a job fighting off the bachelors in this town. No means nothing to them."

"That could be a problem." Paul tapped his pen on the edge of his notepad. "Can you step out of the car?"

"Am I under arrest, detective?" She moved her head off the steering wheel as she stared at Paul. With a quick laugh, she slid out of the car, straightening to her five-foot-six height.

"Of course not. I'm leaving for vacation tomorrow, so my partner will take the lead on your case." Paul motioned for Zach to approach the car.

Blond, silky curls, deep soul-searching eyes, flawless skin. It can't be her, could it? Four years. He hadn't seen her gorgeous face since … it didn't matter; he was clearly seeing things. No logical explanation for her being here.

"Zach?" All color drained from her face as she took a wobbly step away from the detective.

Same voice. It had to be the product of his nightmares. Four years had been good to her. She looked the same besides breathtaking beauty replaced her girlish charm.

"K-Kayla." Never in his wildest dreams did he ever expect to see her again. Didn't mean he didn't want to see her. He just wasn't expecting it. And if her unreturned phone call was a sign, she wouldn't be happy about this at all. So, he only called her once, but that was enough. Behind her innocent face raged a warrior. He'd seen it on multiple occasions. Never wanted to feel her wrath again. God had to be behind this sick reunion. And he didn't know if he appreciated God's intervention. Life was smooth without her back in it.

"You two know each other?" Paul raised his eyebrows, confusion etched on his tan face.

"Uh, something like that." Zach gazed at the broken concrete. Anything to focus on besides her sweet, kissable lips and body that just contoured to his side, like a perfectly fit puzzle piece.

Kayla rolled her eyes at Zach's nonchalant words. "Paul, can I speak to you privately?"

Paul looked at Zach, then at Kayla. "I don't know what's going on, but if I don't get answers, I'll arrest both of y'all for obstructing the peace."

Zach ran his shaky fingers through his blond hair. Why was she here? Didn't their past torment him enough? He prayed for rectification and forgiveness, but not face-to-face. God had a funny sense of humor.

"I'm waiting." Paul's tone turned stern, like dealing with his four children.

"Kayla's my wife." Zach chewed on his bottom lip, letting out an enormous sigh. This was supposed to be a routine, by-the-books case. Not something out of a horror film.

****

"Estranged wife." Kayla shot her eyes at him, knowing he could probably see the fire spewing out. Why was he here, in her little town? She never wanted to see his face again. Who cares if they were married? He sure didn't. Did he have to look so charming in his blazer? His Southern drawl always made her heartbeat quicken. She could feel his gentle touch and his loving words as he … No, she buried those memories years ago. He meant nothing to her. Then why had she never filed for divorce? Having grown up in a Christian home, divorce felt like she was betraying God. Not that she cared anymore. She was His estranged daughter. Besides, it never felt like the right time. College, internship, life. The life they vowed to share. Kayla shook the thoughts out of her mind. No turning back, ever. No matter what a flimsy marriage certificate said. She was Kayla Smith, not Kayla Rivers. That would never change. Those dreams died after his rejection.

"That explains a lot." Paul's hard stare bore into his partner's face. "Should I say welcome to the family or deck you for hurting my cousin?"

"Listen, man, this happened five years ago. I'm not that same emotion-led kid anymore." Zach nervously slid his fingers through his hair. Kayla had seen him do it on multiple occasions when the heat got too hot.

"Nothing surprises me anymore." Paul's eyes softened a bit as he stared at his cousin.

"I know what you're thinking. No, my mom doesn't know the entire story. And you're not telling her."

"Fine, I'll leave that to you."

"Not gonna happen. I've moved on. No point in drudging up my past failures." Her mother would kill her and never forgive her. Okay, that's harsh. She'd spend her prayers praying for a marriage that failed before it ever started. No point in offering the hope of more grandkids or any of that. She'd never raise a family with an incompetent heart breaker like Zach. And because of him, she'd never be free to marry and have her own family with someone else. Maybe if she burned the certificate, that bond would dissipate. Who was she kidding? Zach Rivers was a thorn in her flesh, and as long as they were married, she'd never be free.

"I feel like I'm dealing with two five-year-olds." Paul's stern eyes darted to Zach and Kayla. "How did this happen?"

Zach ran his foot over the cement, avoiding eye contact. "We were high school sweethearts. After graduation, we ran off and got hitched."

"We obviously didn't think it through. We were stupid and in love." Kayla stared at Zach. He looked like the guy she fell in love with, but his twinkling eyes held a sadness that others wouldn't notice.

He had blinded Kayla's love-struck heart so much that she didn't see the holes seeping out of their spontaneous marriage. At eighteen, they both knew everything, and love convinced her their union could withstand anything. Foolish. It didn't take long for the rose-colored glasses to disappear.

"How did you fool your parents?"

"You make it sound like we purposely deceived our parents." Zach shifted his body, staring into the parking lot.

"Was that your plan all along? Never giving me an opportunity to seek my mother's wisdom?" Kayla chewed on the bottom of her lip, frowning. Could this day get any worse? She needed a bigger carton of ice cream.

17

"We both know no one can talk you into doing anything you don't want to do." Zach glared at her. His blue eyes darkening with each word, throwing daggers at her heart.

"How about you? You…"

"Settle down and play nice." Paul cut Kayla off, throwing his hands in the air. "How did your parents never find out?"

"We both had summer jobs on campus. So, we got married and left two days later for NC State," Zach said.

"We lived in student housing for married couples. Our schedules were crazy. We barely saw each other until one day, I came home expecting to find my husband, and all I found was an empty apartment and a lame note explaining his departure."

"You make it sound so…"

"Hateful? Foolish?" Kayla could spit fire. No way was her estranged husband standing here, justifying splitting from their marriage. Forever actually meant something to her.

"No, innocent. You're no saint, Kayla." Zach's smirk didn't match his icy eyes.

She stepped closer to him, wanting to knock the smirk off his handsome face. The face that ruined her life. "At least I tried to make our marriage work. Was that your plan, after all? Get me off the market and spit me out like yesterday's leftovers?"

"Believe what you want. *I* wanted our marriage to work." His voice held a fiery edge to it. "Besides, Adam Fisher and Donny Davis sure got a lot of your attention."

"Whatever. I couldn't care less about either of them." Kayla took a deep breath. Why was she wasting her sanity arguing with a man too hotheaded to admit his mistakes?

"I heard all the rumors," Zach said dryly.

"Why did you leave? I deserve that much."

"I don't have to explain anything to you." He crossed his arms over his chest, shaking his head.

"How do I know you're not my stalker?"

"Unbelievable. I didn't even know you lived here until five minutes ago." Zach took a couple of deep breaths.

"Estranged spouses are high on the suspect list." Paul shrugged his shoulders as the words tumbled out of his mouth.

"If I wanted her back, I wouldn't have to attack her or even scare her to get my way."

"You're so full of yourself." Kayla wanted to explode. Why did he have to ruin her semi-peaceful life? Not like he didn't already control her dreams or nightmares.

"Kayla, I'm gonna be the adult here and step away. No more fuel for your fire." Zach threw his arms in the air as he turned around and walked off. Exactly what he did best. He walked away when things got too hot.

"I can't do this." A tear escaped from Kayla's eye. "Please tell me you were only joking about going on vacation?"

"I realize how awkward this is, but he's good at his job."

"When you come back, one of us might not be alive. And this has nothing to do with a stalker." Kayla glanced in Zach's direction. His body leaned over the car like he was praying. Maybe if he would have done that years ago, they'd still be together.

"Kayla, I've never seen you act like this. He's my partner, but you are family." Paul pulled her into a brotherly hug. "Don't let him destroy your good-natured personality."

"He doesn't have any power over me anymore." Doubt seeped through her mind as she glanced his way, trying to

19

stop the floodgates of memories attacking her. She would have given anything to make their marriage work, but not anymore.

As if God just wanted to make her suffer, Thomas swaggered himself to her side, throwing his arm over her shoulder. And if looks could kill, Zach's piercing glare would have dropped her dead right in the school parking lot.

"Thomas, what are you doing here?" She moved out of his arms. One man was enough of a headache. Two men were enough to admit her to a psych ward.

"I was grading papers in my room when I heard a screaming match." He touched the top of her arm, looking her over. "You okay?"

"Someone assaulted Ms. Smith in the hall? Know anything about that?" Paul crossed his arms over his chest, never breaking eye contact with Thomas.

"Why would I? When I'm in the zone, my music is loud and nothing else matters but grading papers."

"Are you hurt?" His eyes held a coldness that didn't match his words.

"Just shaken up." Nothing two cartons of ice cream and a long bath wouldn't cure.

"Is that guy the creep?" Thomas stalked off in Zach's direction, ignoring Kayla's pleas to stop him. Just great. Two-over-the-top charmers and hotheads clashing.

"What did you do to Kayla?" Thomas's height matched Zach's, but his build was the opposite. He was skinny, with no bulging muscles.

"What's it to you?" Zach's gaze looked him over like sizing up the competition.

"She's my … friend." The way Thomas said the words sent goosebumps popping off her arms. She was not his anything, but Zach didn't need to know.

"Real innocent, Kayla."

"You're impossible." Kayla threw her arms in the air, deciding she'd rather take her chances with a stalker than either man.

"I'll give you a ride home and call someone to pick up your car." Thomas stepped closer to Kayla in a protective stance.

"Not happening. I'll escort her home. For all we know, you're her stalker. You had an opportunity."

"And you had a motive." Thomas smirked as he stepped away from Zach, facing Kayla, before walking off. "Call me if you need anything. You know my number."

"You dating that loser?"

No way would he waltz back into her life after being absent for four years and demanded access to her social life or lack of one. Kayla rolled her eyes and mumbled under her breath. She did not need him or any other guy to complicate her life. She walked off wondering what sin she was being punished for. Because she couldn't accept that coincidence had this much power over her life. She wasn't on speaking terms with God, but if He could get these insane men out of her life, she'd start listening.

****

"Earth to Zach." Josh, Zach's older brother by a year, nudged him on the arm. "Bro, hand me the chips."

Zach stared off into space, clutching the bowl of chips with his palms.

"What did the chips ever do to you? Besides, maybe raise your cholesterol?" Josh's hearty laugh got Zach's attention.

"Great game. Which team are you rooting for?"

"Uh … the Bears." Not like he was even watching. How could he when his wife, that he thought he'd never see again, popped back into his life?

"Dude, that team's not even playing. What's wrong with you?" Josh snatched the bowl of chips from Zach's grasp, setting it on the couch away from Zach. "Long day?"

"You could say that." Zach stared at the television, frowning. Of all the people in this world, it had to be Kayla. What he wouldn't give to go back in time and fix his jaded departure. Okay, maybe departure made it sound like a scheduled event. He let his bullheaded jealousy cause a drift between them, and instead of discussing his accusations, he bailed. Going back in time, he'd probably not marry her to begin with. Save his sanity and his future. No, he loved her before. Honestly, he still loved her. How could he not? In five years, he never even peeked at another female, besides Sarah. And what they had was just a shallow relationship. Kayla was in a league all to herself. Five-feet-six, with the most mesmerizing brown eyes he could get lost in. If he stared close enough, he could spot a speck of gold mixed in with the chocolate brown.

"It's a woman, right?" Josh propped his feet on the coffee table, staring at the men cheering across the room.

"It's complicated." Zach didn't want to think anymore. Just watch the game and zone out. Or sit outside a beautiful woman's house, trying to get one glimpse of her, passing by the window. If that didn't scream stalker, he didn't know what did. It didn't matter he was not stalking her. Probably that loser, Thomas, that seemed too friendly with his wife. Loser? Was he like in the first grade or a mature law enforcement detective? Being the lead detective, he couldn't go around calling over-zealous suspects losers.

"Always is when a woman is concerned." Josh patted his brother on the back, smiling. "That's why I'm here with you instead of at home with my overly emotional, pregnant wife."

"You dog." Zach playfully punched his brother on the arm. He envied his brother's marriage to his high school sweetheart. Josh and Britney worked hard to make their marriage work, something Zach couldn't do. Marriage wasn't for him. Not anymore.

"Who are you swooning over, little brother?" Josh tossed a chip in his mouth, glancing at the television. The guys sitting on the couch, oblivious to their conversation, jumped up cheering. "Wait, don't tell me. The new pianist at church. She couldn't keep her eyes off you for the whole service. I didn't notice, but you know how perceptive my wife is."

Who was Josh even talking about? He couldn't even remember what the pianist looked like.

"Or is it a pretty girl from your past?" His brother shot him a knowing look.

"Kayla. You've seen her? And you forgot to mention it?" Zach jumped to his feet, throwing his arms in the air, wanting to punch something. Maybe even his brother. "My wife is in the same town and no one told me."

"Your wife?" A smile tugged on the corner of Josh's lips, causing his blue eyes to twinkle with mischief.

"Did I say that out loud?" Now, his brother knew his fool-hearted past regret. He didn't regret marrying her. At least, he wouldn't have if the marriage hadn't ended before it even started. His fault not Kayla's.

23

"No matter. I knew you were married this whole time." Josh leaned closer so the men watching the game wouldn't hear. "Kind of disappointed in you, though."

"Britney." Zach felt like an idiot. Of course, Kayla would have confided in her best friend, now his sister-in-law. And his role in their broken marriage disappointed him too, just not enough to do anything about it.

"Marriage is forever, bro. Not sure why you walked out on her."

Zach puffed out a flow of hot air. His brother would take Kayla's side. From a bystander's perspective, he'd take her side too. But he knew the secrets she hid all these years. Kayla drove him away. She was to blame for their broken marriage as much, if not more, than he was.

"Y'all talking about Kayla Smith?" Silas Clover, an acquaintance of a friend, shoved a handful of popcorn in his mouth. Dude had no manners.

"What's it to you?" His hard detective persona flashed before his face. Everyone was a suspect.

"We live in the same apartment building. Keep trying to get her to go out with me, but she keeps turning me down." Silas wiped a crumb from his face.

He'd applaud her for that. The guy looked like a slob.

"Only a matter of time. Women can't resist my charm." Zach wanted to punch the guy in the face. He was trying to charm Kayla. His wife. Which meant she was off limits. Yeah, right? If he acted like a husband, none of this would have happened. No stalker or relentless male attention.

Zach couldn't help himself. He stared down the man after his wife, knowing at any time he'd be ready to throw some blows at his opponent. "Where were you yesterday at four o'clock?"

"Why you want to know?" The light came on in Silas's dull mind as he crossed his arms over his chest. "Are you interrogating me?"

"Just a friendly conversation between two of Kayla's admirers." Zach spoke through gritted teeth. He wanted to throw this guy to the curb.

"Are you stalking her?" Silas raised his dark eyebrow, sizing up the detective. "I don't take kindly to predators."

Was this guy serious? He was a more likely candidate for being a stalker than Zach was. "I'm a detective."

"And?" Silas stepped in front of Zach. His garlic-scented breath made Zach want to gag. "A pretty woman and an infatuated detective. You couldn't get the girl, so you went crazy. I've seen it before. Just know if you hurt her, you won't be walking away unscathed."

This dude was really threatening him. And of course he got the girl. He just couldn't keep her.

"Break it up, guys. I think this party is over." Josh stood between Zach and Silas, flipping the television off as groans sounded around the room. "We're not in high school anymore. Both of you grow up." Josh grabbed his keys off the kitchen counter and stormed out of the house, followed by the rest of the men.

Zach felt bad about his immature behavior, but Kayla brought the worst out of him. She always did. But she also brought out his gentler qualities like compassion, love, kindness. Without her, he turned into a caveman, beating his chest and looking to whoop anyone who gave him a wrong look. Pathetic.

God, what's wrong with me? You've changed me, but I'm acting like the old Zach, full of himself and angry.

His ring tone, the theme song to *Rocky,* pulled him out of his daze. He glanced at the unknown caller. If this was another prank call, he might actually punch something.

"Zach speaking." He couldn't hide the agitation in his voice. He needed sleep to clear his annoyances and put him in a better mood.

"Zach?" The soft female voice choked out all the anger in his body. No one had ever said his name like she had.

"Kayla, what's going on?"

"I-I think someone's in my apartment." Fear laced her words as her voice trembled over the phone.

"Where are you at? Are you alone?" Zach snatched his keys off the counter, running into the muggy evening air. Spring in Tennessee boasted of beauty and new life, but this evening felt like someone left the heater on full blast. Sweat poured down his face before he got to his car.

"My sister left a few minutes ago. I'm in my bedroom. Of course, you probably already know that." Her voice quivered, and he knew she was chewing on her fingernails. A bad habit she couldn't break. Why would he know anything about her sister's location? What had she heard? At that moment, he wanted to pull her into his arms, shielding her from the evils of the world. Being her protector, friend, husband.

"I'm on my way. Go into your bedroom and lock the door." Zach floored the gas pedal, leaving a cloud of exhaust behind his truck.

"Zach, I'm scared."

With each soft-spoken word, the layers of anger striped away from his heart. "Sweetie, I'll be there soon." He knew where she lived. As lead detective, he needed to know everything about her and her admirers. Was she the same Kayla that craved honey on her peanut butter sandwiches and ate ice cream from the carton? Of course, she ran the extra calories away the next morning. "I'll be there soon."

God, help me get to her in time.

Chapter Two

"Yum. Something smells amazing." Kayla tossed her purse on the couch and stepped into the kitchen. Her sister Sarah, with her messy red hair in a bun, wearing a sauce-stained apron, pulled a pan out of the oven.

"New recipe; tomato Rigatoni. And homemade bread sticks to freshen up any dish." Sarah blew at a strand of hair that fell in front of her eyes.

"You'll get the promotion to head chef with dishes like this." Kayla fell onto a kitchen stool, fidgeting with a place mat. "Tell me we still have cartons of ice cream in the freezer?"

Sarah turned away from the oven, her green eyes resembling the ocean waves after a storm. She glared at Kayla. "Ice cream before supper? It'll ruin your appetite."

"Yes, mother." Kayla rolled her eyes as she took two steps to the freezer, pulling out a new mint chocolate chip carton. She opened the lid and dug her spoon inside as a minty scent teased her senses. The cool dessert rolled around on her tongue, soothing away a fraction of the day's stress.

"What happened?" Sarah turned the oven off and tossed her oven mitts on the counter with a thud. "You sulk into a carton of ice cream every time something stressful happens."

"Let's see anonymous flowers, nearly attacked, flat tires, Thomas, and my estranged husband lives in the same

28

small town." Kayla spooned another bite of ice cream into her mouth. "I might need two cartons this evening."

"I'm speechless." Sarah rubbed her fingers over the granite countertop, frowning.

"You knew Zach lived here, and you never told me?" Kayla tossed the empty carton into the trashcan and glared at her twenty-two-year-old sister. Whose side was she on? Sarah always liked Zach, maybe even had a crush on him in high school. So, probably on his side. Kayla could see Sarah weaseling her way into Zach's life. The years had only added to his good-looks. Sarah was single and an incredible, easygoing woman. If she would have married Zach, maybe he would have stuck around. *Don't go there, Kayla.*

Her relationship with her sister, Sarah, started out pleasantly, but as the years passed by, they became strained and distant. If not for her baby sister, Rachel, she wouldn't be living with Sarah or even talking to her. Sarah always looked out for herself, never Kayla.

Sarah threw her arms in the air, looking like the mischievous, fiery redhead she used to be. "In my defense, how do you tell someone their husband that they hadn't seen in four years lives in the same town?"

"You're right." Kayla glanced down at Sarah's phone as a text popped across the screen. Kayla's mouth twitched as Zach's name flashed across the screen. "Are you seeing him?"

Sarah nervously shoved her phone into her pocket, busying herself with preparing the food. "It's not what it looks."

"I don't have time for this. You've always wanted everything I've had." Kayla stomped out of the kitchen, stopping in the hall. "You can have him. Maybe he'll stick around for you." How could she? How could he?

"Sis, come back."

Kayla, seething with anger, forcefully slammed her bedroom door, the sound reverberating through the room. She sank into her plush feather-top mattress, feeling its softness envelop her body. The sight of her sister, Sarah, resuming her one-sided rivalry with her, brought out Kayla's buried anger amidst this storm of emotions. Thoughts of Sarah cooking Zach's favorite dish, rigatoni, filled her mind, the aroma of the Italian food lingering in the air. Images of her beautiful sister, cuddling Kayla's estranged husband, flashed before her eyes, causing a wave of bile to rise in her throat. Apparently, Zach had no conscience, obvious by his ability to date whomever he pleased, as the marriage certificate held no value to him. He had not fought for her or their marriage, leaving Kayla feeling betrayed and abandoned.

Needing an escape from her tumultuous thoughts, Kayla decided a bath would help clear her mind. She took three deliberate steps; the floor creaking beneath her as she entered her master bath. She had installed a claw-foot tub, its elegance standing out against the simplicity of the toilet. To Kayla, that was all that mattered. Being a teacher, she couldn't afford much, unlike her sister Sarah, who made a decent living as a chef. However, Sarah selflessly helped pay for their younger sister Rachel's college education, adding to Kayla's feelings of resentment.

Just as Kayla climbed into the soothing effects of a hot, bubbly bath, the front door slammed shut, jolting her attention to her phone. A text from Sarah informed her of her delayed return, causing Kayla to hope that a sudden power outage would ruin her sister's dinner date. Living in

East Tennessee, the unreliable power grid often failed for no apparent reason. Guilt clawed at Kayla's gut as she realized how unfairly she had treated Sarah. Despite her own anger, Sarah didn't deserve Kayla's wrath. Even if they were together, cuddling each other on the couch and sharing laughter over Sarah's jokes, accompanied by the mouth-watering aroma of rigatoni.

Five years ago, Kayla and Zach had vowed to support each other unconditionally. A solitary tear slid down Kayla's wet face as she lowered herself into the steamy water, feeling the warmth envelop her body. The absence of Zach's embrace, the safety it once provided, left a void in her heart. Why had he walked out on her four years ago? She had tried to balance college and their marriage, but it had never been enough for him. In his eyes, she was never enough. His decision had shattered her heart and destroyed her future. Kayla knew she could never go back, never forgive him. Nostalgia, rather than love or affection, tinged her heart, leaving her longing for a past that she could never recapture.

Feeling utterly alone, she wanted to pick up the phone and call someone, anyone. Her contact list was full of people, but none knew about her impulsive marriage besides Sarah and Britney, her best friend, but Zach's sister-in-law. Against better judgment, she called her friend. What if her alliances laid with her brother-in-law? Before she could hang up, Britney's soft voice floated through the phone.

"Kayla, I've been thinking about you." *I'm sure you and Zach have been talking about me, too.* Kayla shook her head at her crabbiness. Apparently, bubble baths did nothing for awful attitudes. She slid further into the water as bubbles clung to her chin.

"Oh?"

"I haven't heard from you in a while. How's everything going?" Her friend's cheerful voice sounded forced.

Let's see a stalker, my absent husband, and now my little sister. Life couldn't get any worse. But she would not tell that to anyone. "Fine. I'm looking forward to spring break next week."

"Listen, Josh told me you ran into Zach. I'm sorry I never told you. I tried staying out of it. My best friend and brother-in-law it's quite a precarious situation."

Kayla loud out a whimper at the mention of Zach's name.

"Honey, are you crying?" Background noises shuffled in the background. "I'm on my way."

"No, please. I just want to be alone…" The sound of the squeaky front door heightened Kayla's senses. Rachel wouldn't be home until next weekend and Sarah was probably snuggling with Kayla's husband. Her low opinion of her sister shocked her. What was wrong with her? Jealousy? Beginning stages of a mental breakdown? She'd have to talk to Stephen and Lily at the birthday party tomorrow. They were doctors, and she needed something.

"Are you still on the phone?" Britney's worried voice blared into the phone.

"I think someone's in my house." Kayla climbed out of the tub, throwing her clothes on, not bothering to dry off.

"Call Zach."

"I have to go." Kayla looked around the room for a weapon. Grabbing the first thing she saw, a blow dryer.

"He still cares for you."

"I'd hate to see how he treats his enemies." Kayla ended the call, sliding into her bedroom.

An eerie silence filled her small apartment, broken only by the distant sound of faint footsteps drawing nearer to her bedroom. Kayla bit her lip, her eyes wide with fear as she desperately tried to suppress a scream. She was fine. Of course, past fatal victims of stalkers probably thought they were fine, too. The chilling reality smacked her in the face. She was going to die at the hands of a crazed stalker.

Kayla gripped her phone in her hand, hitting the first number she saw. Zach.

"Zach speaking." His Southern drawl was more pronounced when agitation coursed through his body.

"Zach?" she mumbled the words, fearing the intruder would hear her and find her location.

"Kayla, what's going on?"

"I-I think someone's in my apartment." Fear laced her words as her hands trembled, barely holding the phone steady.

"Where are you at? Are you alone?" Zach's voice was a surprising welcome that calmed her erratic heartbeat.

"My sister left a few minutes ago. I'm in my bedroom. Of course, you probably already know that." Kayla double-checked the lock on her door, as she pressed her face on the cool wooden surface. Silence. Was she going crazy? No, she had heard footsteps. Whoever it was, didn't want to be heard.

"I'm on my way. Say in your room."

"Zach, I'm scared." Kayla chewed on her thumbnail, listening for anymore noises from the intruder.

"Sweetie, I'll be there soon." Her heart skipped a beat at hearing him call her sweetie. She never tired of his pet names for her. How amazing it'd be to rest in his arms, hiding from the danger that seemed to haunt her. Only, she hasn't that foolish, love-struck eighteen-year-old anymore.

And he would not sweet talk his way into her heart again. Ever.

****

Zach took a calming breath, knowing he couldn't rush into a crime scene full of built-up emotions. He was a professional, not a hotheaded rookie. No matter who the victim was, he had to remain in control. He couldn't let unresolved feelings for his wife skew his investigation. Over the years, he begged God for a second chance with Kayla, never thinking it would actually happen. But here they were, a psycho throwing their lives back together. No matter, Kayla hated him, and the bitterness that laid dormant for four years spewed out of his heart. Zach loved her. He always would love her, but they were terrible partners. Best to keep it professional and keep her where she belonged; in the past.

He yanked his keys out of the ignition and ran his fingers over his gun, feeling the security and confidence that came with it. After another breath, he walked into Kayla's two-story apartment building. No security code or any type of barrier between residences and trouble. He'd have to talk to the property manager later.

His shoes echoed on the white-tiled floor, reminding him of high school and all of its glory. Mostly a beautiful blond with hypnotizing chocolate-brown eyes. He'd go back in time if it meant rekindling a love most people never experienced. But he blew it. Or maybe he could say she blew it. It didn't matter who was at fault; they were pretty much enemies, making his job almost impossible.

Focus Zach. No time for daydreaming. A victim needs you. Not his wife or a woman he'd never stop loving. Just a victim.

He took the stairs two at a time, his long legs coming in handy. Her apartment, on the second floor, last door on the right. Not the fanciest complex, but he'd seen worse. How far could her salary go? Teachers weren't raking in the cash. But her financial status was none of his business. Right now, she needed Detective Rivers, not a curious estranged husband.

Finding her door, he noticed someone had left it cracked open. Not willing to alert the perp, he stealthily slid into the living room. The aroma of Italian food caused his stomach to growl, reminding him his supper of chips didn't last long. Did Kayla cook? When they were married, she never did besides awful microwaveable meals. To this day, he couldn't bring himself to eat one. Too many memories and the thoughts were suffocating.

Zach glanced over a traditional-looking living room. Two love seats rested on the beige carpet, separated by a coffee table. An over-sized portrait of a stallion caught his attention. Kayla had an infatuation with anything equestrian. Blinking back the nostalgia, Zach noticed a full-sized mirror covered in red lipstick. He hoped it wasn't blood.

"Home-wrecker. You will die." Zach mumbled the words under his breath. Not typical of an obsessed stalker. Maybe they had the stalker thing wrong, or more than one person was after Kayla. He stepped into the hall, his heart racing as he glanced into two empty bedrooms. Where was she?

A faint scuffle noise alerted him to her location. The sound of muffled footsteps echoed through the tiled bathroom. He held back a gasp as a smaller-framed, hooded figure forcefully shoved Kayla's head into a tub of water. The splash reverberated through the room, accompanied by the scent of an acidic chemical. Kayla's arms were tightly bound behind her back, her body restrained. The dim lighting made it difficult to see any details, but he could sense her calmness in the face of imminent danger. That was his girl. Well, not really.

"Police! Let Ms. Smith go." His voice quivered with a mix of fear and determination. Or did she go by Mrs. Rivers? In this moment, it seemed irrelevant. He took a cautious step closer to the figure, his heart pounding in his chest. Kayla's head skimmed the top of the water, her body motionless. Had he arrived too late? The air felt heavy as he inhaled deeply, trying to steady his nerves. Suddenly, the hooded figure hurled a bowl of liquid in his direction. It splashed against his face, sending a searing pain through his eyes. He blinked rapidly; his vision clouded by the burning sensation. The sounds of hurried footsteps echoed in the distance, signaling the escape of the assailant. Zach berated himself for letting his guard down, allowing the suspect to blind him with what he suspected was acetic acid, also known as nail polish remover. What an idiot.

"Kayla?" His voice trembled as he rubbed his stinging eyes, reaching out to grab the back of her shirt. He pulled her face out of the water, desperate to save her. *Please God, don't take her away from me. Correction, God, don't take her away from her family.* Zach carefully laid her cold, blue-tinted skin on the bathroom floor, his fingers brushing against the wet streaks on her face. He tilted her head back, preparing to administer CPR. With a sense of urgency, he pressed his lips firmly against hers, willing to do whatever it took to revive her. After two breaths, he began the rhythmic compressions on her chest.

"Twenty-five, twenty-six, come on, sweetie." Urgency and hope filled his voice. He continued the compressions, praying for a miracle. Finally, Kayla coughed, expelling a stream of water from her lungs.

"Thank You, Jesus." Zach's voice rang out in relief as he carefully shifted her onto her side. With trembling hands, he reached for his phone, dialing his partner and urgently requesting an ambulance.

"Zach." He had never heard sweeter words. Like he had so many times, he scooped her body into his arms, staring into her glassy eyes. Her erratic heartbeat pulsed through his chest, reminding him how close she had come to death.

"It's okay, sweetie." He ran his trembling fingers through her messy hair. In that moment, his heart yearned for her with such passion that he bent over, brushing his lips over hers. No matter the status, he was holding his wife, the woman he loved, and she had almost died. Maybe he'd regret it later, but right now, he threw all defenses out the window. Leaving a man desperately in love with a woman. His woman.

Kayla returned his kiss for a split second before she scooted out of his arms. A pang of rejection and hurt shot through his heart. He couldn't go kissing her like past mistakes didn't control their lives.

"Zach." Her color had returned mostly, and he knew God had saved her life.

He chewed on the bottom of his lip, staring into her golden-brown eyes. What he wouldn't give to erase every heartache and hurtful decision, going back to man and wife. The simple life that lasted two glorious days before college and real life tore them apart.

"Did you catch her?" She looked up at him, her eyes holding too much trust and dependence on him. He was, after all, the man that walked out on her, barely looking back.

"Her? How do you know it was a woman?"

"She smelled like burned roses and her hands were small like a woman's." Kayla climbed off the floor, sitting with her legs pressed against her chest. Her pajamas covered in water. "Besides, why would a man accuse me of being a home-wrecker?"

She had a point. The body type looked like a woman's. But what about the accusations? Was Kayla trying to steal a married man from his family or flirting with the wrong man? Any man was the wrong man, seeing as how they were still married. But that fact aside, who was she involved in? Someone could equate Kayla's overly friendly personality as flirtatious.

"Kayla, are you seeing a married man?" Just rip off the love-colored glasses and get to the truth. Professionalism aside, he wanted to know for personal reasons too.

"How..." Fire burned in her brown eyes as she glared at him. Whatever they shared seconds ago disappeared from reality. She could never be his again, no matter how much he wanted her to really be his wife.

Footsteps sounded outside the door as Paul dashed into the room, taking in the scene. He gave Zach a disapproving look and stepped to Kayla's side, helping her off the bathroom floor. "I'll help you to the ambulance. And no arguing. Your mom will have my hide if I don't make you get checked out."

Zach stared at the tub of water. Unbelievable. His partner thought he was an unstable, estranged husband. No, he wasn't, but he was her husband and no one would keep him out of that ambulance next to her.

****

"Stop looking at me like that. I'm fine." Kayla popped a grape into her mouth. The ER wanted to keep her for a twenty-four-hour observation. Like that was happening. She felt ninety percent better. Physically, she healed fine. But emotionally was a different story. Every time she closed her eyes, she could feel steamy, tub water suffocating her. A favorite, calming mechanism, no more. She had to force herself to step into the tub and shower before the party, almost hyperventilating.

She glanced over the sea of familiar faces as her eyes stopped on a good-looking detective. His laughter sounded like music to her ears. In less than twenty-four-hours, he had bitterly confronted her, not hiding his contempt of seeing her again. But reminding her of the old Zach, he cradled her body in his, kissing her gently. Saving her wasn't surprising. That was his job. Staying by her side, pulling the husband's card, had surprised her.

Not like she wanted to mend fences with the man who broke her heart, leaving and never looking back. Oh, he had made one lousy phone call to clear his conscience, but no explanation for his abrupt departure. Kayla ran her fingers over her plate of finger foods. Honestly, she had always loved him, but their spontaneous kiss quickened her dead heart, reminding her of all the emotions Zach always brought out of her. Maybe they could have a second chance. But since the hospital, he had been avoiding her

39

like he would her gourmet cooking or lack thereof. And there was the minor issue of her sister. Was Zach seeing her sister?

"I'm a doctor, right?" Lily wiped crumbs off her one-year-old daughter's face. Her body squirming in her mother's arms.

Kayla let out an enormous sigh. Maybe coming to her cousin's birthday party was a terrible idea. She couldn't look at Zach and not want to feel the warmth from his nearness and smell his woodsy cologne entrapping her senses.

"I don't think physically you should be worried about her." Belle grabbed her niece from Lily's lap, planting a kiss on her black curls. "Heart matter is a different story."

"What are you talking about?" Was her infatuation so obvious? She was gawking at a married man. But she had a flimsy certificate to prove that under normal circumstances, she could gawk all she wanted. Being her husband and all.

"You haven't stopped looking at the handsome detective since we got here." Belle, Kayla's cousin, nudged her on the arm. "You're blushing."

"I'm gonna cry." Lily patted Kayla's arm, offering moral support. "I knew this day would come. Now I sound like Stephen."

"You're awfully emotional." Belle raised her eyebrow at her sister-in-law. Leaning in so no one else could hear. "Are you pregnant?"

"We just found out yesterday." Lily took a sip of her water. "Promise you won't tell anyone."

"You have my word." Belle beamed as she bounced the baby in her lap.

"Kayla?"

"Yeah, sure." Kayla stabbed a meatball with her plastic fork. Jealousy pricked her heart as she glared at her husband flirting with a pretty redhead. What was her sister doing here? She never went to family gatherings. Her job kept her busy. And why was she making a fool of herself in front of everyone?

"Hon, go talk to him." Belle glanced through the crowds of people. Probably trying to locate her four children.

"I might leave after the presents. I'm not feeling well." Kayla's heart sunk as Zach patted his hand on Sarah's shoulder. Her sister was a home-wrecker. Maybe the assailant confused her with her sister.

"What did that meatball do to you?" Lily's wide-grin spread across her olive-tinted face.

Kayla rolled her eyes as she jumped to her feet. "I need some air. I'll be back in a few minutes."

She deftly navigated her way through the bustling crowd, a sea of people with their eyes fixed on her. With a forced smile plastered on her face, she greeted her family and friends, concealing the turmoil within her. The Walkman residence, standing tall as the largest house in their quaint town, exuded an air of opulence. The scent of dogwood trees wafted through the air, mingling with the unmistakable aroma of wealth that permeated the grandest homes in the vicinity. From the back deck, a picturesque view of a wooded lot stretched out before her. As she ran her fingers along the smooth, cherry-stained railing, her gaze fixed on nothingness, desperately seeking solace. She refused to let Zach, the man who had once promised to love her forever, only to flee, shattering her dreams, sway her. Kayla was determined not to let his presence awaken the emotions she had painstakingly locked away in the darkest recesses of her heart. Zach Rivers, a heart-breaker. Perhaps they could have made it work, but his choice of her unblemished sister over her spoke volumes about his character. What kind of man flirted with his own sister-in-law?

The back door slid open as her cousin Stephen stepped onto the deck. His blue eyes glistened with concern. "Lily told me you were out here, alone."

"Why are men such jerks?" Kayla pounded her fist on the railing, not stopping when pain shot up her arm.

"Age-old question." Stephen pulled Kayla into a bear hug, being more like a brother than her cousin. "Say the words and I'll go deck him right in the middle of the party."

Stephen's protectiveness sent a smile across Kayla's face. If only she could fight her problems away.

"I know y'all are technically married. Paul told me. No one else knows. I won't lecture you about your impulsive, idiotic choices. You already know, or you'd be by his side and not your sister." Stephen squeezed his arm around her shoulder. "You were always my favorite cousin. Sarah is like chewed-up baby food compared to you."

"Thanks. I think." Kayla pushed out of her cousin's arm, feeling overwhelmed and alone. She couldn't escape to home without her sister's smug face entering her domain. Could things get anymore awkward? "I'm gonna head home. Give the birthday girl a hug from me."

"If you insist. I won't even try to talk you out of it." Stephen patted her arm, giving her a steeling look. "If you need me, call me."

"Thanks. And congrats. You're a top-notch daddy."

Stephen's lips turned into a smile, lightening his ocean-blue eyes. "Thanks." He stepped back through the sliding door, leaving Kayla alone.

Kayla patted her pockets, searching for her keys. *Oh, right, I got a ride with Aunt Lea.* She slid her phone out of her pocket, scheduling an Uber pickup. She wouldn't bother her aunt, and Kayla couldn't go back inside. Too many emotions that she didn't care to deal with.

The door slid open again. Only this time, the guy who stepped onto the porch wasn't a friendly sight. Kayla took a deep breath, trying to still her jumbled nerves. What did he want? He made his intentions crystal-clear. Her sister, not her, intrigued him. Once a player, always a player.

"I ... um, saw you step outside." He ran his fingers through his golden hair.

"I'm surprised you could see anything with Sarah hanging on your arm." Kayla could spit fire. Why was he even out here?

Zach rubbed the sides of his forehead, something he did a lot around her. Like she caused him tension headaches. "About that…"

She threw her arms in the air, taking a step away from him. "I don't need an explanation. We only have a relationship on paper."

"Kayla." He took a step toward her, an unreadable flicker in his eyes.

"Please don't." What was he even doing? Trying to charm her? Put two sisters against each other? It didn't matter. She needed to get away from him. Her heart yearned for this man, who clearly wasn't worthy of her love.

"Can we talk?" He gave her a puppy-dog look that always melted her anger away. *Not this time, buddy.*

43

He reached for her arm, sending awareness pulsing through her body. How easy it would be to lean into his secure embrace, forgetting everything besides the love they once shared.

"Out of all the women in this town, did you have to pick my sister?" Kayla stepped off the porch, noting the car pulling into the driveway. Her ride. Did he want her blessing or something? Because that wasn't happening.

"Kayla come back."

Ignoring his pleas, Kayla ran to the car, stopping only when the driver climbed out of his car. "Kayla."

"Thomas, what are you doing here?" Awkward.

"I am an Uber driver on the weekends. My teacher's salary barely pays the bills. But you know that already." Thomas stared at Zach on the porch. She thought they were gonna have a brawl in the driveway.

"Let's get out of here." She glanced at Zach. He had perfected the death glare over the years. It didn't matter. He was interested in her sister, and she couldn't fall prey to his charm again.

****

"I can't eat another bite." Zach raised his hand in protest as crumbs fell out of his mouth.

"What do you think?" Her green eyes twinkled with amusement.

"That you're the best chef in town." Zach wiped the corner of his mouth with a napkin, smiling. "And a man could get used to eating your cooking daily."

"Like a domesticated life together?" Sarah's soft whispers sent a cascade of prickling sensations up his arms, causing goosebumps to form on his skin. As he sat there, reveling in the company of a Smith girl, he couldn't help but realize the gravity of his mistake in marrying the girl he married. Kayla, with her icy demeanor, felt like ice on a freezing winter day. Sarah radiated warmth and sunshine, like a sunflower basking in the golden rays of the sun. Previously, he had never truly taken notice of Sarah's beauty, although she was not as striking as her sister. Yet, her physical allure was undeniable. The way she looked at him, with a mixture of desire and affection, sent a thrilling jolt through his veins. The only thing holding him back was the piece of paper, the marriage certificate that bound him to Kayla. However, their relationship had been over for years. Yes, he had foolishly kissed Kayla, allowing himself to feel emotions he had long forgotten. But that chapter was now closed. He would never travel down that treacherous road with Kayla again. Never. And if need be, he'd officially end their marriage. Then Kayla could run off with loser Thomas. The jerk was relentless, showing up innocently, everywhere she was. Yeah right, and he could do ballet. Didn't matter though. Kayla Smith was not his problem anymore.

"Um, yeah, I'm sure your future husband would gain ten pounds the first week of marriage." Zach took a swig of juice and jumped to his feet.

"Do you picture that man being you?" Sarah ran her finger along the top of his forearm, sending warning bells screeching through his mind.

Innocent flirtation, maybe, but he wasn't ready for marriage again. Especially with his wife's sister. Awkward.

Zach could feel his face turning five shades of red at her presumptuous ways. His heart quickened as he ran his fingers over Sarah's much smaller, calloused ones. How would he get out of this situation?

Before he could run through scenarios, a deep voice cleared his throat, causing Sarah to jump back in surprise.

"We need to talk." Paul grabbed Zach's shirt, leading him further into the backyard. "What are you doing?" His cold-as-steel eyes bore into Zach's soul, making him squirm under the intensity.

"What are you talking about?" Zach hit his partner's fingers off of his shirt, straightening his clothes.

"Don't play coy with me. What are you doing with Sarah?" Paul folded his arms over his chest, scolding.

"My personal life is none of your business. Off limits." Zach ran his fingers through his hair, like he did in uncomfortable situations.

"True, but you're at my house, surrounded by a bunch of kids. Keep the atmosphere G rated." Paul's gruff voice held an underlining warning that Zach didn't miss.

"You're off base, man." They were partners, nothing more. And if Paul didn't keep his nose in his own business, Zach didn't know if they could be partners. Partners equaled trust, which was lacking since Kayla showed up.

"Should I remind you of your marriage status?" Zach felt sorry for Paul's kids. The guy was a bulldog for justice. They wouldn't rebel and get away with it.

"No. I don't need you or anyone else throwing my past mistakes in my face." Zach's fingers curled into a fist. "I married the wrong girl."

"Are you sure about that?" Paul raised his black eyebrow mockingly. "Maybe you married the right girl, but your arrogant, flirtatious ways sliced through the marriage before it had time to stake into a solid foundation."

Ouch! Zach jumped to his feet. "Before you accuse me of destroying our marriage, how about you look at your cousin? Her innocence doesn't run deeper than surface level."

Paul let out a deep sigh, frowning. "Man up and fix your mistakes. God's giving you a chance of restoration. Don't blow it on a cheap side dish, when you could have the steak and everything with it."

Zach didn't know if he should punch Paul for stepping into his business or bust out laughing at his awful metaphors. "As of this minute, my love life is off the tables. And so is the God talk." Although he had a relationship with God, he didn't need preached at or condemned. Zach was not the bad guy in this situation.

"Whatever, bro. Just remember, you're the lead detective in my absence. Don't mess it up." Paul stomped back to his house, mumbling under his breath.

The dude was probably praying or something. A chuckle escaped Zach's lips at the thought. Maybe if he would have done that, he wouldn't be in such a precarious situation.

Within minutes, Zach was traveling down a country road, back into town. Cautious of deer or possums, Zach slowed his car down, glancing into the fields.

The peaceful countryside snagged on his heartstrings. What he wouldn't give for peace. He was a Christian, but after two years on the force, his relationship with God plummeted. Not entirely his fault. Did he blame Kayla for everything? No, but she deserved the blame, having destroyed his life. And any hope for the future. A green-eyed redhead floated in his mind. It really felt good being the recipient of someone's affections. At twenty-four, he couldn't bury his attractions, and die an old bachelor. He'd casually get to know Sarah. Nothing wrong with that.

Something bigger than a deer darted in front of his car. With tires squealing, he slammed on the brakes, stopping inches from the figure. He jumped out of his car, gun in hand. That's when he noticed a woman crouched in a fetal position on the curvy country road. Blood splattered on the side of her cheeks.

What in the world happened?

"Ma'am? I'm Detective Zach Rivers." Zach inched closer to the trembling figure. Zach stepped closer, locking eyes with the woman he kept running from, but couldn't seem to flee from. "Kayla?"

She froze at the mention of her name. What was she doing out here? Disoriented, ripped clothes, bloody face. Thomas. If he did anything to her, he'd … What, take the law into his own hands, beat him to a bloody pulp? No, Zach was better than that.

He kneeled on the warm asphalt, staring into her lifeless eyes. "Kayla? Can you tell me what happened?"

She straightened her body, her dark brown eyes piercing into his, before wrapping her slender arms around his muscular neck, snuggling into the warmth of his broad chest. He stiffened at her gentle touch, his heart pounding in his chest. She felt so right in his arms, her soft scent of lavender filling his nostrils, but he could never go down that road again. Patting her on the arm, he reluctantly pushed her out of his grasp, a deep sense of emptiness and regret washing over him as her body became absent. His sweet Kayla. No, that was years ago. She was only his in pretense, bound by a marriage certificate neither wanted. He led her to his sleek car, the engine humming softly, and helped her into the plush passenger seat.

He watched her figure fade into the seat. She had left the party twenty minutes before he had. What had transpired in that fleeting time frame?

"Kayla, can you tell me what happened?" He leaned back in his seat, staring at her.

"Why do you keep calling me Kayla? That's not my name." Agitation rolled through her words as she curled her legs into the seat.

Was she joking? Not normally one for dramatics or pranks, something must have fogged her memory. "What do you remember?"

Swallowing hard, she fought back a flood of tears. Her blond hair was disarrayed, with strands sticking out in every direction, giving her the appearance of someone who had just engaged in a brawl. "Someone shot at me and I took off running."

Where was Thomas? How had she stopped the car? And who had shot at her, attempting to abduct her? Nothing made sense. "Can you tell me anything else?"

Zach's gaze fixated on Kayla, her body slumped against the worn seat, her delicate features hidden beneath a curtain of closed eyelids. A surge of emotions welled up within him, a mixture of concern and frustration at the sight of Kayla, vulnerable and disoriented. Why had fate brought her back into his life? It had been so much simpler to ignore their troubled marriage when they lived hundreds of miles apart.

Suddenly, Kayla's body convulsed, her lips releasing unintelligible words in a trembling whisper. With careful hands, Zach secured the buckle over her chest, mindful not to cause her any further harm. In haste, he dialed his partner, his voice laced with urgency as he relayed the situation. Racing against time, Zach sped towards the hospital, his rapid heartbeat piercing through the silence.

As he navigated the curvy roads, Zach couldn't help but wonder what had happened. But he trusted Paul to uncover the truth, to delve into the depths of what had transpired. Kayla needed immediate medical treatment, her well-being hanging in the balance. In a moment of desperation, Zach silently pleaded to God, praying for Kayla's recovery. He couldn't help but feel like a hypocrite, praying for her well-being when he himself had been a catalyst for her suffering.

Chapter Three

Kayla blinked her eyes, struggling to focus as her vision blurred, the world around her a hazy mess. A gnawing feeling twisted in the pit of her stomach, spreading unease throughout her body. Where was she? And more importantly, who was she? Pain throbbed relentlessly in her head as she shifted on the bed, desperate to escape the darkness and find answers.

Suddenly, a woman's sing-song voice pierced through the fog of confusion. "Whoa, Ms. Smith. Any more tossing and turning under those covers and you'll end up on the floor," the voice teased.

Kayla's body froze as her vision slowly cleared. She found herself in a sparsely decorated room, the scent of cleaning supplies overwhelming her senses. Who had brought her to the hospital? And why couldn't she remember anything beyond the terrifying image of a man chasing her with a gun? Fear gripped her stomach as she reached up to touch the bandage on her head.

"Now, now, Ms. Smith, if you keep fidgeting with that bandage, your stitches might come undone," the nurse, a kind-looking woman with gray hair, gently cautioned, patting Kayla's arm. Her eyes exuded warmth and compassion. "Oh, how rude of me. Let me go get your husband."

"I have a husband?" Kayla blinked, confusion clouding her thoughts, her fingers absentmindedly tracing the bandage on her head.

The door creaked open, revealing a tall, muscular man with a boyish face. His piercing blue eyes flickered with a mix of emotions as he entered the room, fidgeting nervously with something in his pocket. He took a hesitant stance against the farthest wall, his expression etched with concern.

The nurse's laughter filled the room, booming and infectious as she adjusted Kayla's IV. "Ah, young love. Boy, come over here and give your wife some comfort. Stop acting like an awkward schoolboy."

Zach hesitantly obliged, Kayla's heart pounding in her chest with each step. He crossed his arms tightly over his chest, the fabric of his shirt looking like it might rip. Standing just inches from the bed, Kayla took deep, shallow breaths. He tried to keep his distance, careful not to touch her, and that didn't seem very loving. What kind of marriage did they have?

Kayla fought back tears, her breaths coming out in shaky exhales. She could hear the hushed sounds of her own sniffles, trying to hold back the overwhelming wave of emotions. She glanced at Zach, hoping for comfort, but he seemed uncomfortable with her nearness. Doubt creeped into her mind - what kind of wife was she?

The nurse's voice broke the silence, her words cutting through the tension. "That's all you got?" The nurse paused, peering at Zach with a scold on her wrinkled face. "Y'all get in a fight or something? You do this to her?"

Zach looked up, meeting her scolding gaze. Deep lines etched on her wrinkled face, a testament to years of caring for patients. Her voice carried a mix of authority and concern.

Zach shook his head, his voice filled with sincerity. "No, ma'am, I'd never lay a hand on Kay … my wife."

The nurse's eyes narrowed as she assessed the situation. She didn't hold back her judgment, her voice sharp and filled with disappointment. "I see that. I've seen dogs with more affection than you. Now quit being a jerk and comfort your terrified wife." The sound of her pen scratching against the dry erase board echoed in the room. "In case you need me, sweetie. I'll check on you in a few minutes." With a final pointed glare, the nurse turned and stepped out of the room, leaving Zach to confront his own guilt and uncertainty.

Zach reached down to touch her, his fingertips grazing her skin before quickly retracting, as if a surge of electricity had jolted through him. The room felt cold and lonely as Kayla, engulfed in misery, yearned for his touch. With a glimmer of hope, she reached out, entangling her fingers with his. The sensation of his touch sent tingles cascading up her arms, but Zach's body tensed in response.

Confusion etched across her face, Kayla questioned, "Why are you afraid to touch me? Aren't you my husband?" She shook her head, attempting to brush aside the stray bangs obscuring her view.

Zach's gentle touch brushed away the hair from her face, his teary eyes shimmering as bright as a cloudless sky. "Yes, I am. But it's complicated," he murmured, his voice filled with pain.

Locked in a gaze, Kayla felt an overwhelming rush of love coursing through her veins. "Then make it uncomplicated," she pleaded, her pale face displaying both confusion and determination. "Because all I remember is the sound of the gunshot. As my husband, you can fill in the gaps."

Taking a deep breath, Zach visibly struggled with the weight of his emotions. "What do you want to know?" he asked, his expression filled with anguish.

"Everything," she replied, her confusion giving way to a faint smile. The sound of her laughter resonated in the room, causing a momentary ease for Zach. He sat down on the edge of her bed, finally allowing himself to relax.

"You always were curious," he chuckled.

"What's my favorite food?"

"Is this amnesia-related or a test to see how well I know you?" His eyes twinkled with amusement.

"Guess you'll have to find out." Kayla breathed out the words as she ran her finger over the stubbly side of his chin. She admired his strong jawline and the dimple almost hidden. His touch felt so familiar, yet so wrong. "Are you sure we're married?"

Zach straightened his back, moving an inch away from her. "Yeah, why? You remember something?"

"No, I just wanted to make sure before I do this." She pulled the top of his shirt, making his body close enough to feel his breath on her lips. She leaned forward, planting her lips on his, claiming her husband's kisses for herself. Unsure why, but she felt the need to embrace him before someone snatched him away.

Zach wrapped his arms around her waist, pulling her body closer to his chest. She marveled at the security and emotion packed in one kiss. She couldn't remember him as her husband, but she was thankful he was.

He pulled away from her embrace, staring longingly into her eyes. "I-I shouldn't have done that."

"Why?" She rubbed the spot where his lips touched hers.

"I've loved you for so long, but I can't take advantage of you. Especially when you can't remember our past."

Kayla's head pounded at the hurt and regret plastered on his creamy-white face. What was he talking about? He loved her, but not anymore? That kiss was definitely from a man in love with his wife. Fear pricked her body. Although she didn't remember their past, she knew him now. He couldn't leave her. Not when everything seemed foreign besides his touch.

"Don't leave me?" She reached for his hand, clinging to the top of his fingertips.

Zach leaned over like someone had stabbed him with a knife. His face turned ashen white. "You don't know what you're asking me."

"Of course, I do." She scooted her body to an upright position, frowning. "Our past doesn't matter right now. I just want you."

Zach stepped away from her. Anger spread across his face at her words. "I've never been enough for you. I won't pretend I am now."

"I can't answer for the Kayla of the past, but right now, I want and need you." She opened her arms, hoping he'd accept her invitation and cling to her, allowing her to bask in his familiarity and security.

With a puff of air and a few mumbled words, he stepped to her side, wrapping her in his arms. "Kayla, what if this is a mistake?"

"All I know is we vowed to share the good and bad times together. I won't regret leaning on you in my time of weakness." She laid her head on his chest, wondering what the Kayla of the past did to wound this wonderful man in her arms. And vowing to love and cherish him from this day forward.

****

Zach wrapped his arms around her, inhaling the sweet scent of lilies that emanated from her hair. He marveled at how perfectly she fit against his body, like the missing piece of a puzzle. The softness of her touch made him never want to let go. But deep down, Zach knew this wasn't reality. Once her memory returned, their complicated past would surely hinder any chance of a future together. What was he even thinking? He had promised himself to resist her enchanting ways. Yet here he was, unable to forget the woman in his arms. Emotions and logic battled within him, a constant tug-of-war. And let's not forget, she had made him leave her. Kayla's facade of innocence was nothing short of shameful. What could he possibly do? Her warm brown eyes drew him in, just like they did back in high school. But he was a grown man, immune to the allure of beauty. And oh, she was undeniably beautiful, with flawless skin, lips that begged to be kissed, and captivating chocolate-colored eyes.

And then there was Sarah, her sister. In high school, she was a mere annoyance, always trailing behind them. Zach hardly noticed her, except as the kid who wouldn't leave them alone. Why would he have paid any attention to her? Sarah was awkward and lacked personality, a far cry from the woman she had become. Now, her mesmerizing green eyes sparkled with mischief and adoration whenever he met her gaze. And she could cook mouth-watering, hearty meals, unlike Kayla's burned TV dinners. The best part was that the marriage certificate hadn't scared her off. She knew that the marriage he had with her sister meant nothing. Honestly, he enjoyed the attention she gave him.

But now, Kayla's eyes shone with love and trust, replacing the cold, piercing look she used to give him. She resembled the girl he had fallen in love with, the one who still held the keys to his heart. Although he would never admit it, Paul believed God had given him a second chance to mend their broken marriage. It was possible, but did he truly want to tread that bitter path once again? He needed to get rid of her and place a barrier around his heart, one she could not chisel away.

"Zach?" Kayla's amusing voice broke through his thoughts. Her brown eyes danced with pleasure. *Don't stare into her eyes, man. It's a trick.* Too late. He held eye contact with her, searching for something beyond the playfulness that flashed in her eyes.

"Y-yes?" He swallowed the bile rising in his throat. The tiny room was closing in on him. He needed air and distance, not to mention a reality check.

"We'll go home together, right? You won't leave me?" Her innocent question smacked him on the side of the face. They hadn't had a home together in years, and even then, he wouldn't have called it a home. Campus housing wasn't the charming, newlywed home he would have chosen. Too much distractions and enticements. Avoiding her question, the door swung open as a group of people crammed into the little room. As if the day couldn't get any worse, her family walked in, and he wasn't high on any of their lists.

Zach's closeness to Kayla earned him a scolding glare from Stephen. Oh well, he would not let looks intimidate or threaten him. She wanted him here. Even if he wanted to flee and never look back.

"Honey, how are you feeling?" Belle leaned on the side of the bed, grabbing her cousin's hand.

"I've been better." Kayla pulled the covers to her chin, staring blankly at Belle. "Who are you again?"

Belle's soft laugh cut through the awkward silence in the room. "I'm your favorite cousin." She gave Stephen a playful wink.

"Don't listen to her. I've always been your favorite." Stephen leaned in, patting her on the arm. "When your memory returns, you'll remember all the crazy pranks we did. Like the time…"

"Babe, maybe she should forget your mischievous years. Quite the influence you had on her." Lily playing punched him in the side as his face mocked the pain.

"When will my memory return?" Kayla's quivering voice sounded over the playfulness of the room.

"Post-traumatic amnesia can last mere minutes to months. You banged your head pretty good, hence the stitches and mild concussion. Don't stress, your memory should return in due time." Stephen's lips curled into a smile at Kayla's surprise. "I'm a doctor and so is Lily."

Lily smiled, her eyes sparkling with warmth as she spoke. "Which is why you're coming home with us until you recover."

Yeah, like he'd let her family come in here and snatch her from him, brainwashing her with lies about him. The sterile hospital room smelled faintly of antiseptic, and he could hear the rhythmic beeping of the machines monitoring her vital signs. He was just her husband in the eyes of the law, but he hoped she would choose to stay with him.

"Kayla's coming home with me." The room fell silent, all eyes turning to him. It felt as if the air had turned heavy, laden with tension.

"No way." Stephen's defiant voice shouted as he crossed his arms, his gaze piercing like laser beams. Zach remained steadfast, refusing to show any signs of weakness or fear.

"I'm her husband. My title trumps y'all any day." A smirk tugged at the corners of Zach's mouth, but his eyes remained distant, not fully connecting with the amusement he tried to convey.

"What? Y'all are married?" Belle gasped in surprise; her reaction almost comical if Zach had been aiming for surprise.

"Now you want to play husband. I don't think so." Stephen took a step closer, his gaze never wavering from Zach's. His eyes held a steely determination. "Where were you the last four years? Playing house with someone else?"

Lily, sensing the escalating tension, quickly intervened. She entwined her arm with her husband's; her touch was a gentle attempt to calm him down. "Babe, not a good time."

"You want to settle this right now, doctor?" Zach's voice held a firm resolve. He didn't want to resort to violence, but he knew he could hold his own against a man who expected him to cower in his presence.

Kayla's screams suddenly pierced through the room, her body trembling with fear and distress. "Stop!"

"I'm about to stop him." Zach clenched his fist at his side, his words muttered under his breath.

"That's it. In the hall with me, now." Paul's grip tightened on the side of Zach's shirt, forcefully dragging him out into the sterile hallway.

59

"Get your hands off me." Zach brushed his partner's fingers off his shirt, frowning.

"Now's not the time to show yourself. You can prove yourself by being the man Kayla needs, not landing yourself in jail to cool off."

He had a point.

"Maybe I shouldn't go on vacation." Paul's words held an edge to them and a challenge.

"I can handle everything." Zach ran his fingers through his hair, willing himself to cool off. "Did you find anything out about Thomas or the shooter?"

"No. The shooter got away, and Thomas was nowhere to be found." Paul took a deep breath, sighing. "Your brother is a patrol cop. Call him if you need him. And don't let pride ruin this investigation."

"Don't trust me?" Peter, his brother, always had Zach's back. But his partner didn't trust him.

"I have a bad feeling about this case," Paul said.

"I'll call him if I need backup." Zach stepped out of the waiting area, back to Kayla's room. *Be cool, man. Kayla needs you.*

Zach took a deep breath, feeling the cool air fill his lungs as he slipped back into the dimly lit room. The soft glow of the overhead lights illuminated the worried faces of Kayla's family. He didn't care if they didn't welcome him; their opinions didn't matter. All he cared about was Kayla, and her warm smile greeted him as he moved towards the opposite wall where her family stood.

A bright-eyed redhead, her fiery hair catching the light, watched his every move from the corner of the room. The sight of her presence felt out of place, her presence unsettling. She was Kayla's sister, but she didn't come here for concern for Kayla.

"Hey, handsome." Sarah's voice slithered up next to him, her breath tickling his ear. He leaned away, feeling a shiver run down his spine. The room fell silent as every eye turned to him, their gazes filled with curiosity and judgment. Sarah's scandalous glare held him captive, branding him as hers. Conflicting emotions swirled within him, unsure of how he truly felt about that.

"Can we go soon?" Kayla's voice broke the tension, her body shifting in the hospital bed as she clutched a bouquet of roses in her trembling hands.

Sarah raised an eyebrow, her perfectly plucked brow furrowing. "Is she going somewhere with you?" Her disapproval hung heavy in the air.

"Kayla's going home with her husband until she recovers," Stephen spoke up, his voice laced with anger. He flexed his fist, a threatening gesture directed at Zach. The tension in the room intensified.

"Really, Zach! How could you?" Sarah stepped into his personal space, her enticing perfume filling his nostrils, clogging his airway. He struggled to maintain his composure as her words stung. "I thought you were better than that and finally picked the right sister." With a final glare, she stormed out of the room, slamming the door behind her.

"What's her problem?" Kayla's tear-filled eyes searched for answers as she fidgeted with the roses in her hands.

Zach closed the distance between them in two long strides, taking the roses from her trembling fingers. He glanced at the card, anger coursing through his veins. What kind of idiot stalked someone in the environment of the ER, surrounded by concerned family members?

Paul, his partner, snatched the card from his grasp. "Care Bear, we were so close to starting our lives together. Why did you run from me? I'm the only man you'll ever love." The words on the card sent a chill down Zach's spine. He exchanged a worried glance with his partner, knowing they had to stop this creep before he could hurt Kayla again.

****

"We live here?" Kayla grazed her finger over her bandage, wincing as a sharp pang of pain trickled down her forehead. The little house exuded a cozy-cottage vibe, enveloping her in a sense of warmth. The living room boasted of smooth wood paneling, emitting a faint earthy scent, and featured a masculine color scheme; a deep forest green and a rich tree-stump brown. The sight was not attractive, lacking any feminine touches that would show her presence. Her eyes scanned the outdated kitchen, the appliances emanating a faint hum of their ancient mechanisms. She searched for any hint of a feminine touch, but there was not even a dainty throw pillow to be found. It puzzled her. If they were truly married, why was there a lack of any pictures showcasing their wedding or their life together? As if sensing her thoughts, Zach leaned against the worn leather couch, his gaze fixed upon her.

The realization struck her suddenly she had a deranged admirer. Her family's disapproval of Zach had reached a boiling point, almost resulting in a physical altercation in the ER room. Could he be behind the unsettling flowers and cryptic cards? No, there was something about his demeanor that triggered a flicker of recognition within her heart. She couldn't quite grasp it, but she knew she had to stay close to Zach.

With a heavy sigh, Zach pushed himself off the couch, avoiding her gaze. The sound of his movements filled the room, mingling with the distant chirping of birds outside. "I live here, remember?"

"But we're married. That makes no sense." Married couples were supposed to share their lives and live together. Something didn't add up.

"It's complicated," Zach mumbled, running his fingers through his tousled hair, his eyes still evading hers.

Sounds like more than that. Like a nightmare. Maybe she didn't want to remember her former self if her presence brought frown lines etched across his handsome face. Tears sprang up in her eyes as she blinked back the realization that this arrangement was only temporary, and soon, she'd go back to her life, that didn't intersect with his.

"Kayla, don't cry." His words were soft, but he still kept his distance, like a man afraid she'd devour him if he got too close? No doubt she wounded him. But how? And did she have invisible scars from his hurtful words or actions? Buried in the depths of her memory were secrets, waiting to come out and destroy whatever second chance they had. Was this a road to a new beginning together? Or did he just feel obligated to look out for her until her memory returned and she could go on with her life?

"Our marriage makes no sense. You cower across the room from me, like I'm poison or something." Kayla wiped a fallen tear from her cheek, feeling heat creep up her face. "And who was that girl at the hospital? The one who seemed a little too friendly with you?"

Another sigh. "Your sister."

What? Kayla bent over like someone punched her in the stomach. "You're seeing my sister? No wonder my family doesn't like you. You're cheating on me with my sister!"

Zach raised his arms in the air in a surrender motion. "It's consensual. We're married in name only. I hadn't seen you in four years. Just so you know, I haven't dated the whole time. But your sister and I reconnected a couple of weeks ago. We're just friends."

Kayla couldn't breathe. She needed air fast, or she'd pass out. Maybe she shouldn't stay here. She ran to the door, opened it, leaning over as the breeze cooled her fiery face.

"Don't act all innocent. I've met your loser boyfriend, Thomas." Zach threw the words out like venom. Her heart pounding in her chest at his forceful words. She had a boyfriend? And a husband? What was wrong with her?

Zach stepped up behind her, offering support without touching her. "I'm sorry. I'm acting like a jerk. Let me show you to your room so you can rest."

Kayla followed him down a small hall, noticing the three closed doors. "Do you live here alone?"

Zach opened a door to a small, clean room. The room exhibited a hint of feminine touch. The walls were pale purple, matching the ancient looking flowery quilt. A tiny white dressed rested against the wall opposite a large window. A lily-scented candle burned on the nightstand.

"My younger brother, Peter, stays here with me. He's an officer in the city. Peter didn't want to work for the Sheriff's office like I do. He's forging his own path in law enforcement."

"Did he decorate this room?" If he took after Zach, she doubted it.

A deep chuckle floated through the small room. "No, he can barely match his socks. Britney, your best friend and my sister-in-law, took it upon herself to spruce up the room."

She had a best friend. Maybe Britney could shed some light on their past and why Zach refused to look her in the eye.

"I'll leave you to rest." He turned to go, but paused at the door. "I have some leftover Rigatoni. I can heat for supper."

"Thanks." Kayla shut the door, falling on the old bed. She felt so alone as tears poured from her eyes. She didn't like the person she was or that Zach perceived her to be. Could things get any worse? She closed her eyes, drifting to sleep, dreaming of a life with Zach. Not in pretense only, but a joy-filled marriage with no past or present obstacles standing in their way.

Kayla's hand shot out and yanked the pillow away, her fingers gripping it tightly. Her eyes darted around the dimly lit room, trying to make sense of her surroundings. A faint rustling sound echoed in her ears, causing her heart to race. It took a moment for her to realize that she had dozed off and slept through the day, awakening only when night had fallen.

Suddenly, a sharp popping noise shattered the silence, jolting her senses into high alert. Reacting swiftly, she rolled out of bed, narrowly avoiding the explosion of glass that erupted from the shattered window. Panic surged through her veins as she realized someone was shooting at her.

Her screams pierced the stillness of the night, a stark contrast to the violence unfolding around her. Another bullet whizzed through the broken window, missing her by mere inches. Desperation filled her as she frantically searched for an escape from this deadly ambush.

"God, help me," she whispered, her voice barely audible amidst the chaos. Crawling over the shards of glass strewn across the floor, she made her way towards the bedroom door. The unfamiliar sensation of praying felt strangely right in this dire moment.

"Kayla!"

The door swung open, revealing the strong, protective figure of Zach. His muscular arms swiftly pulled her out of the bedroom, shutting the door behind them. Safety was fleeting, and time was of the essence.

"I know. We need to get out of here," he said, his voice steady. His touch on her cheek provided a momentary reassurance. "I need you to be brave."

A knot formed in her throat as her body trembled with fear. Summoning every ounce of courage, she uttered, "I can try."

"We can't wait for the assailant to find us. That would sign our death warrant," Zach explained, his tone resolute. Taking hold of her hand, a sense of familiarity washed over her, but now was not the time for such thoughts. Zach's gaze locked with hers, his finger grazing her bottom lip. In an instant, tenderness vanished, replaced by a steely determination.

"Let's go." With a firm grip on his gun, he led her towards the front door, plunging into the enveloping darkness of the night. Gunshots reverberated through the air, each one a menacing threat. She bit down on her screams, placing her trust in Zach. Running behind him, she cared not about their destination, as long as she remained untouched by the piercing bite of a bullet.

****

Zach glanced back as a bullet ricocheted off the tree behind him. He wasn't a rookie, but he felt like one. He should have been patrolling the perimeter, knowing wherever Kayla stayed, danger was close by. Instead, he battled with his emotions, fighting off nostalgia and the butterflies swarming in his stomach from Kayla's closeness. He never expected being in the same town, let alone a house as his estranged wife. God had a funny way of doing things. Part of him wanted to bury past disappointments and secrets and start over. He would always love her, not be in love with her, though. But, if he let himself, those emotions could surface again. He glanced at their clasped hands, feeling a small tremble from her arms. Her closeness fogged his mind and destroyed his logical brain. How would he get out of this ambush alive if he couldn't focus beyond the feel of her skin on his?

Tears streamed from her face as another bullet zoomed over their heads. Whoever was after them was persistent. Zach didn't know if he could trust her ever again. Protect her? Yes. It was his job. Trust her and move on together? Probably not a smart move. Old, buried feelings of betrayal and anger would always stand between them. Best just to protect the victim and move on. Keep it professional.

Kayla's fingers tightened around his, her grip becoming desperate as she stumbled over a gnarled root jutting out of the ground. With lightning reflexes, he reached out and grabbed her arm, steadying her before she could collapse into the muddy terrain. The heavy rain had turned the once solid red clay into a treacherous mush, making their progress almost impossible.

"We have to keep moving." He helped Kayla through the sludge of muddy clay as they walked deeper into the woods.

As they trudged deeper into the woods, he could feel the squelch of the mud beneath his boots, each step a struggle against the suction-like pull. These woods, where he used to go hunting with his brothers, felt foreign and menacing now. The sanctuary of his stomping grounds had transformed into a nightmarish battleground. Hunting here would never be the same. Would he ever be able to hunt in these woods again?

Josh burned with contempt for Zach, the revelation of his shattered marriage breaking their brotherly bond. Eventually, Josh would get over it. He didn't hold grudges beyond a reasonable amount of time. But he'd always have Zach's back, even if he couldn't stand to look Zach in the face.

Peter, like Zach, possessed a similar personality - too focused and stubborn to maintain a lasting relationship. His charm and looks drew many college-aged females to him, but he had no time for romance. His professional aspirations took precedence, his goals of becoming a detective by twenty-two and a sergeant by twenty-five consuming his every thought. Nothing else mattered until he achieved them. Unrealistic? Maybe, but goals kept him out of trouble.

The distant sound of snapping twigs shattered his thoughts, jolting him back to reality. Awareness surged through him like an electric shock. Kayla stood hunched over, gasping for breath, her scratched and red-streaked arm trembling as she rubbed it. Mud covered her exposed skin, accentuating the exhaustion etched into her features.

The emptiness in her eyes spoke volumes - she wouldn't last much longer.

"Kayla, please, talk to me," he pleaded, finally realizing how consumed he had been with his own thoughts, neglecting her well-being.

"I'm fine," her breathy voice shook with each word.

Zach leaned in, wiping a smudge of mud off her pinkish cheek. Her golden-brown eyes locked with his, reminding him of all her love-filled looks that swelled his heart. The feeling of oneness and genuine joy stabbing him in the heart. They weren't leisurely hiking through the woods as a couple in love. No, they were running for their lives, thrown together by a job he was failing at. Best he remembered that. No turning back. And no going forward with a woman that destroyed his past and future with a few thoughtless acts. Sure, she looked the same, especially because she couldn't remember her contempt for him, but time would reveal her true thoughts and feelings she had for Zach. And no matter of playing pretend would change that. God hadn't entwined their lives or future together. If so, they'd be a couple.

"I'm gonna get us out of here." *Think, Zach. Where can we hide or go to lose the assailant?*

The sound of footsteps grew louder as someone angrily sloshed through the muddy ground behind them, cursing without a care for who could hear. Bullets zoomed wildly around their heads. Zach's grip tightened around Kayla's hand as he swiftly guided her behind a tree, his finger gently hushing her with a touch to her lips. Zach's body shivered as the guy's proximity sent icy pricks coursing through him. The urgency of the situation became clear - if he didn't take immediate action, one of the stray bullets would hit him or Kayla. Finding out what the assailant wanted was his priority, but he refused to put Kayla's life in danger to do so.

Zach leaned over, whispering in her ear. "When I return fire, run through those trees. Beyond the creek is a tiny cave. It's covered with trees, and hard to find, but I know you can do it."

Kayla's hollow eyes welled up with tears as she peered through the dense foliage. Distant sounds of a gunshot reverberated in the air, causing her to stumble forward, propelled by the forceful push from him. Urgency to keep her safe consumed him. The damp earth beneath his feet squelched as he raised his gun, ready to employ his hunting skills. The woods enveloped him, the scent of pine mingling with the adrenaline coursing through his veins. He knew he could remain undetected amidst the trees for hours, waiting to ambush the assailant and uncover their identity. Thoughts raced through his mind. Could it be a married man, driven by jealousy? Or perhaps Kayla's own missing memories held the key. He couldn't shake the nagging question about Thomas, Kayla's past acquaintance. Was he behind these attacks? The guy was a loser, but would he stoop so low as to harm her? If he couldn't have her, would he resort to such violence? Suddenly, Kayla's piercing scream shattered the silence of the woods. His concern outweighed the risk of exposing his position. He charged forward; the branches slapping against his body and his feet propelling him over the uneven ground. His heart pounded in his chest, a reminder of his recent lack of physical activity. But nothing could deter him from his sole mission—finding Kayla.

Chapter Four

"Ugh." Kayla swatted at a mosquito the size of a hummingbird. She glanced down at her mud-laced jeans, feeling itchy all over. She had no memories of trekking through the woods, so she couldn't be sure if this was a favorite pastime, but she doubted it. Nothing about this sweat-infused weather made her jump for joy. What she wouldn't give for ice cream? Ice cream? A memory popped into her mind of her downing a carton of minty-green goodness while sitting alone in an equestrian-decorated room.

Kayla hit a dangling tree branch out of her face, stepping into a sticky spiderweb unawares. "Yuck!" What if the eight-legged creature feasted on her for supper? Were there poisonous spiders in Tennessee? It didn't matter. This total nightmare would haunt her for a long time. Not to mention, a bad guy's bullets almost snatched her life away. She needed to remember that an armed assailant was determined to silence her. From what? She couldn't remember.

Kayla touched her forehead as a pounding headache shot through her head, glancing behind her. A sloshing noise jumped through her ears, making her heart drop. What was that noise? A deer? A hungry-looking bear? Lions? Which should she be afraid of more? The guy with the gun or the creatures with sharp teeth?

"Just keep moving," she mumbled under her breath. Why did Zach have to act all macho-protector? He wasn't bulletproof. If anything happened to him, she'd never forgive herself. What was it about this man that quickened her heart and caused flutters in her stomach? She couldn't remember anything about their marriage. Probably a good thing, considering how standoffish Zach seemed. One minute, she could see inside his guarded heart, the next second he locked his emotions away, leaving no hints to the man behind the badge. Was she just an assignment to him, or did their past matter?

A fuzzy scene popped into her mind as she stepped near a tiny, flowing creek, feeling the cool water splashing over her face.

"Kayla. I've loved you since we first met in algebra. I never knew running late for class would change my life." He ran his finger over her red-tinted lips, smiling.

"Besides the demerit, you added to your impressive collection." Her laughter floated through the muggy summer air. *"I stole your desk, not knowing it belonged to anyone."*

"They didn't call me demerit guy for nothing." He leaned over, brushing his lips over hers. *"You stole my desk and my heart. I knew my life would never be the same."*

"My mom made me so angry, uprooting my freshman year of high school and moving to some rural town in North Carolina." Kayla traced the outline of his faint mustache with her fingers. *"You're the reason I forgave her."*

"And you're the reason I survived high school." Zach kneeled on the pavement, pulling out a small velvet box from his pocket. *"I love you, Kayla Smith. Will you marry me?"*

Her mouth dropped open, staring at the nonexistent diamond ring. "Zach?"

"I know it's impulsive and we have our whole lives ahead of us, but I don't want to live if it's not with you."

"Tomorrow's graduation." Tears welled up in her eyes.

"Let's run off after graduation and get hitched. No one has to know." He slid the ring on her finger, kissing her knuckle. "Your parents are so busy with your younger sisters to even care. And my dad hardly calls to check on me since he moved to West Virginia. My mom has too many jobs to notice anything. What do you say?"

"Yes." Kayla jumped into his arms as they tumbled into the grass. "I'll love you forever."

"My sweet Kayla, forever seems too short." He kissed her on the forehead, his eyes twinkling. "I love you."

A snapping branch echoed through the dense forest, abruptly stealing the memory from her mind. She stood there, surrounded by towering trees, their leaves rustling in the gentle breeze.

"Hello?" she called out, her voice laced with a mix of curiosity and caution.

Lost in a blissful memory of laughter, she had momentarily forgotten her mission to find the hidden cave. Instead, she found solace by the gurgling creek, the cool water caressing her bare feet.

Suddenly, a surge of urgency jolted her, and she leaped to her feet, scanning her surroundings for any signs of another person. Maybe Zach had finally caught up to her, she thought. He was supposed to be following close behind, yet he was nowhere to be seen.

Before she could resume her search for the elusive cave, a strong, calloused hand covered her mouth, cutting off her air supply. Panic surged through her veins as she

73

struggled to break free. With a surge of adrenaline, she sank her teeth into her assailant's finger, her desperate yelp barely escaping her lips.

"Stop!" the raspy voice warned her. She turned around, staring at a familiar face. His handsome face lined with pops of purplish-blue bruises. His dark eyes were icy cold as he glared at her. Who was this guy? Friend or foe?

"Wh-who are you?" Kayla spit the words out, though her body couldn't stop shaking.

"Like you don't know. Stop the act." He gripped her arm, squeezing too forcefully. Pain shot up her arm, causing tears to form in her eyes. "We need to leave now."

Kayla forcefully pulled her arm away from the stone-eyed man, the roughness of his touch sending shivers down her spine. She couldn't shake off the feeling of familiarity, a nagging sense of recognition. "What are you talking about?" she questioned, her voice tinged with confusion.

Leaning in closer, the man whispered urgently, his eyes darting around the dense woods as if expecting trouble. The rustling leaves and distant sounds of wildlife intensified the tension in the air. "You're not safe here," he warned, his words barely audible. "We must leave before Detective Rivers arrives."

A surge of unease twisted in Kayla's gut, causing her to instinctively step back from the stern-faced man. The stench of manure clung to his clothes, making her stomach churn. Despite her discomfort, she mustered the courage to stand her ground, crossing her arms protectively across her chest.

"Stop!" Kayla's voice quivered slightly, betraying her apprehension. "I won't go anywhere with you."

With an exaggerated sigh, the man's lips curved into a frown as he closed the distance between them. The intensity of his dark brown eyes bore into her, raising goosebumps on her skin. She knew she couldn't trust this man to be alone with her. "Explain yourself," she demanded, trying to appear stronger than she felt.

"Kayla, we're running out of time," he insisted, his voice laced with urgency. The weight of his words hung heavily in the air. "If I have to forcefully take you with me, I will."

She couldn't deny the man's capability to overpower her. Though not heavily built, his physique suggested strength and agility. Frustration creeped into her voice as she attempted to stall for time, hoping for Zach's rescue. Kayla shook her head, her heart conflicted by the reliance she had on Zach. Trust was a delicate thing, and in her current predicament, feelings could be deceptive.

"Why are you trying to abduct me?" she questioned sharply, her eyes locked with his. She needed him to keep talking, to distract him long enough for help to arrive.

A deep, booming laugh erupted from the man, startling nearby birds into flight. The sound reverberated through the silence of the woods, leaving an eerie echo in its wake. "I'm one of the good guys," he chuckled, his finger tracing a muddy streak on her cheek. "I like the whole outdoorsy look. It's attractive."

A wave of revulsion washed over Kayla at the thought that she had chosen this man over her own husband. Bile rose in her throat, threatening to escape. How had she become a person who had both a boyfriend and a husband? "Are we...?" she began, her voice trailing off, unable to form the words.

His laughter continued, the mischievous glint in his eyes betraying his intentions. "I'm not the settling down type. But you, my dear, are my favorite teacher," he confessed, his voice tinged with a hint of seduction. "Our flirtatious banter is quite enjoyable. One of these days, I'll sweep you off your feet."

Kayla shook her head, trying to maintain her composure in the face of this unsettling revelation. She felt like a deceitful, heartless player. No wonder Zach had kept his distance. "I'm married," she stated firmly, hoping her words would deter him.

His discomfort was obvious as he shifted his weight, his gaze scanning the dense forest. "I've known you for years, and you've never mentioned a husband. It's rather peculiar." He remarked, his unease palpable in the surrounding silence.

Kayla opened her mouth to speak, but what could she really say? I'm a traitorous woman. No, a traitorous married woman. Stay away from me.

"Kayla, someone is stalking you. But it's not that innocent anymore." He touched her chin, tilting her face to look up at his. "He attacked me and would have killed me if not for my amazing karate skills. I won't let him harm you, especially in your confused state."

"God, I don't know what to do," Kayla mumbled, taking a step away from the man, her shirt snagging a low-lying tree branch. "God, help me."

****

Of all the idiotic things he could have done, letting Kayla stumble off in the woods alone was top of his list of the foolish things he'd done. The old Kayla would have bucked at his command, reminding him he was her husband, not her drill sergeant. Faced with an abductor, he had no time to coddle her with sugar-laced words. One bullet was all it took to end a life. He'd seen it before. The haunting memory, a regret he could never reverse. Zach's arrogance cost a life. Not just any life, but his partner's life. He left behind a wife who never got to embrace her fallen husband again or a child begging God to bring his daddy home, only to be disappointed. Zach blinked back a stray tear. He failed before; it couldn't happen again. Different state, same story.

His commanding officer, his father, all but begged him to leave the force or face reprimands. Zach wanted to walk away from his failed career like he had done for his wrecked marriage, but he had clung to the only thing he had left—his job. Pulling some strings, his father helped him transfer to East Tennessee, where his brothers lived. Working for the sheriff's office had its perks, and small-town living screamed a false sense of security, but time made him wiser. He wouldn't go into a situation being led by his hothead and arrogance that had no place in a law enforcement's life. He used to pray before running into an unknown, dangerous situation. Even though he had tried rekindling his faith and still went to church, the desire to seek God wasn't there. He didn't want to ask God for safety. Zach wanted to blame God for abandoning him and snatching a life away prematurely. Life wasn't fair. God wasn't fair.

Zach's insides burned with contempt as he swiped back a branch from his face. Now wasn't the time to be playing hide-and-seek with his estranged wife and an assailant. His gunfire had held the perp up, but what if the guy had fooled him all along and his gun show was just a rouse, waiting for his partner to grab Kayla? If so, he fell for it. Like an idiot.

He paused, listening for any signs of a struggle. Nothing. Not even a peep from the heavily populated wildlife that claimed these woods as their own.

"Why did you send a terrified, amnesiac woman into unknown territory? How did sending her away protect her?" Zach clinched his teeth together as the words punched him in the gut.

Zach stomped past the overflowing creek, kneeling down, searching for any clues of Kayla. She was here. He glanced at a set of muddy prints, likely belonging to her. But another set of larger shoe prints sent him rubbing the top of his gun for reassurance. Someone ambushed Kayla. The assailant had a partner.

If only his partner hadn't left town. Zach shook his head as he stepped near another muddy print. *Is this your way of handling it? Rivers, you endangered the life of a civilian. What is wrong with you?* His father's deep, piercing voice popped into his mind. His father's voice, a voice tied up around his failures, never a welcomed sound.

Zach yanked his phone out of his pocket. He needed backup. Fast. He dialed his younger brother's number, willing him to answer his phone.

"What's up, bro?" Peter's smooth, tenor voice floated through the phone.

"Where are you at?" Zach's husky voice came out hoarse and raw.

"I may or may not be eating a bag of chocolate candies while flipping through a stack of reports," Peter laughed. Zach imagined his brother's legs propped on his cluttered desk, bluegrass music humming in the background, shifting through endless piles of desk work.

"I'm in the woods behind our house. One, possibly two perps after us. Shots fired, need backup."

"On it." He heard shuffling in the background, likely his brother running out of the police station. "Who's with you?"

Zach slid his gun out of the holster, spotting the tiny cave under a canopy of tree branches.

"Bro, answer me," Peter's voice sounded distant. He probably put Bluetooth on. "Are you alone?"

"No, my wife is somewhere in the woods." Now wasn't a good time to bring up his secret wife. Never was a good time to bring up his wife. But his brother needed to know what the stakes were. Besides, he'd find out eventually, anyway. Being his roommate and all.

"Your what?" Peter growled into the phone.

"Look, I'm not proud of past mistakes. I'll explain later." Or if I'm lucky, you'll never bring up this conversation again.

"Married? Where has your wife been all these years?"

Zach blew out a harsh breath. His brother would never understand. Peter was a spokesman for Christian living. His biggest sins were tossing his candy trash on the ground, forgetting to throw it away. "Drop it. What's your ETA?"

Peter sighed into the phone. He knew his brother wanted to chunk Bible verses at him. As kids, while Peter memorized verses for church, Zach read comic books, drifting farther away from the faith his mother tried to instill in her boys. No surprise when Zach stopped going to church at a ripe age of fourteen. If he would have heeded his mother's warnings, maybe his life wouldn't be in a mess.

"Ten minutes."

"No sirens." Zach slid his phone in his pocket, listening for any hints to Kayla's location. The wind carried a soft whimper, a voice he could never forget. Kayla needed him.

Without considering the danger, he burst into the cave, drawing his weapon. Frozen in fear, he stared at a man, arms wrapped around Kayla's wrist, pulling her farther into the cave.

"Police! Stop!" Zach pointed his gun at the perp. Small beads of sweat poured down his forehead. He stepped closer, eying the suspect. "Thomas Holmes?"

"Back up." His voice shot up in a harsh tone, fingers trembling. "Kayla is coming with me."

He stared at Thomas. The guy was a loose wire. His hands tightened around Kayla's wrist, producing faint pleas from Kayla's stony face. "I won't leave her with you."

"Thomas, I'm one of the good guys." Zach felt dumb, trying to explain himself to an unstable loser. Thomas didn't appear to have a weapon, but he didn't know what he carried in his pockets.

"Not likely." Thomas fixed his icy glare Zach's way, pulling Kayla closer to his body. "She has amnesia or something and you preyed on her weakness by bringing her home and playing house? What twisted fantasy motivated you?"

Was he serious? Zach wasn't taking advantage of Kayla at all. In fact, her presence bordered on an awkwardness that he'd rather forget. Yeah, sure, he could have let her go home with Stephen and his wife. They were family and doctors. But some selfish motive drove him to prove his worth to her family, maybe erase the guy they saw him as. Maybe feed the part of him that wanted her in his life. What did it matter? Kayla wasn't his anymore. Never truly belonged to him.

"Let her go." Zach inched closer, noticing the bruises on Thomas's face. Something didn't add up. Where had

Thomas been after the thug had tried abducting Kayla? Was he working for the assailant? Who beat him up?

"I won't let you take advantage of her." Thomas's unwavering stance caused Zach's pulse to beat a little faster.

"Man, let her go and we can discuss this rationally." Zach stood closer, close enough to pry Kayla out of his grip. He gazed into her deep brown eyes. The trust and admiration flashing back at him nearly toppled him over. After four years of distance, or rather, hiding, she looked at him like he could do no wrong. Amnesia, nothing more, caused her starry-eyed appearance. None-the-less, he didn't deserve her silent encouragement. He didn't even want her adoration. That would take them down a traveled road that ended at a dead end, like their past and future. No. He needed to wipe her love-filled look off her face. He didn't want her love. She broke his heart and her actions drove him to walk away four years ago. No innocent gaze would change that.

"No."

"Fine. Take her. I never wanted her anyway." Definitely not true. Kayla was his world. He loved her. Maybe after all these years, he could admit infatuation, not love, pushed every decision he had with her. Love would have hankered down, pushing through the problems, not walked away.

Kayla's eyes filled with tears as she chewed on her bottom lip. He could only imagine the thoughts going through her pretty head. He just crushed her dreamy-eyed gaze in a second. Replaced by a fire that reminded him of the woman he left behind. The woman he could never reconcile with.

"Thomas. I can decide who I go with." She jerked her wrist out of his grasp, giving both men the death-glare. "Right now, it's neither one of you."

Thomas backed up like her words had physically pinched him in the gut.

Zach yanked his cuffs out of his pocket, slapping them on Thomas's wrist. "Let's take a little walk and figure out what's going on."

"I'm not the thug that's after her." Thomas pulled his arm, trying to break free. "I'm protecting her from you."

Likely story.

A bird chirp floated through the woods, alerting him that backup had arrived. His brother's secret call. With help, he'd figure out what was going on.

****

Their resemblance was uncanny. Same bright blue eyes, wavy blond hair, left dimple, a smile that could light up the world. Peter Rivers was an attractive man. Only thing, his eyes danced with a twinkle, whereas Zach's eyes were dim, to the point of lifelessness. Clearly, Zach's haunted past had wiped the boyish mischief out of his deep-closed off eyes. Did she have a part in stifling out the light in his eyes?

"Are you listening or gawking at my little brother?" Zach's words held no amusement. His blue eyes bore into her soul, making her squirm.

Kayla's face turned five shades of red. Busted. *Focus Kayla on anything but the tender-eyed man next to you.* It wasn't attraction, just a curiosity for the guy sitting next to her. She glanced to the side, catching a side glance of Peter, a smile plastered on his face.

"I remember you in high school." Peter's laughter floated in the air like a melody. "All of my friends had a crush on you, including me. Why did you end up with this loser?"

Good question. But Kayla suspected underneath Zach's hard core laid a vulnerable, loving man. And the woman who peeled away the layers of his heart received a treasure that never faded. Had she been that woman before? She knew she wasn't now. Zach barely looked at her, but when he did, she didn't like his steely gaze. Oh, to have the tender love and affection from Zach Rivers.

Zach rolled his eyes at his brother's words. He leaned in the chair across from Thomas, getting into his personal space.

"I can't remember, but I'd take his hard-core self any day. Your flirtatious ways produce nothing substantial that lasts." She smiled innocently as her words caused a slight smile on Zach's face.

"Not true. If I were your husband, I'd cherish you, and never let you go." Only if Zach had felt the same way. Kayla slouched on the couch, wanting to be anywhere but in the same room with these three men. Why did Zach leave? He obviously didn't cherish her, but why? Was Kayla Smith a terrible person? Or was Zach playing her being an award-winning actor? She shook her head, hoping the memories would seep back into her brain from the vigorous shake. Besides a headache, it did nothing for her memory.

"Mr. Holmes, start at the top. What happened when you drove Ms. Smith home?" Zach sat upright in his chair, the sound of his pen tapping against the edge of his notebook filling the room. Despite the tension in the air, he appeared relaxed, his jaw set firmly.

Thomas cleared his throat, shifting uncomfortably in the creaking wooden chair. "We were joking around, having a good time. The atmosphere was light, but I couldn't shake the feeling that something was off." He cast a sly glance towards Kayla, causing her heart to quicken. Doubt filled her mind as she found it difficult to look at him without getting the creeps.

Zach ran his fingers through his tousled blond hair, a habit that Kayla quickly picked up on. His disheveled locks tempted her to reach out and feel their texture, wondering if they were silky or coarse, much like his personality. Lost in her thoughts, she must have been gawking because Peter tapped her on the shoulder, winking mischievously.

Zach's hard glare snapped her back to reality, a clear warning to behave or face the consequences. As if there would really be any consequences. What could he do? Send her to bed without dessert? She scoffed at the thought, reminding herself that she was a grown woman, not a child. His looks may intimidate criminals, but they held no power over her.

"Facts. Get to them," Zach muttered under his breath, his voice low and gruff. The way he spoke reminded Kayla of a bulldog, and she never wanted to be on the receiving end of his scolding. But it seemed like that's where she always ended up.

"Deep in conversation, I didn't notice the car tailing us. Suddenly, it rammed into us, forcing us off the road." Thomas's voice softened as he glanced towards Kayla, his concern obvious. Maybe her first impression of him was incorrect. Maybe he was more than the self-centered jerk she had pegged him as. "Kayla hit her head on the dashboard and blacked out for a minute."

Zach leaned forward, his eyes narrowing with intensity. "Description of the perpetrator?"

"He wore a mask, his presence mirroring my own in physique and height. No tattoos or distinctive marks adorned his body." Thomas fidgeted with his handcuffed wrists, the cold metal biting into his skin. "We traded blows, and I left him worse off than he left me. Unaware of his accomplice, he seized me and tossed me into the back of his car. As the engine roared to life, a gunshot pierced the air, and I glimpsed Kayla sprinting into the dense woods, desperate for escape. Before I could react, the perpetrator sped off, leaving Kayla and his partner stranded amidst the trees."

"Do you have any recollection of the car's make and model?"

Thomas moistened his dry lips, wincing at the pain. The bruises on his face seemed to amplify his discomfort. "It was a dark, compact car, but I focused my attention elsewhere."

"Where did the assailant take you, and how did you break free?"

"We ventured about three miles from the crime scene. I maneuvered my hands to loosen the restraints and leaped out of the moving vehicle." Thomas gestured with his hands, the clinking of the handcuffs resonating throughout the room. "Just before I made my escape, I overheard the assailant mentioning your name and engaged in a conversation that I couldn't quite decipher."

"So, because of that, you assumed I must be involved with the attacker?" Zach's eyes blinked, his stoic expression unwavering. Did he ever allow himself to smile, or was he forever entrenched in his role as a police officer?

"My friend's husband, who I never knew about, waltzed back into her life simultaneously as a stalker and assailant tried to destroy her. Admit that doesn't sound sketchy?"

He had a point. And his testimony left more questions than answers. Like, how did she know Thomas? What really went on between her and Zach? Was her stalker and abductor the same person? When would her memory return?

"Why didn't you go to the police?"

"Too scared. I got out of town for a couple of days. Then looked for Kayla," Thomas said.

From his expression, he wasn't buying it. Zach closed his notebook shut, leaning over and taking the cuffs off of Thomas's wrist. "You're free to go, but don't leave town."

Thomas glanced Kayla's way, signaling her to come to him.

"What are you doing?" Zach stood to his feet. Crossing his arms over his bulky chest.

"I'm taking Kayla with me."

"I don't think so. You're still on my suspect list." Zach stepped to her side, daring the man to touch her.

"And Detective Rivers, you're on mine." Thomas stomped to the door, staring at Kayla, deciding if he should take her or not.

Kayla had had about enough of this macho man persona. She didn't need either men dictating what she did or who she stayed with. "Just so you both know, I'm not a helpless female who can't decide for herself. I have amnesia, but I'm not crippled. Fight it out. I don't care, but if I had a choice, I'd ditch both of you." She stormed from the room, slamming the guest room's solid door.

Of all the nerves, they treated her like a helpless child. She was many things, but a helpless child she was not. Kayla paced back and forth in the small room, working off some of her steam. Both men seemed to care, or rather just want to control her life. She didn't need a man to feel safe. Kayla was sure her old self would agree with her thoughts. Kayla stopped pacing, falling to her knees as the cold hardwood seeped into her bones. *God, what do I do? I'm at a disadvantage here. Who am I? Where do I belong? Who is after me? I have a gaping hole in my memory, and I'm not sure what to do.* Tears fell from her eyes as peace flooded her soul. It was as if God audibly told her to be still and wait where she was. With Zach.

****

"So, what do you think?" Zach leaned against the rough, textured wall; his gaze fixed on Peter.

"That you're an idiot." Peter sunk into the plush, over-sized recliner, the fabric creaking under his weight, as he casually threw his hands behind his head.

"What?" Zach shook his head, his brows furrowing in a frown. His younger brother never held back his opinion. Nor did he know anything about tact. But Zach valued his professional opinion. His personal one, not so much.

"Kayla Smith?" Peter let out an exaggerated sigh, the sound echoing through the room. "How in the world did you swoon her and con her into marriage? A marriage that doesn't even exist."

Zach didn't want to discuss his wife or failed marriage with anyone, especially his by-the-book brother. The harsh fluorescent light overhead cast a sterile glow on the room, intensifying his discomfort. Peter wouldn't understand, nor did he care to share his raw emotions with a man who looked up to him as a moral leader. "What do you think of Thomas Holmes?" he asked, his voice tinged with desperation, hoping to guide the conversation back to a safety zone.

"He's hiding something. I'd keep him on the suspect list." Peter's words hung in the air, a heavy silence filling the room.

"My thoughts exactly." Zach's eyes roamed to the closed bedroom door in the dimly lit hallway. The faint scent of lavender wafted through the air, a lingering reminder of Kayla's presence. Should he go after her, offering a shoulder to cry on, or in her case, a face to pound on? With conflicted emotions, he reluctantly stepped away from the door, sinking into the worn, comfortable embrace of the couch. The cool leather fabric provided a soothing touch, easing the tension in his weary body.

"You gonna tell me how my brother won the heart of the only girl my buddies and I ever crushed on?" Peter blinked his eyes, a mischievous twinkle flashing in their depths.

Zach had hoped his brother would drop it. Fat chance of that. Fine. He'd give him an abbreviated version, enough to get him off his back. "I don't want this new revelation to mar your high opinion of me. Since I'm your favorite brother and all." Truth be told, all three of the Rivers brothers were close. Which is why his secret marriage made it awkward with his brothers, since he kept nothing from them. He even told them about his shattered career and how hard he fought to keep it together after his partner's murder.

"Yeah, sure you are." Peter rolled his eyes, lowering his voice. "Seriously, if I had married Kayla Smith, I'd be in there comforting her instead of looking at your ugly mug."

"We ran off right after graduation and married. Our love being too strong to stay apart any longer." A smile played on Zach's face as memories from their early days together attacked his mind. No doubt he loved her and wanted their marriage to work, but reality sank in fast. Marriage was extremely hard. He didn't have the stamina for it.

"I'll buy your love-sap story. She's still the prettiest woman I've ever seen." Peter moved his legs to the floor, the thump vibrating the wooden floors. "What I don't get is why you messed it up."

Zach ran his fingers through his hair, needing something to do with his nervous energy. "I'm not proud of my failure as a husband. But I could chalk it up to our terrible role model of a father who walked away from Mom and us when he couldn't take the heat."

"You could, but that'd be lame. You're nothing like our father."

Warm, fuzzy feelings replaced the bitter chill of his heart as his brother's words bandaged up his aching heart. Zach compared himself to his father a lot. He never quite measured up to his stellar law enforcement career, but his personal life was a mess. Zach wasn't anything like his father, but maybe he really was. He left Kayla in the heat of the moment, licking his pride, just like his father had.

"I know that wounded-puppy-dog look." Peter climbed out of the chair, moving to the couch next to his brother. "You're nothing like him, Zach."

Easy for him to say. He didn't know the grueling details of how he left his wife, blaming her for his choices. "I never wanted to be like him. I hated him for destroying our home. His monthly child support helped pay the bills, but that's as far as his reach went in our lives."

"But?"

"When I left Kayla, he's the guy I ran to. I needed consolation, and who better to get it from than the man who walked out on us?" Zach punched his fist into the arm of the couch, wishing it was his father's face. "He convinced me that Kayla was at fault. That sometimes men walked away. It didn't make us horrible people, but wise, knowing when to call it quits."

"Don't beat yourself up about it. God's given you a chance for restoration. March into her room and beg for forgiveness. She's worth it. You're worth it. And your marriage is worth saving."

Was Peter right? Could he really seek forgiveness and try to repair their marriage? His heartbeat quickened at the thought. He had loved Kayla with more passion than should be legal, but it didn't save their marriage. "I appreciate your pep talk, but there's no going back."

"Bro, what is wrong with you?"

Good question. "Realizing I'm just like the man I've despised all these years hits home the fact that I'm awful at relationships. There's no point going down a dead-end road."

"Zach, you're nothing like him." Peter glanced at his phone as he stretched to his feet.

"Maybe, maybe not. It doesn't matter. Nothing changes why I left. My ... Kayla wasn't innocent and I can never take that mistrust back. I appreciate the counseling session, but this conversation is over."

"Bro..."

"Drop it, Peter. I don't want to hear another word."

"You still love her?" Peter stepped into the kitchen, grabbing a bottle of water, chugging down half the bottle.

"My love for her died four years ago." Anger flowed throughout his body. She destroyed their marriage more than he had.

"I wouldn't be so sure about that. Neither one of you signed the divorce papers."

He had a point. For some odd reason, they stayed married through the years. But it didn't matter, he would never go back.

"Zach, remember, there's always hope." Peter stepped to the door, saluting his brother before slipping out of the house.

Easy for him to say. He hadn't destroyed his past and future with one lousy action.

Before he knew what was happening, the guest room door creaked open, sending a trembling Kayla rushing into his arms. His mind screamed to disentangle her from his body, stepping away for his own sanity. But he couldn't do it. It felt so nice feeling her body close to his. Her heartbeat echoed through his chest as he ran his fingers through her blond, silky strands. Her vulnerability chiseled away the stone around his heart, bringing to life a longing he thought died years ago.

On impulse, he brushed his lips over hers, taking in the sweet taste of her chocolate lips. Her body fit against his like God had designed her as his other half. The half he let get away four years ago. Panic mixed with a deep, buried emotion overwhelmed his senses.

Could they really go back and start over? Did he really want to? If the intensity of the kiss was any clue, Kayla still loved him. But She didn't deserve his forgiveness. Wrapping her tighter in his arms, he rested his face in the crook of her neck, sampling the exotic scent of her hair. It was so wrong, but it felt so right.

"Zach?" her shaky voice whispered his name as someone pounded on the front door. Exactly what he needed, distance and a distraction. Reluctantly, he peeled her body off of his, regretting the loss of their closeness.

He ran to the door, flinging it open, wincing as the red head pushed past him into the house, carrying a covered dish. The aroma of Italian food made his stomach growl. She shoved the dish at him, taking in the scene before her. As if life couldn't get any more complicated, he squirmed under the intense glare from his wife's sister. The woman who was offering him a second chance at life and maybe even love. Zach whispered a silent prayer and slammed the front door. He needed God's direction more now than he had in years.

Chapter Five

An eerie silence filled the room, broken only by the soft ticking of the clock on the wall. Kayla's eyes glared over her sister's sharply defined face, her beauty holding a mysterious and unconventional allure. There were no memories of sisterly bonds or late-night chats, only the lingering bitterness of her sister's attempt to steal her husband. The air was thick with tension, making Kayla feel like an outsider.

She could almost taste the awkwardness in the room, like a bitter aftertaste. The piercing glares sent her way felt like sharp daggers, as if she were the one guilty of betraying a marriage. Her sister's presence seemed to cast a dark cloud over the room, amplifying the discomfort. Kayla wondered if she should leave, allowing them a moment alone, but the hostility directed towards her made her hesitate.

Before her sister's intrusion, she had shared a vulnerable moment with Zach, feeling the depth of his emotions in a single kiss. With unresolved feelings for her, it puzzled her why he would pursue her sister. Maybe her amnesia was playing tricks on her, making her search for something that wasn't there. She longed for her memories to return, hoping it would bring clarity to their twisted relationship.

"Don't you need to rest? You look pale and sick." Sarah's voice broke the silence, her words laced with false concern. The sound was like ice cracking, sending shivers down Kayla's spine. Her sister sliding onto the couch next to Zach, their legs almost touching but not quite, made Kayla's skin crawl. The air felt heavy with deceit, as if a storm were brewing beneath the surface.

"I feel peachy. What are you doing here?"

Sarah's icy blue eyes bore into hers like a laser slicing through an object. "Just checking on my big sister."

Liar.

"Which is why I think you should go lay down." Sarah tapped her fingers on the cushion between her and Zach. Her finger grazing the edges of his leg.

Kayla's gaze shifted to Zach; his discomfort was obvious in his eyes. Did he want her to leave, too? The conflicting emotions swirling within her made her regret not leaving with Thomas. The room seemed to close in on her, suffocating her with its palpable tension. She longed for an escape, a respite from the torment that surrounded her.

She jumped up from the creaking wooden chair, the force almost causing it to tip backward, her hand grabbing the covered dish from the coffee table. Kayla needed something to occupy her restless hands and racing mind. The air carried a faint hint of spicy cologne, mingling with the scent of the dish's warm contents. "I'll heat this up," she said, her voice laced with determination.

"Can you even turn an oven on?" Sarah's voice taunted. Her words sliced through the air, laced with a bitter edge disguised as a joke, and they pierced the depths of Kayla's heart. The room suddenly felt suffocating, as if someone had sucked all the oxygen out.

Kayla shot Zach a disapproving glare, her eyes filled with a mix of hurt and anger, before seeking refuge in the kitchen. Her hands shook slightly as she shoved the glass dish into the oven, the metallic clink of the oven door closing, providing a brief distraction from the chaos in her mind. Leaning against the cool granite counter, she longed for the solace of open space and fresh air, but for now, the confined kitchen would have to suffice.

Her pulse quickened, pounding in her ears like a relentless drumbeat. The events of the day replayed in her mind like a horror movie on a loop. First, the sound of gunshots reverberated through the air, jolting her into a state of panic. Then, the memory of Thomas's attempt to abduct her flooded her thoughts, leaving her feeling vulnerable. And now, her own sister shamelessly flaunted herself in front of Zach, using her mysterious allure to entice him. The combination of emotions threatened to overwhelm her, leaving her lightheaded and nauseous. She desperately needed fresh air, the cool breeze against her skin to ground her.

Sarah's venomous words slithered into the kitchen, her presence suffocating. "Cut the act. He's my man, now. You're old news. Save yourself the embarrassment and let him move on."

Kayla took a deep breath, trying to calm her racing heart, but the smell of Sarah's overpowering cheap perfume assaulted her senses, adding to the tension in the room. "We're married," Kayla mustered, her voice steady but tinged with a hint of vulnerability.

A mocking laugh escaped Sarah's lips; her face contorted with contempt. She moved closer, invading Kayla's personal space, her breath heavy with the stench of bitterness. "Like that worthless marriage certificate means anything to either of you," she spat, her words dripping with malice. "He's mine, and I'll do whatever it takes to keep it that way."

Kayla's patience snapped. Without a second thought, she stormed out the back door, her footsteps echoing on the wooden porch. The distant sound of leaves rustling in the wind provided a momentary respite from the chaos inside. She rushed towards the edge of the woods, not caring that danger lurked in the shadows. The taste of fear lingered on her tongue, but the thought of confronting her sister was far more terrifying. Perhaps Zach, with his flirtatious subtleties and her conniving sister, was supposed to be together. Kayla would rather face the possibility of a bullet than the destruction her sister threatened to bring upon her life.

"God, I doubt I'm a good Christian woman. Especially with this web of entanglement I'm ensnared in, but please get me out of this mess. I need Your help." Her whispered prayer floated to the edge of the woods, drifting off toward the heavens.

"Ahem."

Kayla jumped at the sound of someone behind her. Arms pulling her away from the woods. "You shouldn't be out here."

"Don't touch me." The nerve of this man. Did he think he could charm both sisters?

Zach dropped his arms, raising them in the air in a surrender motion. "Why are you out here alone?"

Oh, I don't know giving you and my traitorous sister time alone. The house isn't big enough for both of us. "Felt like I was in the way."

"Kayla..." He grabbed the top of her shoulder, turning her to face him.

"Stop. I don't need to hear any lame excuse for you and my sister. Frankly, I feel like a fool. Having amnesia will do that to a person." Kayla ran her tongue over her lips, feeling the gesture comforting. "I barged back into your life, unaware of the status of our marriage."

"Kayla..."

"When I woke up in the hospital room, and the nurse informed me I had a husband, I knew everything would be okay, because I had someone who would love me back to health. Your title as husband deceived me. This whole twisted web has destroyed everything good in this world."

"Please, just come back inside with me." He reached for her hand, stopping short of actually touching her.

"No. I won't be the third wheel here." Kayla pointed her finger at his face, her finger trembling with anxiety. "Nor will I pretend like life is dandy."

"Calm down."

Kayla felt on the verge of exploding. "Calm down? You are seeing my sister. Of all people. You're destroying our marriage vows for a cheap relationship. I'm so stupid."

"It's not like that." Zach ran his fingers through his hair again, his voice just above a whisper.

"I have amnesia, but I'm not naïve." She pretended to throw glasses off her face. "My love-covered glasses are gone. I see how you really are."

"Sweetie, you're overreacting." His sweet as sugar words would not diffuse the fury in her heart. She couldn't look at his handsome face and not remember her sister's threatening words.

"You don't get to control how I feel." Kayla stomped away from him, feeling a chunk of her heart shatter into hundreds of pieces at her feet. "I'm leaving. And I never want to see you again." Who cares if bad guys were hunting her? She'd find another way to protect herself. Because staying with Zach made her long for things that would never take place. Like an honorable marriage and an oasis away from the stress of the world. Staying any longer would destroy her heart to the point of no return.

"Kayla, it's my job to protect you."

"Obviously, you're not talking about your role as a husband. So, as a detective, you're fired," she yelled over her shoulder.

"It doesn't work like that. I don't work for you." A barely audible chuckle escaped his lips. "You're a piece of work, Kayla."

It took all her self-control not to walk back to him and wipe his smirk off his face. Knowing he was trying to rile her up, she ignored him.

A dark car pulled into his driveway. Kayla ran off toward the car, needing any means of escaping Zach and her sister.

"Kayla, don't get in that car."

Ignoring him, she opened the passenger door, jumping inside before he rounded the corner into the front yard. As the car sped out of the driveway, Kayla's anger mixed with regret, hoping she made the right decision.

****

Kayla gripped the edges of the coarse seatbelt, running her fingernails through the rough material. Not one for impulsiveness, she stared at the locked passenger door, praying her decision to flee from Zach wouldn't cost her life. Willing to calm her erratic pulse, she cast a sideways glance at the guy driving the car. The one she ignorantly jumped into. His midnight black hair stood straight in the air like an electrical current zapped it minutes before. He smelled of fast food and an overpowering spicy cologne that made her insides queasy. Despite his ruffled appearance, his glassy eyes held a kindness that Zach lacked. Maybe a personality.

"Um ... where are you taking me?"

He turned down his classic music, fingers drumming the steering wheel, acknowledging her for the first time. "I haven't decided." His deep voice threw her a web of sticky silk that she couldn't break through. What did he mean by that? Did she jump into the car with a psycho?

"Meaning?" She gulped down the bile rising in her throat. She glanced out the window, contemplating escaping through the locked door. He didn't have a gun that she could see. So, Kayla could easily unlock the door and dash off into the woods. Story of her life.

"You got in my car, remember?" He glanced her way. His glassy, brownish-black eyes coursed over her body, making her queasy stomach revolt. Who was this guy? His intentions seemed less than honorable. How did he know Zach? Would Zach even come looking for her? She told him to leave her alone, and she prayed he ignored her angry words.

"What's your name?" Let's put a name to that dirty, creepy looking face.

"Not important." He turned down a country road, taking the curve a little too fast for Kayla's queasy stomach.

"I'm gonna be sick. Can you pull over?" She gripped the cold metallic door handle, knowing she couldn't keep the vomit down much longer.

A sly smirk spread across his uneven, tan face, the corners of his lips curling up like a predator closing in on its prey. His bug eyes bulged out of his head, their intense gaze fixated on her, sending a wave of unease through her body. The creepy grin on his face sent shivers down her spine, as if she had willingly entered the car of a deranged nightmare.

"I have a bag on the floor," he said, his voice laced with a hint of malice. She glanced down at the takeout bags littering the floor around her feet, their greasy contents inching closer to gobbling up her shoes. The stench of stale food filled the air, mixing with the sickly sweet scent of his cologne. Clearly, this guy had no life, surrounded by the remnants of his meals.

"What will you do with me?" Kayla voiced, the burning question flashing in her mind, her words catching in her throat as she tried to suppress the urge to vomit. No way would she touch a greasy, stinky bag by her feet.

His crooked grin pierced through her heart, his yellowed teeth glistening under the dim light of the car. "Looks like you could use a good time. I don't get female company much," he replied, his voice dripping with a mixture of anticipation and desperation.

Obviously.

"I'm exhausted, and would be terrible company," she retorted, her voice shaky as she ran her tongue over the rough edges of her chapped lip. "Besides, my detective friend is probably looking for me."

"Nice try. The way you reared into him, I doubt he'll have anything to do with you," he sneered, his icy glare intensifying as the high tempo music blared from the car's speakers. The pounding beat seemed to synchronize with the rapid thumping of her heart, causing sweat beads to pop out on her face. "This couldn't have worked out better. I've dreamed of having this close encounter with you."

Dreamed? More like obsessed. Did she get into the car with her stalker? Or just some lunatic looking for a good time?

"Who are you? How do you know me?" Her amnesia was putting her in awful predicaments. Okay, maybe that had nothing to do with her memory loss, but her quick temper.

"Let's just say you've flirted with me enough for me to claim what belongs to me," he whispered, his finger inching closer to hers, the touch sending warning flares bursting in her brain. It felt slimy and repulsive, making her wish she had taken her chances with her scandalous sister. At least Sarah wasn't pretending to like her. Although Sarah could have poisoned the food, she brought to Zach's house.

How unruly her life was going. She couldn't deny her sister having a motive to get rid of her. Could she trust anyone? How about the doctor and his wife? What was his name? Steve? No, Stephen. His honest face and loving, protective eyes wedged a flutter in her heart that she could trust him. But how could she find him? Kayla stared at her purse, hoping for a solution to reveal itself. Her cellphone. If she could just slide her fingers into her purse, turn on her phone, find Stephen's number and call without the creep finding out. And miracles happened every day.

"Can I get a rain check?" Kayla's fingers rummaged through her bag, feeling through the unknown items for her phone.

"No can do, baby. I've got everything planned out. Good thing I'm an impulsive man. Let me reassure you, I'm single, but after today, I'll never let you go." He ran his fingers through his disheveled hair, smiling.

Kayla let out a deep, not calming breath. Her trembling finger ran against the comforting lifeline as she pressed a button, hoping she was making a call. "You can't keep me."

"Ha. You'll enjoy our time so much. You'll never leave me and forget all about Zach Rivers." He slowed his car down a country road as a deer sprinted across the deserted road. "I'm a real man."

Sick.

"You know what you're doing is kidnapping." She tried neutralizing her voice. No need to panic and let anxiety take control of her senses.

A wicked, low-pitched laugh vibrated through the car, making Kayla's head spin with dizziness. "Listen, a detective saw you willingly climb into my car. You could never prove that I held you against your will. And frankly, that's not what I'm doing. You want our little rendezvous as much as I do."

Was she sending mixed signals or was this creep a good manipulator? "No, I don't want to go anywhere with you. I want to go home." Wherever home was.

"And you will." He tapped his fingers on the steering wheel again. "It's not like I'm gonna tie you up in my bathroom and hold you as my prisoner."

What sane person even thinks like that? Kayla needed to escape this deranged man and lie low until she could figure out what to do. "In case you lost my words somewhere between your ears and brain, I do not want to go anywhere with you. Holding me any further is crossing the line into abduction." Or worse. Kayla's body trembled at the thought.

"Relax, baby," he whispered, his finger tracing a scorching trail along the side of her arm, igniting her skin with an intense heat.

"I'm not your baby, and I won't relax. Stop the car right now," she demanded, her voice laced with determination. The weight of the situation overshadowed any inclination for playful banter. Either he would release her, or she would escape on her own terms.

"You're no fun anymore," he retorted, his foot lightly tapping the gas, propelling the car down the deserted country road with alarming speed. "I'll let you go once we reach our destination. I don't want to be held responsible for bears or wolves feasting on your body."

Bears or wolves? The thought of battling savage creatures seemed preferable to enduring this deranged man. "Where are you taking me?" she asked, her voice trembling with a mix of fear and defiance.

"To a secluded hunting cabin, hidden away from prying eyes," he replied, a sinister smirk curling at the corners of his lips. Madness danced in his eyes, sending shivers of dread down her spine.

Warning signals blared in her mind, urging her to take immediate action. With a swift motion, she looped her purse strap over her head and reached for the door handle, manually unlocking it. Without sparing him a single glance, she hurled herself out of the moving vehicle; the asphalt meeting her body with a searing pain. In slow motion, her head collided with the unforgiving road, enveloping her in a darkness she couldn't escape.

****

Zach paced back and forth in the cramped guest room; his eyes fixed on Kayla's duffel bag. The room felt suffocating, the air heavy with tension. He couldn't believe that she would willingly get into a random car just to avoid him. The situation was awkward enough, with her sister openly displaying affection. And based on Kayla's piercing glares, she seemed to think he wanted to take advantage of the situation and kick her out. Did she really believe he had no moral compass?

Sarah intrigued him. Her attention was intoxicating, and he sometimes found himself caught up in her seductive ways. But he was legally married, and that knowledge had kept him from any other female interactions until Sarah came into the picture.

Glancing at the clock, he pounded his fist against the wall in frustration. What did it matter if he put a hole in the wall? He could fix it later. It had been five hours since she left. Five hours without a courtesy text to let him know she was safe. She was the most infuriating person he knew. No wonder things hadn't worked out between them.

As darkness seeped through the sheer window covering, a sense of dread tugged at his heart. Something was wrong. Had her stalker found her? If so, she could be anywhere now. He had failed once again.

Zach tried to gather his thoughts, picking up his phone and tapping his foot on the worn floors. He dialed his brother's number, his smooth voice coming through the phone.

"What's going on?" his brother asked.

"Can you do me a favor? Find out who owns a black Toyota with Tennessee plates, KDR-S17."

"Is this about Kayla?"

"Yes. Text me as soon as you find out." Zach slid his phone back into his pocket and resumed his restless pacing.

God, please protect her wherever she may be.

A loud pounding sound echoed from the living room, startling Zach. With his gun at his side, he cautiously approached the front door and pulled it open. He stared into a pair of icy blue eyes, instantly knowing that trouble had once again found him.

"Where is she, Rivers?" Stephen Smith forcefully pushed past Zach, the sound of their bodies colliding echoing through the living room. The scent of tension hung in the air as Zach braced himself against the impact, his muscles tensing. Stephen's piercing icy blue eyes bore into Zach's, their gaze locked in a battle of wills.

Stephen's accusation sent a wave of anger and defensiveness coursing through Zach's veins. The room felt suffocatingly hot as the intensity between them grew. Swallowing hard, Zach fought to maintain his composure. He needed to play it cool, find out what Stephen knew before revealing anything.

"Against everyone's judgment, she went home with you." Stephen's voice dripped with accusation, his words laced with the threat of violence. Zach could sense the anger radiating off him, like a tangible force. The room seemed to shrink, their personal space becoming a battleground.

Zach couldn't deny the truth in Stephen's words. He knew he was to blame for Kayla leaving the safety of his home. The emptiness and coldness of his house without her presence weighed heavily on him, like a leaden weight in his chest.

"I'm not her dad," Zach replied, his voice laced with a mix of guilt and resignation. The words hung in the air, heavy with unspoken regret.

Stephen stood motionless, his eyes drilling into Zach's soul. The tension in the room was palpable, suffusing every breath they took. Zach could feel the weight of his mistakes pressing down on him, threatening to crush him.

"No, you're her husband," Stephen retorted, his voice dripping with disdain. The accusation hit Zach like a punch to the gut, leaving him reeling. He had let Kayla down, neglected his role as her husband. The guilt washed over him, threatening to drown him.

Zach fought to maintain his facade; his acting skills stretched to their limit. But deep down, he knew he couldn't keep up the charade much longer. Kayla needed him, and he had failed her. The weight of his past mistakes bore down on him, his breath coming in shallow gasps.

"Your silence is all I needed to hear." Stephen's words cut through the air, filled with anger and disappointment. The room seemed to close in on Zach, the walls closing in with every passing second. He could feel Stephen's presence invading his personal space, the heat of his anger radiating off him.

Determined to regain control of the situation, Zach mustered his resolve. "Listen, man, I don't know where she is, but I'll find her." The words came out strained, his voice a mix of determination and desperation.

Stephen's laughter grated on Zach's nerves, the sound piercing through the tense atmosphere. The room seemed to vibrate with the intensity of their clash. Stephen's ability to interrogate and manipulate was clear, matching Zach's own skills.

"I already know that," Stephen sneered, his voice laced with a mix of smugness and superiority. The words hung in the air, a reminder of Zach's failings.

"Why are you really here, Stephen? Couldn't help but gloat at my failed attempt at protecting her?" Zach was losing whatever minuscule patience he had left.

He crossed his arms over his chest, showing off his arm muscles. Intimidate much? "Rivers, I didn't have a problem with you until you crossed my cousin. She and I are tight, and if you won't do your job, I'll push you out of the way and do it for you."

Zach's heart sank as Stephen's words hit him like a freight train. The dimly lit room felt suffocating, the stale air heavy with tension. The sound of their words echoed in the silence, the only interruption being the soft hum of the air conditioner. Zach's fingers nervously tapped against his pocket as he struggled to find the right words. Stephen's words were nothing Zach didn't already know. The Smith men were fierce. He could only imagine what Kayla's dad was like. Thank God a state and hundreds of miles separated them.

"I can handle my job." Could he really? Maybe his personal emotions were messing with his ability to do his job.

"I'm doubtful about that." Stephen ran his fingers through his short hair, never taking his eyes off Zach. "What's going on with you and Sarah?"

His question felt like a sucker punch to the gut. Bring up the other woman, why don't ya? "Uh … I…"

"A married man shouldn't be flirting with a home wrecker like her. Underneath her flawless skin and captivating face lies a seductive spirit that wants everything Kayla has, including her husband. It's always been like that. Watch your back because you're letting her trap ensnare you."

"I'm not having a counseling session in my living room. I'd appreciate you staying out of my personal business." Zach grabbed his phone out of his pocket, staring at his text message. Great. Like he didn't have enough macho men to deal with.

107

"Noted. But if you hurt Kayla, you'll have to answer to me. And your title won't play a factor in my stance."

Zach rolled his eyes, holding back a smirk. Stephen Smith would be a worthy competitor, but Zach wouldn't go down without doing some damage himself.

"Listen, I should have started with this tidbit, but Kayla is in trouble." Stephen's hardened face softened at the mention of his cousin in trouble.

"What makes you say that?" *We've wasted ten minutes arguing when we could have been searching for her.*

"I got a phone call, kind of muffled, but it was from Kayla. She begged someone to let her go, but the male voice continued to ignore her pleas."

The real reason Stephen showed up at his house. "Any names or locations?"

"Not exactly. But she has a locations app on her phone. It pinged a general location of Crawford Road, before the signal went out." Stephen gritted his teeth as he muttered the last words. "Nothing out that way, but fields and woods."

"Okay, go home and I'll let you know when I find her." Zach grabbed his keys off the counter. A million thoughts running through his head.

"No way. I'm your backup." Stephen stepped to the door. He wouldn't let anything deter him.

Seriously? He couldn't get rid of this guy. "Fine, but no going rogue. I'm in charge."

"Deal."

As he shut the front door behind them, Zach slid his phone safely into his pocket, ready for whatever lay ahead. "First, we need to pay a visit to the getaway car she climbed into. Got the guy's information." And it would not go well. It was clear to Zach that the dude's arrogance would be a major obstacle in his quest for information. Should the situation call for it, he would fulfill his duty by apprehending the man and ensuring his presence at the police station for questioning. And once he found Kayla, because he was determined to find her, they were going to have a long, heartfelt conversation. Four years' worth of talking.

****

Zach meticulously checked the chamber of his gun, the metallic click echoing through the tense air. Better to be safe than sorry. He could feel the weight of the weapon in his hand, the cold steel sending a shiver down his spine. He glanced at Stephen, the sound of leather creaking as he adjusted his holster on his shoulder. The scent of gunpowder hung in the air, a reminder of the gravity of the situation.

As they approached Kayla's apartment complex, Stephen's fingers grazed the door handle with a nervous energy, like a caged animal ready to bolt. Zach could hear the distant hum of traffic, a backdrop to the impending interrogation. This was no routine questioning; they were on the brink of something far more sinister. The uncertainty clenched at Zach's gut.

"Why are we at Kayla's apartment complex?"

"Ironically, the suspect lives here," Zach replied, his voice tinged with anticipation. He hoped they wouldn't run into Sarah, the thought of her and her alluring ways only serving as a distraction. He needed a clear head for what was to come.

Stephen gave him a knowing look, his eyes piercing through the tension-filled atmosphere. "Stick to the plan, Rivers. No deviating to visit a certain redhead."

Zach clenched his fist at his side, feeling the release of tension with each flexing motion. "This is my investigation. Remember that."

"Sure, if you remember why we're actually here," Stephen shot back, his stare icy as he gripped the door handle.

Zach ran his fingers through his hair, a nervous habit that helped him think. The sensation of the strands slipping through his fingertips grounded him. "You're silent backup, man," he reminded Stephen, the words laced with a mix of caution and concern. "Men have died from routine checks. Don't play hero. Your wife and child want you to come home."

Zach's words hit their mark, the weight of the situation sinking in. All color drained from Stephen's face as he closed his eyes, perhaps saying a silent prayer. They needed more than prayers, though. They needed to act swiftly to find Kayla safe and alive. The thought of being too late threatened to consume Zach, but he shook it off. There was no room for despair.

He motioned to the door as they quietly climbed out of the car, the car engine humming softly in the background. They quickly entered the dimly lit apartment complex, the hallway bathed in a dull fluorescent light. A spicy Italian scent lingered in the air, intertwining with the musty smell of old carpet, causing Zach's empty stomach to churn and rebel from lack of food. He hadn't eaten since breakfast, the thought of the dish Sarah had made for him sitting on the counter, now likely a rotting mess. He shook off the gnawing hunger, his footsteps echoing softly as he climbed up the worn-out stairs to the third floor. First apartment on the left.

Taking a calming breath, he pounded on the beige-colored door; the sound reverberating through the quiet hallway. Waiting for what seemed like an eternity, the door creaked open; the hinges protesting with a rusty groan. A smug, almost cocky face appeared at the door, a self-satisfied smirk playing on his lips. His stench of garbage mixed with days old fast food attacked Zach's nostrils, making him fight back the urge to retch. He would not lose his breakfast on the grimy-looking carpet. With a sideways glance, Zach could see Stephen beside him, his face contorted in a similar struggle to control his senses.

"Gentlemen. What do I owe the honor of your visit?" His smug words dripped with false sweetness, failing to deceive Zach. Irritation seethed over his too-perfect tan face, causing Zach's brows to furrow.

"Silas Clover, I'm Detective Zach Rivers with the McMinn County Sheriff's Office. This is my consultant, Stephen Smith."

Not even pretending to hide his aggravation, Silas slid his door shut, the sound echoing in the narrow hallway. As he stepped into the hall, his arms crossed over his chest. "What's this about?"

"Do you know Kayla Smith?" Zach's voice remained firm; his gaze locked with Silas's dark eyes. The mention of her name seemed to darken Silas's eyes even further, a flicker of guilt crossing his face. "Our apartment complex is rather quaint. Everyone knows everyone here."

"Have you seen her today?" Zach's fingers gripped his notepad tightly, the texture of the paper providing a minor distraction from the thoughts swirling in his mind. He wanted nothing more than to confront this man, to wipe away the smugness from his face. And to protect his wife. Although their marriage was only a facade, they were still bound by the law. But that didn't stop him from walking away four years ago. Zach clenched his jaw, trying to push away the unwelcome thoughts that threatened to consume him.

"Maybe. What's that to you?" Silas leaned against the door frame, his posture exuding a nonchalant confidence, as if he had all the time in the world.

"Is she in there?" Stephen, as the silent partner, couldn't actually fulfill that role. Zach shot him a warning glare to back off. His words filled the hall with tension, the air heavy with anticipation.

"Wouldn't you like to see? But, no warrant or probable cause to search my home, meaning you'll never know." Silas looked bored as he stood like a frozen soldier. The creaking floorboards added to the eerie atmosphere, amplifying the silence between the men.

Stephen stepped forward, getting into Silas's craw. He laced his voice with determination, cutting through the stillness. "If you lay a finger on my cousin, you'll have to answer to me. And between us, only one of us will walk away, unharmed." The room seemed to shrink as the tension escalated, suffocating them all.

Silas's tan face paled at Stephen's words, fear creeping into his eyes. "Did you hear that threat, Detective Rivers?" His voice trembled, betraying his bravado. The sound of a distant siren added to the unease, a reminder of the outside world.

"What? I wasn't paying attention." A smirk spread across Zach's face, his voice dripping with defiance. He'd throw down his badge and settle the score with Silas if he harmed Kayla at all. Zach already knew Silas had a crush on Kayla. But would he act out on it? The sound of his pounding heart echoed in his ears, drowning out all other noise.

"Here's what I know. If you were half the man you claimed to be, your wife wouldn't come calling on me to perform your husbandly duties." Silas cocked his head to the side, grinning. The stench of stale sweat and unwashed clothes permeated the room, assaulting their senses. "She is one fine piece of work." The words hung in the air, leaving a bitter taste.

Normally even-tempered, Zach bolted forward, his footsteps echoing in the room, grasping the top of Silas's shirt, throwing him against the door. The impact reverberated through the wooden panels, creating a jarring sound. "If I find you touched her..." His voice was low and menacing, filled with a raw intensity.

"Assaulting a civilian? Making accusations you can't back up? You're not having a good day." Silas jerked his shirt out of Zach's grip, smiling. The sound of fabric stretching added to the chaotic scene, a visual representation of their mounting aggression.

"Cool it, Rivers," Stephen whispered, his voice barely audible over the rising tension. His eyes burned with restrained fury; his hands clenched into fists. The hall felt smaller, suffocating them with its intensity.

Focus on your training. Cool and in control. Zach repeated the mantra in his mind, trying to regain his composure. The sound of his own breath filled his ears, a steady rhythm amidst the chaos.

"This afternoon, I witnessed Kayla climbing into your car. No one has heard from her since." The words hung in the air, heavy with accusation. The hall seemed to grow colder, a chill running down their spines.

Silas grimaced like Zach just punched him in the gut. The faint sound of a whimper escaped his lips, barely audible. "Yeah, so I gave her a ride. No big deal."

"No? Abduction is a pretty big deal," Zach said, his voice piercing the silence. "Where is she?" The sound of his own heartbeat thumped in his chest, a thunderous reminder of his urgency.

Silas fidgeted with the hem of his smelly shirt. Did the guy believe in washing clothes? He defined the word slob. The pungent odor of body odor mixed with the musty scent of the room, overwhelming their senses. "I gave her a ride to a friend's house. Don't know or care what happened to her after that. I don't think she's my type anymore." The words dripped with indifference, a callousness that sent shivers down Zach's spine.

Convenient. "Address and name?" Zach's voice was firm, demanding answers.

"I never actually saw her friend. I dropped her off at a house on Crawford Road. Probably four hours ago." Silas's voice trembled, a hint of nervousness seeping through his facade.

Zach wasn't buying it. The creep knew more than he was letting on.

"I have a voice recording of Kayla in distress. A background male voice similar to yours." Stephen gave Silas his intimidating Smith men look. The look that cowered many grown men. The intensity of Stephen's gaze bore into Silas, the weight of his stare almost tangible.

"You're grasping at straws. My country twang isn't uncommon in these parts. You have nothing." Silas opened his door, smirking. "Unless you have solid proof of my involvement, we're done here."

Zach wanted to punch something, preferably the dude's ugly face. It took all of his willpower to back away from the man. He slid a card out of his pocket, handing it to Silas. "If you hear from Kayla, call me."

"Not likely." Silas stepped into his apartment, slamming the door in Zach's face.

"That went well," Stephen mumbled under his breath.

"I have no probable cause to arrest him. But this isn't over. Let's go take a drive on Crawford Road."

"And pray we don't find her body abandoned on the side of the road." Stephen balled his fist at his side, following Zach out of the building.

Zach wouldn't let those dark thoughts invade his mind, eating away at his sanity. They'd find her alive. And when they did, he was sticking to her like glue.

Chapter Six

Kayla blinked back the overwhelming sense to sleep, her heavy eyelids fighting against the exhaustion. She rubbed her throbbing head as millions of jackhammers exploded in her brain, the pounding sensation reverberating through her skull. She winced, feeling the dry, sticky blood clinging to her trembling fingers as she touched the top of her forehead.

Where was she? She struggled to gather her bearings; her surroundings shrouded in darkness. As she climbed to her unsteady feet, her gaze pierced through the blackness, searching for any signs of familiarity. Howls and growls echoed in the night's air, sending shivers down her spine and causing her to tense up. She glared into the darkened night; her eyes fixated on a faint street light that provided a small respite from the utter darkness.

What was going on? Awareness flashed before Kayla's mind like a vivid movie reel, her heartbeat quickening with each passing moment. She stepped closer to the edge of the road, her fingers clutching tightly onto her ruffled purse. Memories of a locked car door, and the haunting laughs from the man who wouldn't let her go. An unwelcome reminder of a terrifying ordeal. Then after a quick escape; jumping out of the car, everything turned black.

But through the abyss, a glimpse of Zach's charming face emerged. Zach, the man she had fallen in love with, but ultimately lost. The pain of their shattered marriage resurfaced, and Kayla's heart ached with the weight of it all. She had desperately wanted to save their relationship, to mend the broken pieces, but he had slipped away in the early morning hours, thwarting her confession and plea for forgiveness.

A myriad of forces had conspired to tear apart their hasty union, and as an eighteen-year-old, Kayla had been ill-equipped to navigate the temptations that surrounded them. Rumors had swirled through their college campus, poisoning their love and causing them to forget their marriage vows.

Kayla's fingers trailed along the bottom of her stomach, the weight of her loss becoming unbearable. Tears welled up in her burning eyes as she thought about all that she had lost on that fateful day four years ago. The loss she felt was twofold - not just the man she loved, but also the cherished connection they had hidden from his awareness. The breath of life had been fleeting, slipping through her grasp despite her desperate attempts to hold on to it. Anger simmered within her, directed towards Zach. She blamed him for wrecking her life and stealing away the precious life that she hadn't even realized she wanted until it was too late.

She slid her phone out of her purse, the cold metal sending a shiver through her fingers, as she looked around in the chilly night air. The faint scent of spring hung in the atmosphere. If she could just get a signal, maybe someone would come to her rescue. Kayla's eyes darted across the screen as she scrolled through her contacts, her finger hovering over Zach's name. She remembered waking up in the hospital, her vision hazy, and seeing her awkward-acting husband by her side. He had been the one to rescue her, taking her to his house until her memory returned. She ran her fingers over her lips, a tingling sensation reminding her of the kiss they had shared. And for one fleeting moment, Kayla wished that a simple act of affection could revive their dead hearts and mend their broken marriage.

But then, Sarah's scandalous smile flashed into her mind, sending a ripple of goosebumps across her skin. In a blatant display of disrespect, Zach openly flirted with her sister, causing Kayla to feel a mix of anger and hurt. Clearly, his heart didn't long for his estranged wife, but for the excitement and thrill of a bachelor's life. Trying to regain her composure, Kayla vigorously shook her head, hoping to clear the deluge of memories. She didn't want to dwell on past mistakes and present heartache. At least for a couple of days, she had escaped the haunting ghosts of her past.

With a determined gaze, she stared at her phone, scrolling away from Zach's name. There was no point in calling him. Sarah probably had him caged up in their apartment, pretending to be the married couple they could never truly be. No matter what Kayla had, Sarah always lusted after it. Her fingers tapped on Stephen's name, the bright screen illuminating the surrounding darkness.

But as she anxiously waited for a signal, disappointment met her. No signal. Just her and the cold, silent night. Her body shivered as the late-night spring air whirled around her, making her wish she wore something heavier than a shirt-sleeved t-shirt. A distant roaring of an engine shattered the silence, causing Kayla's heart to race. She swiftly dove into the dense, shadowy canopy of trees, the damp earth squelching beneath her feet. Ignoring the choir of nocturnal creatures, she fought off the pungent smell of decaying leaves and damp moss. Every rustle of the underbrush sent a jolt of fear through her, as she desperately tried to avoid becoming a midnight snack for some unknown predator lurking in the darkness. But her greatest fear lay in encountering another human, someone with malicious intent.

As the piercing beam of headlights sliced through the inky blackness, the night seemed to amplify its sinister presence. She huddled further into the shadows, her heart pounding in her chest. The car came to a halt on the gravelly shoulder of the winding country road, its tires crunching with an eerie finality.

Friend or foe? Her mind raced with uncertainty. The jingling of keys reverberated through the air, sending a prickling sensation down her spine. That walk, she recognized it all too well. What was he doing here? Was he coming to rescue her? How did he know the desolate forest ensnared her? Nothing made sense. The middle-of-nowhere had become her prison, and she refused to step into the car of a stranger or a man she thought she knew. The consequences of such trust had been disastrous before.

"Kayla?" The deep voice resonated in the darkness, carried by the chilling wind that whispered through the trees.

Her heart pounded in her ears as she weighed her options. Should she reveal her location or play a dangerous game of freeze tag, where her life hung in the balance?

"I know you're here. Come out. I won't hurt you." A nearby branch snapped, causing a surge of dizziness to wash over her.

Breathe. In and out. She focused on regulating her breath, trying to steady her racing heart.

"I'm your ride home." The warmth of his body suddenly loomed behind her, sending shivers down her spine. Willing herself to become invisible, she squeezed her eyes shut.

Calloused fingers closed around her forearm, tightening their grip. Panic surged through her veins. She couldn't let him take her. Trust no one. With a burst of determination, she swung her leg back, connecting with the man's stomach. His deep groan mingled with the unsettling howl of a nearby animal, too close for comfort.

"Let go of me," she hissed, wrenching her arm free from the man's vice-like grip. As she stumbled deeper into the thick, oppressive darkness of the woods, the damp scent of earth filled her nostrils.

"Kayla, don't make me hunt you down. I'm trying to help you for your own good," he pleaded, his voice strained with desperation.

Likely story, she thought bitterly, her heart pounding in her chest. Suddenly, her foot caught on a gnarled tree branch, causing searing pain to shoot up her leg. She winced, knowing she couldn't afford a leg injury that would hinder her escape.

She fell onto the damp grass, her hands instinctively searching for the object that had tripped her. Her fingers brushed against a rough, dirt-caked stick, its surface worn and weathered. It wasn't the best form of defense, but it would have to do.

"Know, I'd never hurt you. You mean too much to me," he whispered, his presence looming just inches away from her trembling form.

Without a second thought, she swung the stick, its woody thud connecting with the side of his head. In the dim glow of the distant headlights, she glimpsed his profile as he crumpled to the ground, collapsing at her feet.

What had she done? Did she just kill a man? Panic surged through her, threatening to overwhelm her senses. She sank to the cool grass, her trembling fingers searching for a pulse at his neck. Relief flooded her body as she felt the steady throb beneath her fingertips.

Running her hands through his dark, disheveled hair, she questioned her own actions. He annoyed her, his persistent pursuit never-ending, but deep down, she didn't believe he would truly harm her. Confusion and fatigue battled inside her, her body aching and her head throbbing fiercely. She knew she needed to rest, to find solace amidst this chaotic, uncertain night. Her feet throbbed with pain, and her mind yearned for a respite from the relentless turmoil.

She stroked the man's rough face, her fingertips tracing the rough texture of his skin, while a knot of anxiety twisted in her gut. She silently prayed that she wasn't losing her sanity, that she wasn't unwittingly placing herself into the clutches of a relentless stalker. "Wake up," she whispered, her voice filled with a mix of desperation and caution.

A few low groans escaped his lips, accompanied by fluttering eyelids, as the man slowly regained consciousness. His brown eyes locked onto Kayla's face, a mischievous smirk spreading across his captivating features. "I always knew that one day you'd cuddle me," he teased, his voice laced with a hint of playfulness.

Kayla rolled her eyes, her discomfort obvious in the grimace that briefly flickered across her face. "There's nothing remotely romantic about this situation," she retorted, her words tinged with annoyance and apprehension.

A playful glint danced in his eyes as he continued to gaze at her, his admiration clear. "You may not see it, but being cradled in the arms of a beautiful woman has its own charm," he remarked, his voice filled with a mixture of admiration and intrigue. After a brief pause, he pushed himself up, rising to his feet. "Your strength and determination are truly captivating," he added, his words heavy with genuine admiration.

Despite the irony of the situation, a faint smile tugged at the corners of Kayla's lips. The roles had reversed, with the hunted now becoming the helper. She could have easily abandoned him, leaving his fate to be devoured by the unforgiving wilderness, but her conscience would have haunted her relentlessly. "We need to find a doctor," she stated, determination lacing her voice. She wrapped her arm around his waist, providing support as best as she could, feeling the weight of his body press against her.

"I understand your lack of trust, but I promise I won't harm you," he reassured, his words carrying a sense of sincerity. Kayla swiftly snatched the keyring from his wrist, feeling the cool metal against her palm, as she fought to maintain her balance under his heavy weight.

With a mix of trepidation and resolve, she reminded herself that she was in control. She was the one driving, the one responsible for their fate. As they embarked on this uncertain journey, Kayla silently prayed that she wasn't making a colossal mistake, that her decision to help this enigmatic man wouldn't come back to haunt her.

****

"How did you do it?" The voice echoed through the truck, bouncing off the dashboard.

"What?" Did he have to ask personal questions? Or questions in general? Couldn't they just ride in silence? Awkward? Yes, but it beat twenty questions. Zach gripped the steering wheel, feeling heat crawl up his face.

"Kayla has always been level-headed. How did you convince her to marry you? And keep it a secret." Stephen's large body shifted in the passenger seat, his eyes glaring at Zach. "Like a sister to me, she's kept no secrets from me, or so I thought."

Was this about his wounded pride, or that Zach wasn't good enough for his cousin? Honestly, Zach never could figure out how he had won Kayla's heart. In high school, all the boys had crushes on her, and the girls aspired to be like her. Zach's home life caused a rebellious streak, and if not for Kayla, God only knows where he'd be. She believed there was more to him than anger and hurt. Kayla made him long to be the man she saw in him. Her love changed his life.

Of course, his mom loved him, but she was too busy filling his dad's role as provider to see below the surface of Zach's needs. Raising three boys who ate like bottomless pits kept her busy. His mom worked as a social worker for the county, saving one child at a time. But she picked up hours at a local diner for extra spending money when his father's child support ran low.

Seeing his mother's passion for civil duty caused a fire in Zach's soul. He wanted to rid the world of the bad guys that inflicted pain on innocent children. Same profession as his father, but he never wanted to be like him. His brothers followed suit. Josh was the assistant district attorney and Peter was a police officer.

"Stop stalling, Rivers." Zach shook his head as the memories flowed from his mind. He looked around, still sitting in his truck, driving toward a desolate road with a beefy man that wouldn't think twice about dumping his body in the dense forest. Okay, Stephen Smith had more character than that, but he acted like a papa bear with Kayla.

Zach bit the inside of his cheek. The moment of truth. "Her beauty captivated me, but her heart reeled me in and won every fiber of my being. When all the other teens were running from me, Kayla sought me out and befriended me."

"Sounds like my amazing cousin." A smile softened Stephen's hardened face. "I guess she didn't reel you in enough to stick around. You conned her into marriage and then ran off when your marriage got heated?"

He did not want to have this conversation, ever. Zach turned left at the fork in the road, driving under the speed limit since deer liked to bolt out in front of cars.

"As a nineteen-year-old know-it-all, I can tell you that jealousy and pride wedged a drift between us, and I stoked the fire, causing her unmerited heartache. I was becoming my worst nightmare—my father."

"So, you disappear in the early morning, and never look back?"

When he put it that way, it sounded foolish, but his wounded heart couldn't take any more rejection. Kayla was his world, and he didn't know how to keep her when the male students gawked at her and made light of their marriage. Zach never witnessed her flirting, but the rumors circulated fast, and he did the only thing he knew how to do—flee.

Zach realized a couple of years later, when he gave his heart to Jesus, that he had put Kayla in the place of God. No wonder their marriage failed. Zach should have tried to reconcile their marriage two years ago, when God nudged him to seek forgiveness, but Zach didn't want to go back to that vulnerable place. Besides, she caused him to leave.

That's what his father convinced him as the truth, and it hurt less to cast the blame entirely on her shoulders.

"Not my smartest move. But, yeah, that's how it went down." Zach cranked the air to full blast. Was it just him or were the temperatures climbing to dangerous digits?

"You're an idiot." Stephen growled the words, not even hiding his hostility.

"So, I've been told," Zach replied dryly.

"How do you plan to fix it? And smooching on Kayla's sister won't win her heart back."

Did Zach want to win her heart back? Or finally end their marriage and move on with life? No more flimsy marriage certificate binding them together. Kayla's bright blue eyes flashed into his mind. The eyes that once caused him to hope and see the world as more than dull and pointless. The man that got to wake up to those eyes and her killer smile every morning had God's favor on his side. That was him. Could still be him, but not without addressing vulnerabilities and past failures. He couldn't go back. Zach wasn't that weak teen anymore.

Memories of Kayla wrapping around his arms, feeling her heartbeat, stroking her silky strands, sharing laughter, stealing her last bite of ice cream whacked him in the face as he choked back a flood of tears. He loved her once, and he buried that love under layers of padlock doors and chains. He could never open that door, never allow himself to love her again. Because losing her again would destroy him and nothing could restore his crumbled life. Not even God.

"Stephen, Kayla and I are old history. We will never be a couple again." Saying the words out loud caused a prick in his shriveled heart. Was he finally ready to close that chapter of his life?

"You're a bigger idiot than I thought." Stephen tapped his fingers on the armrest, looking like he might explode. "Never underestimate the power of God."

"What's that supposed to mean?" Zach pulled onto Crawford Road, hoping they didn't find Kayla's body on the side of the road. "Are you threatening me?"

Stephen's hearty laugh filled the space between them. "It's not me you have to worry about. You're a Christian, although I'm guessing you're skimming on the edge, teetering away from God. But I'll let you figure this one out yourself."

Thanks, man. Zach wanted to slap the smirk off Stephen's face. He didn't want to hear about God right now or a life riddle.

"Stop the car!" Stephen exclaimed, his voice filled with urgency as he unbuckled his seatbelt, leaping out into the enveloping darkness of the night. The sound of screeching tires echoed through the air as Zach quickly turned off the car, his heart pounding in his chest. He swiftly yanked his gun out of the holster, the cold metal sending a shiver down his spine, and sprinted past Stephen. He was the detective, not Stephen Smith.

In the dim glow of the headlights, Kayla's bloodied face came into view, her features illuminated in a haunting manner. With a man's lifeless body clutched tightly under her arm, there was no visible sign of a struggle, but the anguish etched on her face told a different story. A piercing scream escaped her lips upon sighting Zach and Stephen, causing her to drop the lifeless body and seek solace in Stephen's embrace. Zach couldn't help but yearn for the comfort of being the one she ran to, but he chose a life without her. No turning back.

Reluctant to interrupt the family reunion, yet compelled to fulfill his role, Zach approached Kayla cautiously. The stench of dried blood mingled with the night air, the metallic odor assaulting his senses. As he neared her, he noticed the dried blood caked onto the top of her hair, exposing a deep, jagged gash. How could Silas have inflicted such harm upon her?

"Zach," her eyes silently conveyed the message. Her memory had returned, and the look she gave him was a warning to keep his distance. However, he knew he couldn't comply, as his duty was to protect her.

"Kayla, are you injured?" he inquired, extending his arm to brush her hair away from her face, but hesitating just before making contact.

"I'll live," she replied, her voice muffled as she buried her face in her cousin's shirt, refusing to acknowledge the lifeless figure sprawled on the pavement.

Zach moved closer to the motionless body, leaning over to check for a pulse. His own steady breaths broke the silence of the night. "He's alive," he confirmed, his voice barely above a whisper.

"I know. I'm taking him to the ER," Kayla stated firmly, pushing herself out of Stephen's embrace and fixing her gaze on Zach, daring him to challenge her decision.

"Kayla," Zach said sharply, his voice tinged with concern, "that's not smart. I don't know what happened here, but I'll call an ambulance for Silas."

Kayla's eyes narrowed, and she folded her arms tightly over her chest, her face ablaze with anger. The outside seemed to crackle with tension, the air heavy with the scent of adrenaline.

"You don't have the right to dictate what I do," she retorted defiantly.

Zach's gaze flickered to the motionless body on the floor, contemplating the situation. A sudden thought crossed his mind, and he stated, "Maybe I should arrest you for assault."

A bitter chuckle erupted from Kayla's lips, the sound cutting through the charged atmosphere. It landed like a slap on Zach's face, leaving a sting of disbelief. "For self-defense? Not happening."

Interrupting their exchange, Stephen interjected with a lighthearted tone, "Okay, you two lovebirds, let's get this guy to the ER." He effortlessly lifted the unconscious body, gently placing it in the backseat. "He'll be fine, just taking a little nap. I need to examine his head at the hospital. I'll drive him and meet y'all there."

Zach felt a surge of frustration as his control over the investigation slipped away. Stepping forward, he confronted Stephen, his voice laced with determination. "No way. I'm the detective on the case."

Stephen calmly reasoned, "You protect the witness. I'll get the suspect to the hospital. I'm a doctor, remember?" He motioned towards the driver's seat, silently requesting the car keys.

Reluctantly, Zach conceded defeat. "Fine. We're right behind you." He walked towards his car, a sense of irony weighing heavily on him. "I guess Silas came back to finish what he started?"

Kayla settled into the passenger seat, closing the door with a resolute thud. "Silas is a jerk. But that guy isn't Silas. It's Thomas."

Zach's mind raced, thoughts swirling in confusion. How did Thomas know where Silas had left Kayla? Were they working together? The truck seemed to close in, a suffocating sensation gripping Zach. Determined, he vowed to unravel the twisted web of events, refusing to rest until he uncovered the truth.

****

Kayla felt the air slowly evaporating from the small confines of the truck. What was Stephen thinking, sending her off with Zach like their history meant nothing? Lovebirds? As if. She caught a sideways glance at his strong profile, noticing a couple of scars that weren't there years ago. No way around it. Zach Rivers defined the word attractive. He always caused her insides to melt like chocolate. In high school, his rebellious charm attracted her to him, but it was so much more than his bad boy facade. Being the class president and the head cheerleader, she had standards to abide by, which is why she concealed her relationship with Zach. Loving him was against everything she had worked for in life, but he made her feel alive and special, not just a status, but a real person.

A frown covered her face. When he left her in college, she didn't know how to pick up the shattered pieces and move on. He was her everything, and all of her hopes and dreams died that day. Kayla had planned a special dinner hoping to reveal his new title in life, but he walked away and never looked back.

"Um … Are you cold? You're shivering." He glanced her way, centering his baby blues on her. What she wouldn't give to go back in time and make sure their marriage was safe guarded. Would that have changed the outcome of her biggest grief? Maybe. Maybe not. But at least she would have had someone walking through the valley of death with her.

"I'm fine," Kayla whispered, her voice barely audible over the hum of the car engine. She sank deeper into the plush leather seat, the warm material clinging to her skin.

Zach glanced at her; his eyes filled with concern. "I know that look. You're not fine," he murmured, his words blending with the distant sounds of bugs outside.

Kayla felt the weight of his gaze, the intensity of his concern making her palms damp with sweat. She wanted to escape the flood of memories threatening to overwhelm her senses. "What do you want me to say, Zach? That sitting near my estranged husband has no effect on me?" The words caught in her throat, the taste of bitterness lingering on her tongue.

Zach brought the car to a stop at a red light, the darkness of the night enveloping them. His eyes searched hers, searching for answers. "What do you mean by us?" he asked, his voice tinged with confusion.

Kayla clenched her fists, her fingernails digging into the soft flesh of her palm. She fought to hold back the tears threatening to spill over. This was a conversation she didn't want to have with Zach. He didn't deserve to know. "Wrong choice of words," she replied, her voice quivering.

Zach's words hung in the air, a mix of accusation and curiosity. "Yeah, right? You're an English teacher. You don't make simple word mistakes like that." In a moment of familiarity, he reached for her hand, his touch melting her resolve. "What are you hiding from me?"

A single tear escaped Kayla's eye, tracing a path down her cheek. She never wanted to revisit the vulnerability and the unending nightmare that haunted her. "Zach…" she began, her voice heavy with a mixture of pain and longing.

"Kayla, you can accuse me of a lot of things, and you can hate my guts, but I deserve to know whatever secret you're keeping from me," he said, his voice tinged with desperation. As he spoke, he ran his thumb gently over the back of her hand, creating a tingling sensation that sent butterflies swirling inside her stomach.

Right now, she wanted to feel his lips on hers, tasting his minty breath. She blinked repeatedly, trying to clear her mind of such thoughts. Zach was no longer hers, no matter how much her traitorous heart longed for him.

"Open up to me, sweetie," he pleaded, his eyes filled with a mix of longing and a mysterious emotion she couldn't quite identify. Zach had always possessed an irresistible charm, a magnetism that often got him what he desired from her.

"You don't get to call me that anymore," she replied firmly, her voice laced with a hint of sadness.

"Sorry, old habit," he muttered, his voice filled with regret.

Kayla cleared her throat, summoning the courage to reveal the truth. "The day you walked out on me, I had planned a special dinner to celebrate."

He pressed down on the gas pedal, causing the car to speed off down the country road. However, he never let go of her hand, his touch providing a comforting warmth. "Celebrate what?" he asked, his curiosity obvious.

"The tiny life that we created together," she confessed, memories flooding her mind. The positive pregnancy test, the relentless morning sickness, the awe-inspiring first ultrasound—they all came crashing back, stealing her breath away.

"What?" Zach abruptly pulled the truck to the side of the empty road. His eyes locked onto her face, searching for answers.

"We were pregnant. I couldn't believe it at first. I took twenty pregnancy tests before I finally accepted it as true," she revealed, her fingers absentmindedly tracing circles over her stomach, reliving that bittersweet time.

"I was going to be a dad? Or am I a dad?" Zach's voice trembled with a mixture of shock and disbelief. He snatched his hand away from hers, running it through his hair, his gaze turning stony.

"You left, Zach. I couldn't even find you," she said, her voice filled with four years' worth of bitterness and anger. Her arms trembled with the weight of her emotions. "What was I supposed to do?"

"I don't know. But you kept this secret from me for four years. Who does that?" Zach tapped his fingers nervously on the middle console, his eyes welling with tears, distant and lost. "I would have stayed if you had told me."

"Get real, Zach. You were itching to leave even after we exchanged vows. I was never enough for you, and neither would our daughter have been."

He slammed his fist on the steering wheel, the loud thud reverberating through the car. The sound echoed his frustration, a sharp crack in the silence. Kayla could feel the force behind his anger, a palpable wave that filled the small space. She could see the veins on his hand bulging, his knuckles turning white from the impact.

"That's a lie," he seethed, his voice laced with bitterness. "You were my world. How do you think I felt hearing the jocks talk about you like you were a prize to win? No one cared about our marriage, not even you."

Kayla rolled her eyes at the slap in the face, a gesture filled with both annoyance and disappointment. The sight of his anger twisted something inside her. "I touched none of those jerks. I only wanted you."

"Likely story," he retorted, his words dripping with skepticism. "That's not what the guys were saying in the locker room."

"Their words meant nothing to me," Kayla countered, her voice tinged with hurt. "But you believing them sent daggers to my heart. I was never unfaithful to you." She gripped the door handle tightly, her knuckles turning white as well. The cold metal sent a shiver down her spine.

Maybe she should walk to the hospital. She couldn't stay in the car with him. The thought of leaving this suffocating atmosphere consumed her.

"Kayla, they knew things that no one would know," he pleaded, his voice holding a mix of desperation and accusation. "Like your oval-shaped birthmark under your ribcage. Facts are facts."

The words hung in the air, heavy with the weight of betrayal. Kayla's heart pounded in her chest, the rhythm matching the quickening pace of her breath. She couldn't bear to face him any longer.

"I can't do this." With a surge of determination, she jerked open the truck door, the cool night air rushing in to meet her. She stepped out, the darkness enveloping her like a comforting blanket. The distant lights of town flickered in her vision, offering a sliver of solace amidst the chaos.

"Kayla, don't walk away from me," he pleaded, his voice strained. "Tell me what happened to our baby. I deserve to know."

She shook her head, her entire body trembling with a mix of sorrow and anger. Slamming the door shut, she felt the vibrations reverberate through her. It was as if her world had shattered all over again; the fragments piercing her heart.

"Leave me alone, Zach," she whispered, her voice filled with a mix of resignation and defiance.

The slight hum as the window rolled down caught her attention, a soft whir that cut through the silence. "Don't do this."

A smug look spread across her face, an insignificant victory amidst the pain. "I'm acting like you. When the heat was too hot, you left. Bye, Zach."

Kayla ignored his pleas, turning her back on him, and disappeared into the darkness of the night. The unknown scared her, but she couldn't face Zach again. That hurt worse than any blow from any stalker.

God, help me. The plea hung in the air, a whisper carried away by the wind, as she ventured into the uncertain night.

****

Zach anxiously paced the sterile hospital corridor, the harsh fluorescent lights casting a cold, clinical glow. The rhythmic ticking of his watch echoed in his ears, intensifying his growing impatience. He berated himself for his stupidity, allowing Kayla to bolt from the car and vanish into the obscurity of the night. The weight of the baby news had finally hit him, the numbness slowly dissipating. He was a father, or maybe not. For four long years, she had concealed this life-altering secret from him. Any warmth he had once felt for her had plummeted in the wake of her revelation. How could she deny him the chance to be a father? The word "daughter" slipped from Kayla's lips, haunting his thoughts. Where was she? Did she inherit his piercing sky-blue eyes and the faint dimple on his left cheek? Would her innocent lips portray her mother's killer smile? If she was still alive, would he ever meet her? He would fight tooth and nail in court to assert his parental rights if necessary.

Suddenly, Stephen, clad in his pristine white doctor's coat, entered the waiting room. The scent of antiseptic hung in the air, mingling with the faint aroma of coffee wafting from the nearby cafe. His face wore a hardened expression, his emotions indecipherable.

"Thomas Holmes has regained consciousness," Stephen announced, his voice laced with frustration. "But he refuses to speak unless Kayla is present. Where is she?" He scanned the empty waiting room, his eyes brimming with concern.

"How should I know?" Zach retorted, defiance flashing in his eyes, daring Stephen to invade his personal space. The anger within him simmered, urging him to unleash his frustration on something or someone.

"I specifically asked you to bring her to the ER," Stephen exclaimed, throwing his arms up in exasperation. He took a deep breath, attempting to regain his composure. "What is wrong with you? Someone attacked her, almost abducted her. She needed your protection."

"Listen, man, I can't bear to look at her right now," Zach replied, his words betraying his genuine desires. In truth, he would find no peace until he laid eyes on her, unharmed, walking through the doors of the ER.

"Way to be professional. Perhaps I should inform your superiors to remove you from the case. You're clearly not operating at full capacity," Stephen retorted, his voice laced with disappointment.

Zach couldn't argue with the truth. His professional façade crumbled before him, reduced to a pile of ashes at his feet. And he blamed Kayla.

"Your saintly cousin just dropped this bombshell on me, revealing I'm a father, or was a father. I don't even know. Who keeps such a secret from a man for four years?" Zach ran his fingers through his hair, his gaze piercing Stephen's.

"That explains a lot," Stephen muttered, adjusting the stethoscope around his neck.

"What do you know, Smith?" Zach stepped closer, invading Stephen's personal space, desperate for answers to the countless questions swirling in his mind.

"Not my story to tell, bro."

The automatic doors of the ER swung open with a mechanical hum, revealing a scratched up, pale face. Her eyes were red-rimmed and her disheveled hair gave off a faint scent of sweat and desperation. As Zach laid eyes on her, a whirlwind of anger and attraction swirled within him. He longed to embrace her, to feel the rapid thumping of her heartbeat against his chest. But his rational mind urged him to keep his distance and extract every detail about their child.

She stared back at him, her chocolate-brown eyes penetrating the depths of his soul. As the mother of his child, she deserved a measure of compassion. However, Zach's heart burned with contempt, making it impossible for him to extend an olive branch.

Stephen, sensing the tension, pushed her gently into his arms, shooting him a resentful glare, silently pleading for him to postpone the questions. "Are you okay?"

"I'm alright," she murmured, her gaze momentarily flickering towards Zach before sighing as if her entire world had crumbled. "Just exhausted."

"Lily is on her way to pick you up. You can stay with us for as long as you need," Stephen offered, wrapping his arm around her shoulder and guiding her towards Thomas's room.

"You coming, Rivers?" Stephen called from the doorway.

Zach's duty awaited him. He had a suspect to interrogate; nothing else mattered. "Can I speak to Kayla briefly?" he requested.

Stephen gave his cousin some space, entering the examination room to give them privacy.

"Zach..." Kayla appeared worn out, resembling a tattered rag doll. She crossed her arms protectively over her stomach, a troubled frown etching her face.

"I don't think you should enter the room. Thomas is a suspect. It's too risky," Zach cautioned, noticing the subtle shift in her expression, from wounded puppy to fierce warrior.

"You can't dictate my actions, Zach. I'm not yours anymore," she retorted, stepping back, but he tightened his grip on her forearm, keeping her in place.

"What a relief," he replied dryly, pulling her closer so that only she could hear his words. "Just so you know, I will find out about our child and fight you for custody," he seethed, his anger pulsating through his clenched teeth.

A whimper escaped Kayla's lips as she jerked her arm free from his grasp and fled into the examination room.

Perhaps he had come on too strong. Zach entered the room, his gaze fixated on Thomas, who wore a smug grin on his face. He entwined his fingers with Kayla's as she

137

leaned against him on the bed. The fire in Zach's heart threatened to erupt like a volcano. How dare Thomas lay his hands on his wife?

"You two waste no time getting comfortable," Zach blurted out, instantly regretting his words. What was wrong with him? His emotions were chaotic, a tangled mess. If looks could kill, he would have perished thrice over.

Visiting hours were ending, the dim lights casting a somber atmosphere in the hospital room. Stephen's piercing glare sent unspoken warnings to Zach; the tension was palpable in the air. Zach retrieved his notepad from his pocket, the sound of his pen tapping on the surface echoing in the quiet room. He could smell the faint scent of antiseptic, a reminder of the sterile environment they were in.

"Make this snappy. My patient needs to rest."

"How did you know where Ms. Smith was?" Zach asked, his voice breaking the silence.

"Silas called me panicking," Thomas replied, his voice filled with concern.

Zach jotted down a few notes, the scratch of his pen against the paper filling the room. This case couldn't be as straightforward as it seemed.

"You told him you'd clean up his mess?" Zach questioned; his curiosity piqued.

"Not hardly," Thomas mumbled, his voice barely audible.

Zach continued to write, the sound of his pen moving across the page keeping him focused. He needed evidence, not just assumptions.

"Are you working for Silas?" he inquired, his voice steady.

Thomas shifted uncomfortably under the crisp white sheets, the rustle of fabric breaking the stillness. "He's my little brother," he admitted, his voice tinged with sadness.

"What?" Kayla's fingers jerked away from Thomas, the sudden movement causing her to almost lose her balance as she jumped out of bed. The sound of her footsteps filled the room as she hastened away.

"It's not what it sounds like. He has a mental health condition, and when he forgets to take his medication, he turns into an insane person," Thomas explained, his voice filled with desperation.

Zach had his suspicions, but he needed concrete evidence. "Has he been sending Kayla gifts and stalking her?" he asked, his tone serious.

"No," Thomas replied firmly, his voice resolute.

Zach's forehead creased as he rubbed it, the pressure in his temples building. He could feel a headache forming. "How can you be so sure? Only if you're her stalker," Zach pressed, trying to uncover the truth.

"Listen, I find her attractive. Who wouldn't? But I'd never scare her or try to kill her," Thomas insisted, his voice fading as his eyes drooped closed.

Suddenly, Stephen stood at the door, his presence commanding. "Detective, I think you've asked enough questions. You can return during normal business hours," he declared, motioning for them to leave. The sound of his voice was authoritative, leaving no room for argument. "Kayla, Lily is in the parking lot. I'll see you at home." He placed a kiss on top of her head before stalking off down the hall.

Kayla, her emotions in turmoil, rushed out of the ER without sparing Zach a second glance. The sound of her hurried footsteps echoed down the corridor.

Zach felt a surge of frustration, his head pounding. He kicked the side of the wall; the impact reverberating through his body. It felt like he had lost control over his own life.

"You can't keep our daughter from me. I deserve to know," he exclaimed, his voice filled with desperation as he struggled to regain a sense of control.

Chapter Seven

Zach rhythmically strummed his fingers over the warm, swirling steam that rose from his coffee cup, creating a comforting mist in the air. Lost in a daze, he observed the delicate tendrils of steam vanish into the crisp morning air. Despite already savoring his second cup of decaffeinated coffee, he found no solace in the tranquil stillness of his backyard, even as the birds chirped in the distance. Their melodic songs failed to calm his restless soul. The world, with its illusion of peace and unity, offered no respite for his troubled heart.

Throughout the night, Zach had wrestled with his covers, tormented by the haunting echoes of squeaky toddler voices calling out for their father. For him. It was a nightmarish memory that clung to the recesses of his mind, waiting to pounce and attack the woman who had held the answers to his paternal questions.

Contemplating stepping down from the case, he questioned how he could protect Kayla when she refused to meet his gaze and when impurity tainted his thoughts. She had stirred up a wild beast within him, extinguishing any remnants of attraction or longing when she confessed her secret. Deep down, he had yearned for a second chance to prove to her he would never abandon her. But what was the point? He could not go backwards and he could not move forward with a deceitful woman.

"Why are you tormenting me, God?" Zach silently pleaded. "I don't deserve this treatment. I am a dedicated advocate for justice, for Your justice. Why must you unravel every fiber of my being?"

The back door slid open, interrupting his inner turmoil, as Peter skillfully balanced two bags of donuts and a steaming coffee mug. Zach couldn't help but envy his brother's seemingly uncomplicated life, and he would willingly trade places with him in an instant. With a casual toss, Peter handed a white paper bag to Zach, emanating the enticing aroma of freshly baked pastries.

"Thanks, bro," Zach expressed his gratitude, reaching into the bag and retrieving a piping hot, cinnamon-coated donut. As he took a bite, it instantly transported back to his childhood, sitting beside his mother on tall stools, eagerly awaiting his favorite treat. In those innocent days, he had been blissfully unaware of the heartaches and cruelties that plagued the world. He had entrusted someone else to care for him and fight his battles. Oh, to be that carefree boy again.

Peter took a sip of his vanilla-scented coffee, wincing as the warmth coursed down his throat. "What's on your mind?" he inquired.

Zach, his mouth still full of dough, pinched off an enormous piece and tossed it into his mouth. "I don't want to talk about it. Ever."

"Kayla getting under your skin?" Peter propped his feet on the weathered ledge of the back deck, the warm sun casting a golden glow on his face. He couldn't help but smile as he devoured his sugary donut, the sweet aroma wafting through the air.

"I'm thinking about stepping down from this case."

Peter's eyebrows furrowed, his mouth forming a surprised "o" shape. The sound of birds chirping filled the quiet backyard. "Who are you? My brother's no quitter."

Zach clenched his fists, feeling the tension build. He tossed the last bite of his donut into his mouth; the crumbs falling into the crumpled bag with a satisfying crunch. "Thanks for those uplifting words, but I don't deserve it."

"Listen bro, you're not that same nineteen-year-old boy. God has transformed you, and you never have to go back." Peter's words hung in the air, accompanied by a gentle breeze rustling through the leaves.

Zach ran his fingers through his damp hair, feeling the coolness against his skin. He shifted uncomfortably in the cushioned chair, the soft fabric pressing against him. "God and I aren't that close right now."

"I suspected that. But He hasn't left you, Zach. God's waiting in the shadows to pick you up and carry you through this trying time." Peter's donut trash soared through the air, the sound of the bag crinkling as it landed in the trashcan with a thud.

Zach longed for the days when he relied on God for support, feeling His presence like a warm embrace. He missed the comfort of letting Him carry his burdens.

"I'm a dad," he blurted out, bitterness tinged his words.

"You're a what?" Peter's mouthful of hot liquid sprayed onto his khaki pants, causing a sizzling sound. He quickly reached for a napkin, the soft fabric absorbing the mess. "I didn't even know you were married until days ago. You're full of surprises."

"My marriage is nothing more than a legal, binding document. All love and attraction washed away years ago." Zach's fingers clenched into tight fists, the pressure building. He fought the urge to pound something.

"You sure about that?" His brother's voice was hopeful, a hint of longing in his tone.

"Sure, I have to beat down the attraction because she's more beautiful than when we first got married. But there is not even an ounce of love for her in my heart." Zach's words came out dry, void of emotion. He couldn't love a woman who lied to him and continued to conceal a huge part of his life.

"Tell me about my niece or nephew." Peter leaned forward in the chair, his elbow resting on his knee. The sound of a distant lawnmower filled the air.

"That's just it. Kayla threw a bomb in my face and never expounded on it. Do I have a child running around, feeling abandoned by her father? Or is there a grave somewhere with the remains of my child?" Zach's frustration boiled over, causing him to jump to his feet and slap the side of the porch railing, the sound echoing through the spacious backyard.

"It's a good thing you have skills to aid in finding your child," Peter said, his voice carrying a hint of relief, as he stood up from the creaking porch chair. He rested one foot on the weathered ledge.

"I could, but I'd rather watch Kayla squirm and sweat," Zach replied, his frustration obvious in his voice. The urge to rip something in half coursed through him, his hands itching with pent-up anger. He had a tiny part of himself; a small child, running around, oblivious to who her daddy was. Why make anything easy on her?

"Just remember, if there is a kid involved, you don't want to damage the relationship with Kayla so much that she gives you the bare parental rights," Peter cautioned, the words hanging in the air like a warning.

"She doesn't decide what rights I have. I'll leave that to the judge," Zach said, his temples throbbing with a constant pounding pain. He rubbed them, hoping to find some relief. "While I'm at it, I'll finish our divorce. Get a clean break from Kayla."

Peter's hand squeezed Zach's left shoulder, a supportive gesture that spoke volumes about their brotherly bond. The pressure provided a moment of comfort amidst the chaos. "What about Kayla?" Peter asked, concern lacing his words.

Zach brushed off his brother's hand, turning to face him with a piercing gaze. "Are you seriously defending her?" he retorted, his voice sharp with resentment.

"I'm just saying you left her. Not like she could find you. How do you think it was for her going through pregnancy alone? If you have a living child, there's no evidence to show that she's a mommy," Peter reasoned, trying to bring some perspective on the situation.

She only had herself to blame for going through pregnancy alone. He had left, but he wasn't exactly hiding. Kayla could have found him if she wanted to. The thought lingered, mingling with a mix of guilt and regret. At nineteen, he wasn't fit to be anyone's dad, let alone a husband.

"I gotta hit the gym before work. Want to join me? Take your mind off everything?" Peter suggested, his voice hopeful. He walked towards the sliding back door, his fingers tapping impatiently on the cool glass surface.

"Maybe another time," Zach replied, feeling the weight of the day bearing down on him. He pulled his phone out of his pocket, the sleek device fitting snugly in his hand. Glancing at the screen, he saw it was already eight o'clock. He knew he needed to get ready for the day, but a lack of motivation held him in place. Leaning against the sturdy railing, he felt its solid support against his back.

"You behave yourself today," Peter said, a smirk playing on his slightly tanned face.

He wouldn't make any promises. But when he drove to work, he'd take the scenic route, perform a wellness check on Kayla. Not because he cared, but because he needed to extract any information she had. Maybe he could use his Southern charm to get what he wanted. Either way, he was determined to find out about his child.

His phone suddenly vibrated in his palm, causing an exasperated eye roll. He contemplated ignoring the call, wanting to see if she would enjoy being ignored. Professionally, he knew he shouldn't do that. But the inner child within him yearned to push the red button and ignore her. With a deep sigh, he reluctantly answered the phone.

"Zach, here," he said with a tone that screamed annoyance.

"Zach…"

"What do you want, Kayla?" He scolded himself for the way his heart raced when she said his name. How could he find that attractive when he despised her with every fiber of his being?

"A package … Someone is here… I—I…"

"You're breaking up," he interrupted, leaping off the porch and rushing towards his unmarked SUV issued by the state. "I'm on my way. Kayla, stay on the phone."

With a trembling breath and a cacophony of background noise, the line abruptly went dead. Zach slid the keys into the ignition, barely having time to buckle his seatbelt before he sped down the road. He could feel his pulse pounding through his fingertips, the urgency of the situation palpable. Her relentless pursuer wasn't relenting,

146

and they were exploiting his lack of judgment. He had to reach her in time.

God, please protect her.

****

"Stop!" Lily bolted through the house, chasing her one-year-old daughter, brush and hair bows in hand. "I'm gonna be sick." Lily bent over, dry heaving, crunching up her expanded stomach.

With a gentle laugh, Kayla swooped her cousin into her hands, her long black curls draping over Kayla's arm. "I got you, princess." Kayla swung her cousin around as giggles exploded from the toddler's mouth.

"You're a lifesaver." Lily plopped onto the couch, resting her head on a throw pillow. Her olive-tinted skin was a pale-white. "I just need a moment."

"Since I'm already holding Ray-Ray, why don't I fix her hair and you grab some crackers?" Kayla grabbed the brush and bows while juggling a squirmy little girl, her green eyes sparkling with mischief. She was definitely her father's child.

"Can you stay with us forever? At least until the first trimester is over, and I feel halfway human again." Lily nabbed a pack of saltines off the kitchen counter. The sound of plastic crunching open filled the spacious living room. Kayla sat next to the modern-white-sleeked fireplace, glancing at the open-concept living room and kitchen. Decorated in vibrant, ocean-colored hues, the living room had a tranquil feeling like one felt, staring into the rustling ocean waves. Lily's happy place was the coast of North Carolina, and everything on the first floor of her house gave off that vibe, even the shell-shaped throw pillows.

Kayla's laugh mixed with the rustling of the cracker packaging. It felt amazing to laugh again. Maybe distancing herself from her thorn-in-the-flesh revived her mood.

"I'll stay as long as I can. School starts back in a few days." Kayla ran her fingers through Rachel's black curls, braiding half a pigtail.

"One day, you'll make a wonderful mom." Lily took a nibble of her cracker, propping her feet on the coffee table. "Maybe with that handsome detective?"

Kayla almost choked on her saliva, coughing as she swallowed the wrong way. She figured everyone in her family knew about her past mistakes, but apparently, pregnancy fog swiped those memories out of Lily's brain.

"What did I say?" Lily jumped up from her seat, ready to give the Heimlich maneuver.

Kayla blinked back tears. Life wasn't fair. She should have her daughter in her arms, brushing her golden hair, hearing her precious laughter floating through the room. Maybe even basking in the joys of married life with Zach. But he took all that away when he walked out on them years ago. His selfish arrogance still smacked her in the face continually.

"Oh, Kayla. I'm so sorry. Me and my big mouth." Lily leaned against the arm of the chair, scooping Kayla into a loose hug. "Want to talk about it?"

No. She wanted to bury the hurt and pain under layers of dirt, never letting those piercing pains consume her again. But Lily had a way of drawing out the pain with her soothing voice. She should have been a psychiatrist instead of an ICU doctor.

"Whatever you say stays between us." Lily squeezed her arm over Kayla's shoulder. Something her mom always did. Man, Kayla missed her parents. It was almost time for her weekly trips home for a visit.

"Um … You know, Zach and I married out of high school. We lived in student housing at college. We were both so young and unprepared for a future together. I tried making it work, but Zach had a jealous streak that put a wedge between our marriage. He never felt good enough for me, which left me with a lot of insecurities."

Lily grabbed the wiggly toddler out of Kayla's arms, watching her teeter off into her book corner. "Oh, honey."

"When he left me four years ago, I had planned on sharing with him my positive pregnancy test." Kayla swiped at the tears streaming down her cheeks. "At first, shock gripped my heart. We weren't ready for a baby, but I hoped as a couple, we could figure it out. Only, he packed up and left, never giving me the chance to tell him."

Lily squeezed Kayla's hand in a motherly, supportive way. "What happened to the baby?"

Kayla covered her face with her trembling hands, tears sliding through the cracks. "Her name is Annabelle. She has the prettiest golden hair and ocean blue eyes. Every time I look at her, I see Zach and all the past failures engulf me like the waves of the ocean."

"After all these years, you've never hinted at being a mother." Lily jumped up from the chair, taking away the remote from Rachel's busy fingers.

"I wasn't ready to share my story. There's still so much more that I can't tell anyone. The wound hasn't healed. Not sure if it ever will."

"Where is Annabelle?" Lily pulled her daughter off the floor, giving her a bear hug.

"During the week, she stays with my parents. I see her every weekend. I've saved enough money to buy a tiny house, just the two of us." Kayla stood to her feet, stepping to the bay window. "It was a hard decision, but I raised her as a single parent/college student until I graduated college. She's been with my mom since I moved to Tennessee. I needed to get established as a teacher, and I can't wait to bring her home."

"That's the most selfless thing I've ever heard. I just wish you would have shared with us your secret." Lily slid her phone off the kitchen counter. "It all makes sense now. I often wondered where you disappeared to every weekend. Stephen figured you missed your parents so much, you had to drive the four hours' difference to see them every weekend."

"She is the blessing that came out of my heartache." No point sharing the rest of the story. Kayla pulled back the curtain as a dark sedan creeped in front of the house. With sweaty palms, she held the curtain in place, willing for the strange car to drive away.

"We have to finish this conversation later." Lily yanked her purse off the floor. Wiping a smug of breakfast off of her daughter's face. "I forgot about Rachel's checkup. Good thing we live close to the pediatrician."

"Be safe." Kayla locked the door as Lily rushed out of the house carrying a toddler and a diaper bag equal in size.

Seconds later, the doorbell rang, a high-pitched sound that sent a jolt through Kayla's body. Her heart sank as she felt a sudden chill in the air. She tried to calm herself, telling herself that Lily probably just forgot something.

As she cautiously slid open the door, a wave of fear washed over her. The sight before her made her gasp - an enormous teddy bear, its soft fur a comforting shade of brown, and a bouquet of white roses resting against the porch railing. Her stalker's signature—white roses. She scanned the quiet neighborhood, searching for any signs of trouble, but everything appeared normal.

Her trembling hands reached out to grab the bear and flowers, but her nerves got the best of her. The vase slipped from her grasp, shattering on the tiled floor, water flooding the room. The loud crash echoed through the house, adding to the tension in the air. Panic surged within her as she slammed the front door shut, checking the locks twice to ensure her safety.

As she surveyed the mess before her, she noticed a tiny red card floating on top of the water spill. With quivering hands, she reached down to retrieve the card, her eyes scanning the words written on it.

"Care Bear, I can't wait for you to see me. I see you all the time. I know you love me, too." The words sent a chill down her spine, and she felt a knot forming in her stomach. Kayla's pulse quickened as recent pictures of her fell to the floor. Someone was so close, they snapped pictures of her sleeping.

Finding some comfort, she grabbed her phone and dialed Zach's number. The shrill ring tone pierced the silence, causing her heart to race even faster. Just as she was about to speak, an alarm blared throughout the house, alerting her to an intruder.

Fear consumed her, and she knew she had to find a place to hide. With heavy, labored breaths, she dashed for the closet, her footsteps echoing in the empty hallway. It wasn't the smartest hiding place, but at that moment, it was the only option she had.

"Zach, here," his voice came through the phone, filled with annoyance and impatience.

"Zach…" she said, her voice trembling.

"What do you want, Kayla?" His anger was palpable, and she regretted calling him, but she had no one else to turn to.

"I got a package. Someone's in the house," she blurted out, her words rushed and filled with fear.

"You're breaking up," he interrupted, his voice becoming distorted. "I'm on my way. Kayla, stay on the phone."

Before she could respond, the closet door swung open, causing her to drop her phone in shock. A wave of desperation washed over her as she whispered a silent plea for help.

****

"Good thing Paul's coming back in three days. My protecting skills are lacking." Zach shifted the gear in park, grabbing his keys before sliding out of his SUV. He pulled his gun out of his shoulder holster, entering stealth-mode. Zach noticed the blaring alarm, hoping the tripped alarm had alerted the local police. Being within town limits, the jurisdiction fell to the police instead of the sheriff's office. But the two collaborated a lot since the sheriff's office only had two deputies, two detectives, and the sheriff. And the police station had the same number of officers; about four.

The front door, painted in a vibrant aqua shade, stood steadfastly in its frame, its lock secure and no indications of any forced entry. Zach cautiously made his way to the back of the house, his eyes scanning his surroundings. As he reached the back, the door was wide open with a small crack, just big enough for his hand to fit through. The sound of his footsteps echoed through the air, accompanied by the crunching of broken glass under his shoes as he entered the kitchen. Despite the alarming situation, everything appeared normal, except for the blaring sound of the alarm. With a quick text, he got the code and skillfully disarmed the alarm system. As the deafening noise ceased, a sense of relief washed over him, providing a much-needed respite from the constant headache-inducing sound. In this newfound tranquility, his mind could finally think clearly. Stepping over a water spill, he slid his gloves on, retrieving the red card submerged in the water. Through wet, blotchy ink, he made out the words, 'I see you all the time. I know you love me, too.'

What sicko toyed with her emotions and demanded love? The only two suspects, Thomas and Silas, both seemed overconfident and lacking in the female department. Both personalities were not appealing enough to catch Kayla's eyes. He couldn't blame them. Kayla's beauty and personality, though fiery and sassy, were on a field of her own. But clearly, they couldn't measure up to him. Many couldn't. What if the stalker weren't these two losers? A man from her past? College? He knew nothing about her dating history or who she casually flirted with. Might be an awkward conversation, but one they needed to have soon. And if Sarah wanted everything Kayla had him included, would she play the role of a stalker? Hire someone to take Kayla's focus off of Zach? He shook his head at the ludicrous thought. Sarah had a list of faults, but she wouldn't hire someone to stalk her sister or to get rid of her.

Where was Kayla, anyway? He scanned the living room for any clues to her whereabouts. Nothing. She said she was hiding in a hall closet. His shoes bounced off the tiled floor, filling the eerie silence with a beat that matched his pulse; fast and erratic. Zach twisted the closet door handle, sweat attacking the doorknob as he prayed for her to be inside. Alive. He flung the door open as a gush of air swooshed in his perspiring face. Empty. Zach kicked at the pile of clothes on the ground, feeling anger and disappointment travel up his body. He didn't arrive on time. Now, some crazed stalker had his slimy hands on his wife. His MO wasn't really that of a stalker anymore. Casually creepy notes and gifts were more on the level of an infatuated stalker, not abduction or even murder.

He had to find her in time. So, he didn't love her, but he didn't want any harm to come to her. A protectiveness rolled through his body, taking his breath away.

God, I have no right to beg You to protect her, but for her sake, not mine, answer this prayer. Turning to close the closet door, he noticed her brown equestrian phone case lying buried under a jacket, uncovered enough to make out a shiny part of a horse's body. He stared at the text message draft floating on the screen. *School. Female.* He slid the phone into a clear bag, shaking his head at the clue. Or maybe it wasn't even a clue, but a writing prompt for her students. Spring break was slipping away fast.

Zach slammed the closet door, barely noticing his brother standing behind him. "What did the door do to you?" Peter rubbed the sides of his police uniform, straightening out any wrinkles that weren't visible.

Zach jumped at the sound of his brother's baritone voice. How had Peter slipped by him without Zach seeing? Clearly, he was off his game.

"What are you doing here?" Zach knew the answer before he asked, but he needed to make small talk, trying to calm his nerves.

"Jurisdiction." Peter ran his fingers through his neatly combed hair, a habit the River men possessed. "Since you're the detective on the case, my captain said we could work together. No need calling in one of the town's detectives when we are short staffed already."

Great, but he was the lead detective on this case, no matter what.

"Um ... Did you find any clues or Ms. Smith's..." Peter shifted uncomfortably, staring at the floor. Awkward didn't accurately describe the tension in the air.

"Body? Really, Pete?" Zach wanted to keep the case professional, else he'd slug his brother in the shoulder for even thinking about her lying somewhere, the life strangled out of her body. It was a job hazard, and he couldn't keep his mind from going to that dark place.

"Just show me the clues." Peter snatched the evidence bags out of his brother's fingers, frowning.

"It's not much to go with, but we need to canvas the neighborhood and question the staff at the middle school. The crime scene unit should be here shortly to dust for prints, I assume?" He wanted his co-workers out here combing through the scene, not men or women, Zach didn't know or trust. But jurisdiction was a big thing in a small town. So, he'd roll with it. But he called the shots.

"I'll start questioning the neighbors." Peter saluted his brother in a mock way, hiding the smirk tugging on the corner of his lips.

Zach rolled his eyes at his brother's childish tendencies. No time for jokes when a woman's life hung in the balance. Blue lights flashed outside as officers rushed out of their cars. "I'm going to talk to Lily Smith on my way to Kayla's apartment. Maybe I'll find more clues."

"Okay, I got this." Peter motioned with his hands at the crime scene, or lack of one, just broken glass and a water spill. But maybe they'd get lucky and get a print.

Zach crouched down on the newly built back patio, the wooden planks sturdy under his weight. His eyes scanned the area, searching for any overlooked clues in the bright sunlight. A glimmer of teal caught his attention, the earring shining like a tiny jewel against the smooth wooden boards. Carefully, he reached out with gloved fingers, the cool touch of the metal sending a shiver down his spine. Sliding it into a clear evidence bag, he pondered its significance. Could it belong to Lily, or perhaps the perpetrator?

Heart pounding, Zach climbed into his SUV, the familiar sound of the engine rumbling to life. The leather seat welcomed him, cool against his back as he fastened the seatbelt over his shoulder. Thoughts raced through his mind, the weight of his failure to save Kayla pressing heavily on his chest. The uncertainty of the investigation loomed, the lack of solid leads leaving him with a sinking feeling. He knew he had to gather information about his own daughter, just in case anything happened to Kayla. And he couldn't ignore the responsibility of notifying Kayla's parents about her abduction, their anguish mirroring his own. Fear gripped his heart at the thought of contacting Kayla's parents. Did they know about him? If so, their opinion probably wasn't the best. He'd suck it up and put on his big boy pants. Emotions aside, he had a case to run, and a beautiful, amazing woman to find. He admired her, even if bitterness gnawed at his heart over her deception. She could never be his, but right now, that didn't matter. Finding her alive did.

■■■

"Mrs. Smith, my name is Zach Rivers. I'm a detective with the McMinn County Sheriff's Office. I'm calling about your daughter, Kayla…" His voice drifted off as he made the call that always sobered his mood and lit a fire in his heart. Fifteen minutes of torture. Notifying next of kin for any reason, especially abduction or homicide, never sat well with Zach. He, being the bearer or terrible news, often had to learn how to offer hope without sounding as hopeless as most cases were. He also couldn't give a family member false hope, when life rarely produced a happy ending.

Zach turned his SUV off, feeling the heat from the late afternoon engulf his personal space. He swiped his sweaty brow, wondering when spring in East Tennessee became so unbearable. *Focus, man.* Zach shook his head, trying to gain control of his wayward thoughts. Mrs. Smith's words jolted him out of his funk.

"Ma'am, can you repeat that?" Zach ran his fingers through his slightly damp hair, the heat acting like a cruel taskmaster.

"You're the guy that married Kayla?" Uh, he was not expecting that. He didn't think anyone knew about their hasty marriage, but apparently, he was mistaken.

"Y-yes." Was he signing his death certificate? Maybe he should refocus their conversation back to safer ground. Anything but his past relationship with Kayla. "Ma'am, I will notify you with an update once I receive one."

"Wait a minute!" Her voice sounded raspy and urgent. Zach clutched the steering wheel, waiting for a lashing out from his estranged wife's mother—his mother-in-law.

"Ma'am?"

"I'm not condoning you or my daughter for past mistakes. She has suffered enough, and I'm sure you have too."

Where was she going with this?

"I fell yesterday, spraining my right ankle. My doctor expects a full recovery, but recovery time ranges from one week to three or more." Her voice dropped like she was chatting with someone in the background. "I've called Kayla, and now I know why she hasn't responded. But I can't take care of her right now."

"Mrs. Smith, I'm not following you." Zach's eyes rolled through the parking lot, looking for anything suspicious.

"Your daughter!" She blurted out in exasperation.

"My-my daughter?" So, Zach had a daughter that was alive and full of energy. A smile covered his face at the thought of a little female version of himself running around. God, help him because he worried his mom sick, so much so, she had gray hair prematurely.

A deep sigh sounded over the phone. "I guess Kayla never took my advice and filled you in about your daughter?"

That was a nice way of putting it. Deception. Lies. A coward. Those were words running through his mind to describe Kayla. Zach threw his head back in the seat like someone punched him in the face and the shock glued him to the seat.

"I'll fill you in briefly. The rest of the story you'll have to hear from Kayla. God willing, when you find her safe." Mrs. Smith sighed into the phone. Her voice seeming older than her age range of forty to fifty. "Annabelle Rebekah Rivers is an energetic three-year-old. She'll be four in the summer. Annabelle has no filter, but her honesty and innocence add to her natural beauty. I've never met a child so full of love and mischief. She keeps me on my toes, but I'm supposed to stay off my feet, so I'll be bringing her to you until Kayla takes her or I get healed."

Annabelle Rivers. She took his last name. The sound of a child's voice echoed in his mind as Zach, a bona fide bachelor who didn't even own a pet, had a daughter. And her grandmother wanted him to take care of her? The car seemed to spin around him, his heart pounding in his chest. He knew nothing about kids. Was she potty trained? Did three-year-olds wear diapers? Did she drink from a bottle? No, maybe a sippy cup? How was he supposed to brush her hair and cook her meals? The weight of responsibility pressed down on him, beads of sweat forming on his forehead. He didn't even want to think about how you got a three-year-old to sleep.

"I'm not sure this is a good idea." Zach's throat tightened, a sour taste creeping up. He could have a showdown with gun-wielding criminals, but the thought of taking care of an actual human being caused a wave of nausea. His human being. The daughter he never met.

"This is not up for discussion, young man. Man up and take care of your daughter. If nothing else, it'll cause you to find my daughter quicker. Then if you want to be a deadbeat dad, that's up to you."

Ouch, I guess she settled that. The air spun faster, dizziness overtaking his movement. Zach stumbled backwards, reaching out to steady himself against the seat, his eyes closed. *You can do this. It's the chance you wanted—to know your daughter.* The sound of his own heartbeat filled his ears, pounding against his chest. *Don't mess it up.*

"My husband and I will be there in five hours. I'll call you when we arrive." Mrs. Smith's voice trembled, each word barely audible, like she had hung up the phone, but her heavy breaths said otherwise. "Don't tell Sarah."

"Ma'am, why…" Before he could finish his sentence, the phone call dropped. Great, just great. Zach took a calming, deep breath. *Get it together, man. Find Kayla, and fast.*

As he removed his keys from the ignition, he made his way towards Kayla's apartment building, strategizing how he could sweet-talk Sarah into granting him access to search through Kayla's belongings. Without leading her on.

He jogged through the dimly lit apartment building, the stifling heat engulfing his body, causing beads of sweat to form on his forehead. The absence of cool air from the AC only intensified the discomfort of the scorching heat wave.

Zach halted in front of Kayla's apartment door, his eyes fixating on the freshly placed wealth decoration. He rapped his knuckles against the door, hoping to find Sarah at home but dreading the encounter. The door swung open, revealing Sarah, who brushed a strand of fiery red hair away from her eyes. Her disheveled ponytail and smudges of flour on her flawless skin gave her an alluring charm. Her piercing green eyes bore into him, igniting a desire that mirrored his own. If only he had met Sarah Smith before marrying Kayla, everything could have been different.

Despite his buried love for Kayla, Zach couldn't deny how difficult she was to live with. Even after all these years apart, she still brought out the worst in him.

"Hey, Detective. Have you come to investigate my latest recipe?" Sarah's seductive smile drew him into the apartment, her hands gently wrapping around his arm. The tantalizing aroma wafting from the kitchen assaulted his senses, making his stomach protest with a growl. When was the last time he ate? A quick refuel with Sarah's exquisite cooking wouldn't hinder the investigation. After all, a man needed sustenance to stay alive.

As if she could read his thoughts, Sarah tugged his arm towards the kitchen, a mischievous smile playing on her lips. "I've missed you," she whispered. She scooped a generous portion of casserole into a glass bowl, eagerly presenting it to him with a spoon. Brimming with anticipation, she fixed her eyes on him.

The flavors of garlic and onions danced on his tongue as Zach's brain turned to mush in the presence of this stunning woman. He abruptly stood up from the chair, realizing the gravity of the situation. This wasn't a friendly visit. He was the lead detective on Kayla's case, and he was doing her a disservice by flirting with her sister and indulging in a meal while she was still missing, presumably abducted.

"Food not to your liking?" Sarah whispered seductively, her fingers delicately tracing up the side of his arm. The proximity between them was palpable, the heat radiating off her making his face flush. The pounding of his heart echoed in his chest, a mix of desire and apprehension. He knew he had to break free from Sarah's seductive web before it ensnared him completely.

"S-Sarah, I'm sorry. I can't do this," he stammered, pushing her hands away and taking a step back. The air felt heavy with tension as he tried to regain his composure.

"Grow a conscience suddenly?" Sarah's piercing green eyes burned with an intensity he had never seen before. The fire in her gaze stung his soul. "It's because of her."

Ouch. Her words struck a nerve, attacking his integrity and reminding him of his past mistakes. He couldn't deny the truth - what kind of Christian man would willingly play with fire by indulging in a relationship with his estranged wife's flirtatious sister? Despite his faltering faith, Zach still clung to his Christian values. He couldn't continue this dangerous game any longer.

"Sarah, you're captivating, and you make me yearn for things that can never be. But our relationship ends here," Zach said, running his trembling fingers through his hair. Each breath he took came out in short, choppy bursts.

"I know you don't mean those words. We have a connection, and Kayla stood in the way before. I won't let her do it again," Sarah retorted defiantly, her tone laced with a threatening undertone.

A sense of dread washed over him. What was she talking about? He had barely noticed Sarah's presence, his eyes always fixed on Kayla. "Please, don't make this harder for me," he pleaded, desperately trying to shift the focus away from their twisted relationship.

But Sarah wasn't ready to let go. With a chilling smile, she picked up a spatula, the cold metal glinting ominously. The sight sent a shiver down his spine. "I won't let you walk away so easily. You belong to me," she declared, her words dripping with possessiveness.

Suppressing a sigh, he resisted the urge to point out the obvious - that he belonged to Kayla, not her. Now was not the time for semantics. Instead, he swiftly changed the subject, trying to regain control of the situation. "Sarah, I'm here in my professional role as a detective. Your sister is missing," he stated, his gaze darting around the cluttered living room filled with boxes, Kayla's horse paintings leaning against the wall.

A wave of confusion washed over him as he noticed the absence of Kayla's pictures. "Why are you taking down all of Kayla's pictures?" he asked, his voice tinged with concern.

A nonchalant shrug escaped Sarah's shoulders as she sank into a recliner. "She's not coming back," she replied dismissively, the weight of her words hanging heavily in the air.

His mind raced, trying to comprehend the gravity of the situation. "Explain," he demanded, desperation creeping into his tone.

"No, I didn't kill her. But if it would change your mind about us, I'd think about it," Sarah admitted with a mischievous smile playing on her lips. The implication sent a chill down his spine. He couldn't believe his own foolishness - Sarah was not just a potential love interest, she was a suspect in her sister's abduction. He needed to refocus, to get his head back in the game.

As Sarah spoke, her voice echoed in the semi-empty apartment. "Kayla bought a house on the north side of town. Supposed to be her last week in the apartment." She gestured to the boxes along the wall. "Surprised she hasn't picked up her stuff, though."

Desperation filled his voice as he asked, "Can I take the boxes? Look through them?" The air felt heavy, as if holding its breath, waiting for Sarah's response.

"I don't care what you do with them," Sarah replied dismissively, her frustration clear. With a quick flick of her hand, she grabbed a crumpled paper and threw it into one of the opened boxes. The sound of the paper hitting the cardboard was sharp and piercing.

Zach's eyes darted to the box, his heart pounding in his chest. "That's her address. She's probably in renovation mode and tuned out the world." Sarah muttered, her voice trailing off.

With trembling hands, Zach reached for one box near the empty bedroom. The weight of it surprised him, and he struggled to maintain his grip. Silence was deafening as he carried the box towards the door, each step creaking on the wooden floor. The apartment felt devoid of life, as if it had already moved on without Kayla.

"I'll go put this in my SUV and come get the rest," Zach declared, his voice determined, yet filled with a sense of urgency.

"Whatever. I'm late for work. Lock up when you're done." She slipped out of the apartment, slamming the door behind her.

Left alone in the apartment, the lingering aroma of Italian cuisine filled the air, a reminder of Sarah's hurried departure. The scent was both comforting and bittersweet, like a memory fading away.

"God, I'm making a mess out of my life," he whispered, tears welling up in his eyes. "I need Your help and forgiveness. I can't continue down the reckless path I'm on."

With a heavy heart, Zach returned to the task at hand. With teary eyes, he carefully retrieved Kayla's belongings. He prayed fervently, hoping that the key to her whereabouts rested securely in a box. With God by his side, he believed he could find her and begin the journey back to the faith he so desperately needed to cling to.

Chapter Eight

"Hello?" Kayla winced in pain and instinctively rubbed the tender spot on the top of her head. As she blinked her eyes, her vision slowly adjusted, revealing the room she was in. The sight made her question if she was dreaming. Her two favorite things, majestic horses and breathtaking waterfalls, adorned the pink-tinted walls. Although not her own new house, the decorations mirrored the personal touches she had envisioned for her own home. Kayla stepped out of the bedroom onto the narrow hallway. The sound of her footsteps echoed on the polished hardwood floors with each cautious step she took. Her eyes caught sight of a name plaque etched onto a purple-stained door - Annabelle. Tracing her fingers over the coarse letters, a shiver ran down her spine. Curiosity got the best of her as she gently nudged the door open with her foot, revealing Annabelle's room. A gasp escaped her lips as her eyes landed on a disturbing sight. Hung on the center of the wall was a doctored portrait of herself and Annabelle, their faces filled with laughter as they sat outside. The realization sent a wave of revulsion through her. What was more unsettling, a stranger had created this twisted fantasy world or inclusion of her innocent daughter?

"Annabelle?" Kayla's voice, low and filled with concern, cut through the silence of the room. Her eyes scanned the room, taking in the princess-themed comforter on the toddler-sized bed and the dolls lining the wall. A towering dollhouse, a luxury she could never afford on her modest teacher's salary, stood nearby. Panic gripped her as she realized the gravity of the situation. Where was she? And who had abducted her? If Annabelle wasn't present, it meant that the sick individual who had taken her was planning a sinister family reunion. With a sense of urgency, Kayla knew she had to warn her mother and protect Annabelle from the impending threat. But how?

Kayla frantically bolted out of the dimly lit room, her heart pounding in her chest, and stumbled over a smiley-faced rug that felt rough and scratchy under her feet. The sight of it only added to her sense of unease. She needed to escape this place, as if it had invaded her mind and rearranged everything to trap her forever. The feeling of being watched intensified, making her every move feel scrutinized. With a surge of determination, she rushed towards the door, her palms sweaty and trembling as she desperately pulled at the wooden handle, but it remained stubbornly shut. Frustrated, she pounded on the door with her open palm; the sound echoing through the room, but it yielded no results except for a throbbing ache in her hand.

Her eyes then caught sight of a picturesque window adorned with delicate curtains. With a mix of hope and desperation, she grabbed an equestrian-decorated lamp nearby, its weight solid and comforting in her hands, and brought it crashing against the windowpane. She braced herself for the sound of shattering glass, but to her dismay, not even a scratch appeared on the smooth surface. Panic welled up inside her, suffocating her. She couldn't afford to give up. With her heart racing and hands trembling, she dropped the lamp onto the floor, the sound of it shattering into countless fragments filling the air.

God, get me out of here! Her voice filled with anguish and fear. She needed divine intervention to escape this nightmare.

Regrouping her thoughts, Kayla rushed into the modern kitchen, the sleek appliances seeming out of place in this sinister environment. She scoffed at the thought of using them, her focus solely on finding a way out. She grabbed a butcher knife from the wooden countertop, its cold stainless-steel handle providing a small sense of reassurance in her sweaty palm. Determined, she pulled back the blinds, revealing the outside world. Her eyes fixated on the swing set standing against the fence, the metal chains creaking softly in the breeze. Beyond it, a section of dense woods stretched, promising a potential escape route.

Although someone designed the house as her dream house, she had no intention of staying to enjoy it. Gripping the knife tightly, she repeatedly stabbed at the window, the sound of metal meeting glass echoing in her ears. Disappointment washed over her as she let out a primal roar of frustration. The window remained intact, mocking her futile efforts. She ran her fingers over the smooth surface, unable to comprehend why it wouldn't break, a mix of confusion and desperation overwhelming her.

The distorted voice, like gravel grinding against metal, rumbled through the room, echoing off the bare walls. "Care Bear, stop trying to destroy our home. I've worked tirelessly building you a home of your dreams."

Kayla's eyes darted around, her heart pounding in her chest, as she swung the knife through the air, the metallic swoosh cutting through the eerie silence.

"My sweet wifey," the voice continued, its low timbre filled with a sinister sweetness, "your feisty personality is charming. I can't wait to pull you into my arms, never letting go. But our family isn't whole yet. Soon."

"Show your face, you coward!" Kayla's screams, a mix of anger and fear, pierced the stagnant air, mingling with her desperate sobs. Wifey? The word hung in the room, heavy with implications. Was this Zach's twisted attempt to salvage their shattered marriage? Kayla shook her head, tears streaming down her cheeks, refusing to believe it. She longed for the comfort of his embrace, yearned for him to fight her battles for once.

"In due time, my love," the voice taunted, its chilling resonance raising goosebumps on her skin. "You're wasting your energy. There's no way out."

Collapsing to her knees, a sharp pain shot through Kayla's body as she noticed the blinking red light of a hidden camera nestled in the room's corner. Panic surged through her, but so did determination. She would escape, no matter the cost. Even if it meant death. She would protect her daughter with her life.

****

Zach splashed warm water over his face, scrubbing the side of his cheek. He combed his cal-luck, sighing as a single strand of hair stood erect in the air. *Get it together, Zach. You're not going on a date, just meeting the daughter you didn't know existed.* With one last look in the mirror, he switched the bathroom light off. *She has to like you. You're her daddy, who's been absent from her life for almost four years.* He took a deep, calming breath, his nerves on high alert.

He pushed open the guest room door, staring at the toddler bed that took two hours to assemble. A princess doll laid on top of the pink princess-themed comforter. A bag of toys and a few books rested neatly against the kid-sized dresser. The sales clerk at Kids' Depot gave him a list of items he needed for his little house guest. Talk about intimidating. He didn't know so many shades of pink existed. And what if Annabelle hated the color pink? Then he just scarred her for life.

"I can't do this." Zach stepped into the living room, feeling the drowning sensation of a panic attack settling in his body. Why did he let Mrs. Smith talk him into taking Annabelle? He needed someone like Stephen Smith to take care of her, not a clueless detective, who never changed a diaper before. The thought of Stephen playing the role of daddy sent green envy surging through his body.

"Where are you, Kayla?" He rubbed the side of his face, rolling his eyes at the pricks of hair he missed shaving.

Zach walked into the kitchen, noticing a grocery bag he had forgotten to put away: raisins, goldfish, applesauce, fruit snacks. Nothing of excellent nutritional value. But what did he know? He always ordered take out. Maybe Sarah would whip him up a kid-friendly meal. No, he needed to steer clear of Sarah and her presumptuous ways. He'd visit his brother Josh and his wife Britney later. Though they didn't have any children, besides the linebacker, yet to be born. Britney was a preschool teacher.

The doorbell rang as Zach ran to the door, fumbling with the handle. *Be cool, man.* He swung the door open, staring at an older version of Kayla, with pops of gray nestled in her blond hair. He knew where Kayla got her beauty from. Stepping aside, Mrs. Smith let her husband, a tall, red-haired man with big green eyes, step through the door. He carried a squirmy little girl. One look into her baby-blue eyes sent tears into Zach's. Besides her mother's nose, Annabelle looked like a copy-and-paste of him at that age. No doubt she was his daughter.

"Mr. Smith." Zach extended his hand as the couple stepped into his house, closing the door and the heat behind them.

"Call me Howard." Mr. Smith gripped Zach's hand before setting an energetic three-year-old on the ground.

Mrs. Smith hobbled into the room, placing Annabelle's suitcase on the coffee table. With a tear-stained face; blotchy and red. She stared at Zach. Her look hard enough to make a grown man squirm.

"No word from my daughter?" She swiped at the corner of her eyes with a worn-out tissue.

Zach exhaled a steam of hot air. Overwhelmed by seeing his flesh-and-blood running around his house, dizziness almost toppled him over.

"Sit down, young man." Howard tugged Zach toward the couch, his touch friendly but firm. "Martha, give the man a moment to breathe."

"How can he sit and breathe when my daughter is out there in only God knows what conditions?" A sob escaped from her lips as she fell onto the recliner. "What if we never see her again?"

"Martha, how do you think Zach feels? She's his wife." Howard stood behind his wife, stroking the top of her shoulders.

Martha busted out laughing, her voice cutting through the tension in the room. "Howard, you know their marriage is a sham. Kayla's been on her own for four years." She shifted her gaze to him, wagging her index finger in his face. "Where were you when she almost quit college countless times because the morning sickness zapped her energy away? Who lifted her out of depression when we lowered the casket into the ground? Or when she juggled college, a baby, and a job?"

Ouch. Her words stung more than being grazed by a bullet. "Wh-what casket?" Who died?

"Darling. Enough." Mr. Smith's firm but tender words caused the floodgates to open as tears streamed down Mrs. Smith's face.

"Grandma, okay?" Annabelle climbed into her grandma's lap, laying her face on her grandma's chest.

Leaning over, she kissed the top of Annabelle's blond hair. "We made a mistake. I won't leave her with him."

She kept throwing punches Zach's way. He knew where Kayla got it from.

"Darling, we agreed on this. Let the man bond with his daughter. Your ankle needs to heal properly and we need to be here for Kayla when the police find her."

Mrs. Smith wrapped her arms around Annabelle's waist, pulling her into a tight embrace. "Grandma's gonna go bye-bye, but I'll be back. Your dad will take good care of her." After one more kiss, and a stern look thrown at Zach, she set the child on Zach's lap, rushing out the front door.

"Wait! I know nothing about children or Annabelle." Zach awkwardly stood, shifting his daughter in his arms. She weighed more than she looked, which wasn't much of anything.

"There are instructions with a detailed schedule in her suitcase." Howard kissed his grand baby and rushed after his wife. "We'll be in touch."

And just like that, Zach became responsible for someone besides himself. He stared into his daughter's watery eyes, knowing a meltdown was on the brink of existence, not from his daughter, but from him.

"Put me down." She almost jumped out of his arms, running to the coffee table and throwing his sports magazines on the floor. Within seconds, the place looked like a tornado had shot through, leaving disaster in its wake.

"Annabelle, come back." His exasperated plea bounced off the walls as his daughter zoomed down the hall as Hurricane Annabelle.

God, help me. His desperate words tumbled to the floor. Zach didn't know if God was listening, but it'd take His mighty power to get him through this time alone with his daughter.

****

Kayla massaged her achy legs, leaning against the front door. She had spent the entire night sleeping with one eye open, never moving away from the door. Kayla tried for hours breaking the door down, but her attempts were in vain; wasting energy. She had hoped to jump the creep who abducted her and flee outside, but he never came. In frustration, Kayla had destroyed the visible cameras, leaving behind splattered glass and heaps of plastic. Her next attempt would be to burn the house down. Tricky and deadly, but if the sicko cared about his creation so much, he'd save it, giving her an opportunity to escape. She felt like a savage beast, but only the strong ones survived. And giving up wasn't an option.

Annabelle's high-pitched voice floated into her mind, causing tears to swell up in her eyes. *God, You saved Annabelle's life, but took Isabelle's. Please don't let this*

172

sicko rob me of the gift You knew I needed. Protect my baby and make a way of escape.

Tears dropped onto the hardwood floors as scenes from almost four years ago flashed before her eyes. The sound of metal smashing into metal, piercing screams, glass shattering. Kayla touched her stomach unconsciously, remembering the blood that poured down her shirt. The smell of burned flesh and gasoline almost chocking her. Knowing her life was over, but blacking out, waking up in a sterile hospital room, feeling the devastation and life seep out of her.

God, why? Why did You take away one of my reasons for living? Her body trembling at the memory of holding her perfectly formed baby, without the breath of life. A part of her heart died that nightmarish night. Time that she could never get back. God had picked her up out of the trenches, wiping away the tears and sending her forth into the world that she didn't want to face. He didn't let her wallow in her grief, but held her until she could stand on two shaky feet without falling over. Of course, He stood beside her, some days carrying her, but always going forward, never looking back.

If she could survive those hearts wrenching days, this captivity wouldn't destroy her. With determination, Kayla gritted her teeth, waiting for the opportunity she needed to escape.

****

"Sweetheart, I'll be back," Zach said, like he'd been doing this daddy thing for years. It amazed him how fast he picked up and how much his heart soared for the human hurricane.

The first night, he camped out on the floor by her bed, holding her hand and reassuring her that her mommy would be back soon. He had missed so much in this little girl's life. Once he found Kayla, they'd have to work on a custody arrangement. Zach would never leave his daughter again. What about Annabelle's mother? Goosebumps attacked his skin at the memory of her gentle touch. He had loved Kayla with as much love as a teenage boy could give. He still loved her, probably always would. But loving someone and being in love with someone were two different things. Right? He could never go back. She had caused him too much heartache. *Well, what do you think you did to her?* The unwanted voice popped into his mind, making him stumble. He wasn't a saint, but Kayla destroyed their marriage, not him.

"Daddy!" Zach shook the memories out of his mind, staring at his daughter tugging on his pants leg. He'd never get over hearing that name.

"What's wrong?" He kneeled on the carpet, wiping a tear from her rosy cheek.

"I want Mommy!" She stomped her little foot, on the verge of a full-blown tantrum. Zach bit his bottom lip, trying not to bust out laughing at her sassy cuteness.

"Agreed." Zach couldn't imagine caring for Annabelle as a college student with a part-time job. Admiration for Kayla swelled in his heart. "That's why we are here. I need you to stay with Uncle Josh and Aunt Britney while I go find your mommy."

"Promise you'll be back." She wrapped her arms around his neck, forgetting that he might need oxygen to breathe.

In his line of work, that was a promise he couldn't make. Kissing his daughter on the forehead, he tugged her toward his brother. "He will keep you safe."

Annabelle poked out her bottom lip, staring at Uncle Josh. "You smell funny."

Britney leaned over laughing, taking the little girl's hand. "From the mouth of babes."

"Hey, I just ate tuna. I probably should brush my teeth, though." Josh turned to his brother as the front door creaked open. "Go find Kayla. We'll take care of Annabelle."

"You ready to go back to middle school?" Peter stepped into the living room, spinning his keys on the key chain.

"No. I barely survived middle school and without Kayla, high school would have devoured me." That thought punched him in the gut. Kayla. It's always been her. And yet, he pushed her away in college and ruined their marriage. What if they could have a second chance? Now wasn't the time for such thoughts. He had to get his head in the game and focus.

With one last look at his daughter, he stepped outside into the late morning humid air. He climbed into his SUV, being lost in thought, he drove silently to the local middle school. Ten minutes later, he pulled into a parking spot, remembering seeing Kayla again for the first time in four years.

It'd been one eventful week, meaning school started back in a couple of days and Paul would be home from his vacation in two days.

"Come on, bro, let's find your wife." Peter adjusted the badge on his uniform, smiling as he swung open the door.

Zach would let that comment slide. He wanted to find Kayla, but not as a husband searching for his wife, but as a detective finding the victim.

With big strides, they stepped into the office, their footsteps echoing on the tiled-floor. The secretary, a middle-aged woman, glanced up from her stack of papers, frowning. "Officers, how may I help you?"

"Are most of the staff present today?" Zach leaned against the counter, giving the woman his million-dollar smile. He could always get more information being charming than ruthless.

She glanced at the computer screen. Her big brown eyes widened as she scrolled with her mouse. "Yes, sir, every staff member besides our sixth-grade Language Arts teacher, Kayla Smith. I haven't been able to reach her in a couple of days. It's unlike her to skip out on a teacher's workday."

Zach showed his badge, propping his arm on the desk. "My name is Detective Zach Rivers and my partner, Peter Rivers. We are investigating Kayla Smith's disappearance. When was the last time you spoke to her?"

The woman fidgeted with her bifocals, refusing to look him in the eye. A nervous response that came with the job title. "I haven't spoken to her since last Friday. Our relationship is, um … strictly professional. "

Interesting. Why was he getting disgruntle vibes from the secretary? "I don't think I caught your name."

"Marybeth Asher."

"Ma'am, is it okay if we question the staff?" He didn't really need her permission, but she looked on the verge of passing out or giving him a tongue lashing. For what? He didn't know.

"Of course." She jotted down a few words on a scrap piece of paper, handing it to Zach. With a flick of a finger, she had dismissed him and ended the conversation.

"That was odd." Peter grabbed the paper out of Zach's hand, reading the names out loud. "Carrie Walker, fifth-grade science teacher, room twenty-five, Susan White, sixth-grade geography teacher, room one hundred and ten, and Thomas Holmes, sixth-grade math teacher, room one hundred. Potential suspects or friends of Kayla's?"

"Let's go find out." Zach rolled his eyes at his enthusiasm for talking with Thomas Holmes again. The guy had a thing for Kayla, and Zach couldn't tell if she felt the same way about Thomas. The thought of his Kayla in another man's arms made him want to puke, something he'd done quite a few times in middle school. He rubbed his face, trying to get rid of the images of Kayla in his arms. He needed to focus, and he had plenty of time to work on his feelings for Kayla when he solved the case.

"Earth to Zach. This is room twenty-five, and it looks like Carrie Walker is inside." Peter tapped his brother on the arm as he stepped into the science room.

A life-sized poster of the periodic tables lines the wall by the blackboard. Ms. Walker was hanging science vocabulary words and pictures on the pale-white walls. She looked up in surprise as the men stepped to her small ladder.

"I'm Detective Zach Rivers and this is my partner, Peter Rivers. We're investigating Kayla Smith's disappearance." Zach's authoritative voice trailed off as Carrie Walker's face turned into the shade of the white walls. "When was the last time you spoke to her?"

Carrie jumped down from the ladder as her red hair bounced along her chin. Her blue eyes bore into Zach's like

177

a teacher dealing with an unruly student. "It's common knowledge, but she and I are hardly acquaintances."

"Why is that?" Peter crossed his arms over his chest, giving the teacher his intimidating look.

"She's too ... uh, flirtatious with the male staff." Her face reddened at the mention of the male staff. More than likely, the male staff flocked to Kayla and the ugly duckling Ms. Walker sat unnoticed in the background. Could Kayla be a flirt? Yes, but her friendliness was often mistaken as more.

"That affects you how?" Zach noticed the tiny bulging of Ms. Walker's vein between her eyebrows.

"It's common knowledge that I have an interest in one of the male teachers. He may be way out of my league, and Kayla flaunts her scandalous beauty, just as a slap to my face."

Interesting. Would a jealous coworker try to get rid of the popular, beautiful rival? Most definitely.

"Listen, I didn't kill her." Ms. Walker stepped to her desk, falling into her chair.

"Who said anything about murder?" Carrie Walker knew more than she cared to admit.

"I-I assumed. Look, you're wasting your time interviewing me. Her best friend, Susan White, is down the hall. She'd know more than I would."

Was that a way of dismissing the detective and distancing herself from the case? Probably.

"Fine, but don't leave town."

Seconds later, they followed boisterous laughter into room one hundred and ten. A pretty brunette sat behind a desk, playing with the cuffs on Thomas Holmes' buttoned-up shirt. Looking a little too cozy for a teacher's workday.

At the sight of the detective, Thomas jumped back, nearly knocking over a box of pencils.

"Why are you here? Did something happen to Kayla?" Thomas crossed his arms over his chest, leaning against one of the student desks.

"We are investigating her disappearance."

"And you thought I had something to do with it?" Ms. White shook her head as she stepped next to Thomas. "I don't know what Ms. Walker told you, but she has an ax to grind with Kayla. They never got along. But she's my best friend. Why would I harm her?"

The answer to that question stood three feet away from Zach, looking smug and arrogant.

"Detective Rivers, can we talk privately in my room?" Thomas gave a backward glance to Ms. White before motioning to the hall. What was that secret look for? If either of them knew about Kayla's whereabout, he'd find out.

Chapter Nine

Zach leaned against a desk, staring at the mathematical symbols hanging on the wall. Flashbacks from sixth grade and the terror and embarrassment he felt every time he stepped into his math class resurfaced. No one openly picked on him, because, being 'bad boy, Zach', no one would have openly laughed in his face and walked away unscathed. But he heard the silent snickers every time he answered an equation wrong. He felt the eye rolls when his brain wouldn't work quick enough to answer a problem on the chalkboard. Even his teacher did a face palm after some of his ridiculous answers. Mrs. Harriet Oceans probably earned her saintly title that year. It was also the year the elderly grandma retired. He couldn't blame her. Zach had knocked off ten years of her teaching career in one semester.

But to his defense, Zach didn't have help with homework. No one to care about his soaring or plummeting grades. His mom tried, but her jobs kept her busy. Besides, it wouldn't have helped. Zach was rebelling from his dysfunctional family and his deadbeat dad, who ran off years before. Nothing dispersed his anger until he met Kayla years later.

His brothers both were model students and kids. Never giving his mother or teachers a difficult time. Although unspoken, he heard his teacher's admonishments begging him to act more like Josh or even his younger brother,

Peter. They both had met Jesus at a young age, riding the church bus to church. Not Zach. He didn't need God telling him how to live his life. It wasn't until he had already messed up his life with Kayla that God had changed his life. Although, he wasn't the model Christian either. Bitterness at his parents' and Kayla held him back from fully surrendering to God. It was easier blaming others than pointing the finger at himself.

If he hadn't straightened up in high school, prison would have probably been his permanent home. But Kayla believed in the rebellious troublemaker, screaming for someone to throw him the life preserver. Her love and devotion changed his stony heart. He had never felt that deep, without merit, love before. It was why he had never moved on with another woman after breaking up their marriage. And Sarah didn't count as moving on. She was just a distraction.

Peter tapped Zach on the shoulder, a mischievous smirk spreading across his face. Zach could see the determined look in Peter's eyes, and knew he had better focus. "This is your case, Detective Rivers. You better start paying attention."

Zach shook his head, feeling a slight tingling sensation as he tried to clear his mind. He took a deep breath, inhaling the faint scent of chalk lingering in the air. The room felt suffocating, as if all the tension and animosity were weighing down on him.

"As I was saying," Thomas shifted uncomfortably in his chair, the sound of his movements filling the silence, "I'm the most eligible bachelor. Women swoon at me. Most of the single teachers envy the relationship Kayla and I share." Zach could hear the slight creaking of the chair as

Thomas shifted his weight. He was irritating, but he fought the urge to let his frustration show.

Zach crossed his arms over his chest, feeling the fabric of his shirt against his skin. He tried to maintain a calm and composed demeanor, despite the anger simmering within him. The mention of Kayla's name in the same sentence as "relationship" was like a punch to the gut. He clenched his fists, feeling his nails digging into his palms. "Which is?" Zach crossed his arms over his chest, acting like the next words wouldn't be a blow to the face.

"You want me to describe the relationship I have with Kayla?"

"Yeah, my wife," Zach spit the bitter words out like poison.

"Please. I hardly think of Kayla as your wife. You've been absent for four years. What kind of husband does that make you?" Thomas's words cut through the air, their sharpness leaving a bitter taste in Zach's mouth. He took a step forward, his footsteps echoing in the room. The proximity between him and Thomas was palpable, the air thick with tension. "I'd never leave a woman like that. And maybe one day, she'll be Mrs. Thomas Holmes."

Zach could see the smug smile on Thomas's face as he propped his feet on top of his desk. It was infuriating, but he knew he had to restrain himself. He took a deep breath, trying to control his anger.

"Keep your hands off my wife," Zach's voice was low and filled with a warning, his words hanging heavy in the air. The room seemed to grow smaller, the walls closing in as the confrontation escalated.

"Or what? You going to arrest me?" Thomas stood up, his movements swift and confident. Zach heard his chair scraping against the floor. The challenge in Thomas's eyes was obvious. His willingness to engage in a fight was clear. The tension in the room was palpable, a storm waiting to unleash.

"Maybe you should step into the hall. I'll finish his questioning." Peter quickly intervened, stepping between the two men. Zach could feel the pressure on his chest as Peter pushed him back slightly. Zach's pounding heart drowned out every sound. Reluctantly, he conceded and made his way to the door, his hand grazing the icy surface as he pushed it shut.

As he stepped into the hallway, Zach muttered a few words under his breath. The coolness of the corridor provided a brief respite from the heated atmosphere inside the room. He knew his brother was right; he needed to cool off before things escalated further. But Thomas Holmes knew how to push his buttons. And he didn't like the guy.

Moments later, Peter strode out of the room, stuffing his notepad inside his pocket, trying to hide his smile. "How come anytime Kayla is involved you go into protective husband mode and get this close to getting in a fistfight?" He moved his fingers together for emphasis.

Zach huffed out a response, rolling his eyes. "It's not like that. I don't care about her like that. Thomas Holmes just grates my nerves."

Peter brushed past Zach, hitting him on the arm as he walked past him. "I never took you as a coward."

"What?" Maybe working with his brother wasn't the best choice. He didn't need a therapy session or talk about his emotions.

Peter stopped mid-stride, staring at Zach. His playful blue eyes held an icy coolness that showed Peter meant business. "You run into a gun fight without hesitation, yet, you won't man up and admit that somewhere inside your stony heart is a love for your wife that God designed. You turned your back on God and your wife. When will you grow up and work on restoring both relationships?"

Zach stepped back like Peter's words breathed fire, and his face was the target. "Bro, I don't want to talk about this now."

Peter threw his arms into the air in exasperation. "You don't get it. Zach, you need God. From where I'm standing, your life is falling apart. You're responsible for a little girl that you never knew about. Your estranged wife is missing, and you can't investigate without flipping out. God's trying to get your attention. Don't be a fool and reject Him."

He had a point, but the truth felt like a knife slashing his insides to pieces. Zach couldn't do this on his own anymore. Feeling weak kneed, he slid against the row of lockers, head on his knees, tears streaming down his face. A familiar position from his tween days, but this time, he was crying out to God to restore his faith and draw his heart closer to Him.

"Oh, God." With those two words, he gave his heart and life back to the Father that never left him. One whose love ran deeper than the ocean and higher than the mountains. The God of multiple chances. And with Him, Zach would never feel alone again.

****

"Care Bear, I know you're here somewhere." His deep, haunting voice echoed through the dimly lit room. "We can't be a family if I can't find you. And I will find you."

Kayla covered her mouth as sobs escaped her parched lips. Having destroyed all the cameras, the creep couldn't see her cowering behind the bed, but she felt tiny eyes staring at her, taking pleasure in her distraught condition.

"Soon, Annabelle will complete our family." His voice rumbled through the speakers, sending goosebumps attacking her skin. "I'll be the daddy she never had."

At the mention of her daughter. Kayla jumped out of her cowering position, ready to tear the man to shreds for thinking about touching her baby. "If you touch my daughter…"

"Oh, Care Bear, she's my daughter, too." His sickening laughter floated through the room, choking off her air supply. Who was this sicko? With a voice changer, she couldn't tell, but he seemed familiar.

Kayla let out an ear-piercing scream, feeling trapped and unable to save her daughter from this nightmare.

"Don't think your fake husband will rescue you or protect your daughter. I won't let anyone stand in my way of our destiny."

Wait, did Zach have Annabelle? If so, how did that happen? Where were her parents? Did this creep get rid of her parents so he could snatch Annabelle?

Oh, God, I need to get out of here.

"Show your face!" If she could take this guy down, her family would be safe.

"Care Bear, I know your anticipation is bubbling over, but patience is a virtue," he said, laughing. "Soon, we'll be a family, and once you see me, you'll never go back to your deadbeat husband. I'll be your husband, and not just in name."

Her body trembled with anger, a fiery surge that surged through her veins. With a fierce grip, she clenched her hands into tight fists, feeling her nails dig into her palms. The picture on the wall became her target, and she ripped it off with a forceful yank. The sound of shattering glass echoed through the room as jagged shards scattered across the floor, twinkling like stars on a dark night. A sharp pain shot through her as a few of the shards grazed her bare skin, but she paid it no mind. Not even the drops of blood trickling down her arm could deter her. Determined to obliterate this nightmare, she vowed to dismantle it piece by piece. And when she was done, she would set the entire place ablaze, eradicating this sicko's twisted dream.

"My sweet Care Bear, what are you doing? I won't let you ruin our home."

Disregarding his acrid words, she seized the nightstand, forcefully yanking out the drawer and smashing it against the wall. The resounding clatter drowned out his verbal assault, reverberating through the room as she flung the disarrayed wood onto the floor. In mere minutes, she intended to decimate the entire space, leaving no corner unscathed. Before nightfall, she'd fulfill her relentless pursuit—to annihilate the complete house, a symphony of destruction filling the air.

****

"Daddy!" Annabelle's annoyed voice echoed through the house. "Daddy?" Little feet scurried over the hardwood floors as she stopped mid-stride and glanced up, tugging on a man's pant leg.

"You can call me daddy if you want, but I'm Uncle Peter, remember?" He scooped down and picked the little girl off the floor, smiling.

"Where my daddy?" She scrunched up her little nose in a pout.

Zach stepped into the room, carrying a pink sippy cup filled with milk and a box of raisins. He set the snack on the coffee table, grabbing Annabelle from Peter's arms.

"I have your snack, princess." Zach planted a kiss on her awfully braided pigtails, frowning. He needed to find Kayla fast. Annabelle was barely tolerating his lack of experience. Zach's cooking, or fast-food choice, was gross. She obviously liked the finer cuisine. Kayla couldn't cook, so it must be Mrs. Smith's doing. Annabelle complained about the way he tucked her into bed. She had a meltdown at bath time because she could not bathe without her pink sparkle soap and princess wash cloth, both of which were not in her suitcase. He stayed up late last night searching Kids' Depot for sparkle soap and a princess wash cloth. Zach bought five of each, hoping she'd take to one. The only thing he did right was make her laugh during story time. Zach wanted to collapse onto the couch in exhaustion. He needed fifty more cups of coffee to get through the morning. And yet, his heart soared with love for the little munchkin. How had he lived his life without her? Parenting was not for the weak, but he'd never felt so full before.

Annabelle wrapped her skinny arms around his neck, placing a kiss on his scrubby cheek. "I luv you, daddy!" And with that, he knew he'd never let her out of his sight again.

He pulled her close in the biggest hug that melted away the lasting cobwebs of his stony heart. "I love you."

After a second of perfection, Annabelle squirmed out of his embrace, snagging her cup and raisins. Zach turned on her favorite show and stepped to Peter's side at the kitchen table.

"Kayla kept a lot of stuff." Peter set a stack of photos on the table, writing something in his notepad. "I compiled a list of names that made it to my 'person of interest' list."

Zach grabbed the list as nostalgia mixed with a bitter taste filled his mouth. *Donny Davis, Wally Hill, Adam Fisher.* Three college guys that he had considered buddies, but that had used him to get to Kayla. One such episode caused him to abandon his wife of a year and never look back. Peers laughed at him enough in high school, he wasn't allowing it in college.

He blinked his eyes, the bright sunlight from the window blinding him momentarily, as his mind traveled back to NC State. Zach had been running late from class, his heart pounding in his chest, but didn't want to miss his special meet up time with Kayla. He could hear the distant chatter of students around him, the sound of footsteps echoing through the corridors. He had hoped she stuck around, waiting for him. When he finally reached the bleachers, the smell of freshly cut grass filled his nostrils, mixing with the scent of popcorn from the nearby concession stand. Kayla's soft laughs, like a melodic symphony, entwined with a deep male voice, sending warning arrows in his brain. He peered over the bleachers, his heart sinking, spotting his wife in the arms of Adam Fisher. His vision blurred for a moment as tears welled up in his eyes. Seeing red and feeling an explosion building up inside him, Zach turned away, his footsteps heavy on the pavement as he made his way back to student housing. The sound of his own breathing seemed to echo in his ears, his heart pounding in his chest. He packed up his belongings, the weight of his decisions heavy on his shoulders, and waited for the early morning light where he disappeared. It wasn't hard avoiding Kayla, but it broke his heart knowing the rumors of her unfaithfulness were true. The bitter taste of betrayal lingered in his mouth as he tried to swallow down the hurt. He probably should have confronted her, but his wounded heart couldn't handle any more rejection. Walking away from the woman that had showed him unmerited love ripped his heart to pieces. Four years later, he had bandaged his heart up, enough to live, but having Kayla back in his life could rip the bandages off, leaving him vulnerable. The thought alone sent a shiver down his spine, his body tensing up at the mere possibility.

Could he really question these guys that were like wedges destroying his marriage? His wounded pride doubted he could, but glancing at Annabelle, Zach knew he'd do anything to bring his daughter's mommy home.

"These men live in East Tennessee. They own a marketing agency and are all single." Peter's shuffling of papers pulled Zach out of his daze. How convenient was that?

"I'll drop Annabelle off at Britney's, and then we can go." Zach folded the paper, shoving it inside his pocket. "I never thanked you for helping with the investigation."

"No need." Peter's blue eyes lit up like the sky on the fourth of July. "Someone needs to keep you out of trouble."

"Thanks for having my back, bro." Zach pulled his phone out of his pocket as Paul's name flashed on the screen. "Can you take Annabelle to the car while I answer this call?"

Peter's eyes turned an icy shade of blue, and for a split second, he seemed offended about being left out of the investigation. With a shake of the head, he swooped a giggling Annabelle into his arms, grabbing her cup before marching out the door.

"Zach, here."

"Hey, man, checking in on you, and letting you know I'll be ready for duty bright and early tomorrow."

Zach scratched his head as seeds of doubt sprang out of his heart. "Came home a day early because you didn't think I could handle the case?" Paul never leaned toward scrutiny or doubted his skills. But Paul always took the lead in the investigations. Zach couldn't blame him. He doubted his own skills as Kayla's disappearance edged close to three days, with no leads.

Paul's deep laugh echoed through the phone. "Nothing like that. Mary caught a stomach bug, and it's been miserable. Next vacation, we're camping out in our backyard."

The thought of Annabelle coming down with a bug and vomiting made his head spin. "Maybe you should take a few days for the germs to settle before you come back to work."

"Nice try. But Mary has been vomit-free for twenty-four hours, and no one else is sick. A tiny victory for the Walkman clan."

Zach blew out a sigh of relief. He grabbed his keys off the counter, stepping into the afternoon heat.

"I heard about Kayla's disappearance and about your unexpected houseguest." Paul's voice sounded distant and garbled.

"I'd ask how, but you have your ways." Zach laughed at his brother, trying to buckle Annabelle's car seat. Zach displayed the same perplexed look days ago, but thanks to a video hack, he mastered it.

"We'll talk about it in the morning." Zach heard an engine roar to life. He assumed Paul was getting ready to drive. "Guard your daughter with your life."

Did he really need to say that? Zach would use his last ounce of strength protecting her. No one would get close enough to harm her. "On it."

"See you in the morning," Paul said, before clicking the phone off.

He'd protect her even if she wasn't his flesh and blood, but having the same DNA upped his protection detail. With a low chuckle, he stepped to his SUV, taking over buckling his daughter, since Peter still hadn't figured it out.

****

Zach fidgeted with the bottom of his badge, feeling the weight of the metal resting on his leg. He mumbled encouraging words under his breath, trying to get into his detective persona and out of his wounded husband's one.

A low chuckle roared through the front seat of his SUV, causing heat to travel up his pale face. "Giving yourself a pep talk?"

Zach rolled his eyes at his brother's words. Working the case together was the most time they had spent together in years, besides watching sports and eating. He loved his little brother, but forgot how annoying he could be.

"Can I record this for my social media page? A video on how a seasoned detective gets in the zone." Peter reached for his phone, scrolling through his home screen. "Very enlightening content."

"You goofball." Zach lightly punched his brother on the shoulder. "I am reigning in my emotions before I confront the man partly responsible for breaking up my marriage."

"Maybe you should thank him." Peter slid his phone into his pants pocket, moving the seatbelt off his chest.

"What?" Zach did not have time for a sermon about his deprived nature or how Kayla was better off without him. Those words constantly floated through his mind.

"Maybe you leaving was a blessing in disguise."

"How?" Now his brother had intrigued him. Zach turned his head enough to stare into his brother's sky-blue eyes. Eyes that resembled his own.

"From the little interaction I've seen you two have, I'd say your busy college schedule kept you both together as long as you were. Clearly, the sparks are there, but not the compatibility."

No, that couldn't be true. Could it? They were inseparable at first.

"Kayla's league was way above your own. Miss popularity rescuing the lone rebel of the school. Maybe what you had for each other wasn't love but admiration."

"No, way." Zach knew the love that had once burned in his throbbing heart for Kayla was real. Or as real as it got with him.

"Of course, you'd have feelings for someone whose influence set your life on a fresh path. That's understandable. But if what you had was love, it would have stood against the waves of doubt and uncertainties of college."

Wait, he'd never heard this before, but did it have merit? His brother normally spoke the truth, even if he didn't like it or agree with it.

"I say, squash whatever remaining feelings you have for her away." Peter rubbed the sides of his scruffy face. Clearly uncomfortable with his own advice.

"Don't you believe in restoration and forgiveness?"

"Absolutely. But it's not just about you anymore. Think about Annabelle. We know how it's like growing up in a

192

broken home with parents that never should have married. Don't give Annabelle the same baggage that we carry. She deserves better than that."

"You think I should walk away?" Peter's words twisted a knife inside Zach's heart, slicing away the tiny seed that longed for a second chance with Kayla.

"Don't be a deadbeat dad, but don't make their lives worse by claiming something that doesn't belong to you anymore."

Zach nervously chewed on the inside of his lip, feeling the sting of painful memories as his parents' full-blown fights invaded his thoughts. The echoes of their arguments seemed to reverberate through his mind, causing him to contemplate walking away for the sake of his daughter, Annabelle. But the idea of abandoning his role as a father weighed heavily on him.

His mind wandered to the possibility of someone else, like Thomas or even Peter, taking on the role of a father figure for Annabelle. The mere thought sent a surge of bile burning through his throat, threatening to make him sick. Stopping the rising nausea, he hastily swung open the door of his SUV, allowing the muggy spring air to wash over his face.

"We've talked enough," Peter exclaimed, leaping out of the vehicle with a faint smile gracing his lightly tanned face. Sounds of traffic zooming down the main road into town filled the air, horns blaring and loud music drifting by. The cacophony of the bustling street made Zach long for solitude.

Realization of how his lovesick persona had ruined a once wonderful woman's life weighed heavily on him. If it weren't for him, she could have been happily married, surrounded by a houseful of children and basking in the love of her husband. Instead, a flimsy certificate had trapped her in a sham of a marriage. The selfishness he had displayed by keeping her tied to him threatened to consume his being.

Determined to set her free, Zach vowed to find her and sign the divorce papers, relinquishing his control over her once and for all. He knew he had failed in their marriage, becoming more like his father than he cared to admit. With a resolute mindset, he would suppress all his emotions and grant Kayla the freedom she deserved. The mere thought of seeing her in another man's arms caused him to bend over, dry heaving from the sheer agony of it.

Peter, sensing his distress, stepped to his side, offering a comforting pat on the back. "You okay? If it's because of what I said, I take it back."

But Zach knew that once words were spoken, they could never truly be taken back.

Zach led the way inside the one-story industrial-flared building. The air smelled faintly of freshly brewed coffee, mixing with the sterile scent of the clean, straight-lined walls. Sunlight streamed through the row of modern sleek windows, casting a warm glow on the minimalistic space. The sound of muted footsteps echoed in the open area leading into the office. Zach flashed his badge to a receptionist seated in the middle of the room, the sound of the badge sliding against his fingers adding a metallic tingle. Instead of waiting to be buzzed back into the room, he stalked down the hall, the sound of his footsteps resonating with purpose.

"Wait! Detective, you can't go back there." The helpless secretary darted after Zach and Peter, his hurried steps creating a sense of urgency that filled the air. Ignoring the clumsy man behind him, Zach slid into another hall that led to two offices, the sound of his shoes sliding against the polished floor punctuating his confident stride. Zach boasted in the element of surprise.

"Chester, what's the commotion?" The door at the end of the hall opened as a man a few inches shorter than Zach stepped into the hall. His body built like a linebacker. His icy blue eyes sent recognition bells ringing in Zach's ears. *Adam Fisher.*

Adam glanced at the detectives, then waved his secretary off. "Chester, go back to the front of the building. I'll take care of these men." The authority in Adam's voice reverberated through the air, commanding attention.

Zach slid his fingers against his gun, feeling the cool metallic touch tingle his fingertips, a reassuring sensation that reminded him of his readiness for any situation. He wouldn't go down without a fight.

Adam crossed his arms over his broad chest, staring defiantly at Zach and Peter. The intensity of his gaze filled the room, creating an atmosphere of tension. "What do I owe the pleasure of your visit today?"

So, he wasn't a law enforcement fan. Or maybe he recognized Zach and this entire investigation was about to tank. Zach eased up in front of Adam, letting him know, casually, that he was in control. With a slight nod, Adam motioned for them to follow him, the creaking of the floor beneath his footsteps adding an eerie undertone to their interaction. Sunlight cast a beam across his short-cropped blond hair, illuminating his features.

Zach and Peter stepped into a window-lined room; the view of distant mountains etched across the windows creating a picturesque backdrop.

Natural light bathed the room, giving it an inviting and open feel. A single white desk sat in the middle of the scarcely furnished room, its clean surface adding to the sense of minimalism.

"I'd offer you both a seat, but I don't normally entertain in here." Adam ran his finger over his hair, the slight rustling sound of his touch filling the room, before plopping into his desk chair. "How can I help you, gentlemen?"

No need to beat around the bush. "When's the last time you saw Kayla Smith?" Zach's voice held little emotion as he leaned against a windowpane, his fingertips lightly grazing the smooth glass, absorbing the coolness against his skin.

Adam's face twitched so subtly that if Zach weren't watching him, he would have missed it. The tension in the room was thickening with each passing second. Body language was just as important as verbal communication.

"Man, I haven't heard that name since college." He crossed his legs on top of his desk, smiling.

Adam was lying. His tense face screamed of his guilt. He might not be her stalker, but he knew more about her than he wanted Zach to know.

"Ms. Smith is missing and we're trying to uncover her whereabouts." Peter pulled his notepad out of his pocket, waiting to scribble down any information.

"I saw the news report." Adam slid his legs off his desk with a thump. "Wait a minute, you think I'm a suspect?"

"Just standard questioning. Are Wallie Hill and Donnie Davis available for questioning?"

Adam shifted in his seat uncomfortably. "No. They are both out of the office for the rest of the week at a conference."

"Which one?"

"South East Division of Marketing."

Zach nodded to Peter to jot the name down.

"When's the last time you saw Kayla?"

"Man, graduation night." Adam's face lifted into a taunting smirk. Zach didn't like the guy in college and shared the same sentiment four years later.

"Try again." Zach took a deep gulp of air, trying to control his emotions.

"I know who you are. The bozo that left Kayla during our sophomore year of college. Any guy that would abandon her was an idiot."

Maybe, but he didn't need this joke to tell him what he already knew.

Adam went to his desk drawer, eying Zach before he slid his fingers into the closed drawer.

"Hands where I can see them." If this was pay back from abandoning his wife, he deserved whatever was coming. But his brother didn't deserve a bullet. Zach pulled his gun, pointing it at Adam Fisher.

Chapter Ten

"Whoa!" Adam dropped the envelope, throwing his hands in the air. "I'm unarmed."

"You're an idiot Fisher. Who acts conspicuous when a law enforcement officer is inches from them? I thought you had a gun." Through trembling fingers, Zach lowered his gun, feeling his pulse beat through his fingertips.

"What's in the envelope?" Peter asked, trying to diffuse the situation.

In a swift motion, Adam scooped the envelope off the hardwood floor, sliding his fingers inside a bottom drawer. Lifting his body, he stared over the butt of a gun barrel.

"Thanks for the idea." Adam pointed the gun and Zach's chest, his stance that of a seasoned pro.

"What are you doing, Fisher?" Zach was the idiot. He shouldn't have put his gun away. His senses were on high alert for something. He should have trusted his instincts.

"You ruined my life!" Adam stepped closer to Zach. Sweat beads dripping down his face. "You're the reason I'm single."

That was a big accusation. Zach wasn't a Romeo in the love department, but Adam could hardly blame Zach for his own failed attempt at love. Zach felt the gun strapped to his chest. If he could distract Adam enough, Zach could reach for his gun, or give Peter the opportunity to reach for his. Good thing Adam hadn't disarmed them.

"Kayla is all I've ever wanted. But you snatched her from me." His high-pitched voice sent shivers through Zach's body. The dude was crazy.

"Hey, I left, giving you plenty of opportunity to sweep in and steal her heart." Casanova wasn't the ladies' man like Zach had thought. He almost felt sorry for Fisher. Almost. "Besides, I left because of you trying to steal my wife's heart. I saw you two together behind the bleachers." The distant scent of coffee mixed with the bile clogged in Zach's throat almost caused him to vomit. Heat rolled over his face. He needed air fast.

"I made plenty of passes at her, but you always stood in the way." He steadied the small handgun, never wavering from Zach's chest.

Any minute, the loony guy could pull the trigger, ending Zach's life, or at least seriously injuring him. Annabelle's carefree laugh dinged inside Zach's ears. He couldn't go out like this. Not when he had someone else to live for. Peter's speech about walking away and allowing Kayla to start over with a better man made sense, and almost convinced Zach to act like his father and walk away, never looking back. But Zach couldn't do it. He wouldn't do it. He would start repairing the broken pieces of his life, one person at a time. Where did that leave him and Kayla? Could he trust her enough to pursue another relationship with? Zach didn't know, but he wanted to live long enough to find out.

"How?"

Cold hatred filled Adam's eyes as he glared at Zach over the gun barrel. "Loyalty and love. Clearly, we had some attraction between us, but she held to the vows that you broke when you walked away."

Zach almost doubled over, dry heaving. He left his wife because Zach figured she was unfaithful to him, but her loyalty ran deeper than his. Five years of marriage had gone by because of his insecurities.

"Countless nights Kayla cried on my shoulder over your abandonment. I told her to move on, and I thought maybe she would until she told me she was pregnant."

Zach did not like where Adam was taking this story. Speechless, Zach blinked back tears and listened to the man who had destroyed his marriage. But actually, all the years he had pointed the finger at the wrong guy. It was his fault, not Adam's.

"I hounded her to get rid of the baby. Why keep a baby from a man that abandoned her? But she wouldn't do it. Kayla insisted that you'd find yourself and come back. I guess that never happened."

Idiot. All these years, he let self-righteousness keep him away from the only woman he ever loved. "What happened to your relationship?"

"We never had a relationship. But our friendship fizzled away. I walked away just like you, but I didn't have any strings attached like you did."

If Zach could just inch his fingers in his holster and yank his gun out. In a split second, he'd take this wacko down. "Where's Kayla?"

"I don't have her. I'm not her stalker." Adam's fingers trembled as he pointed the gun at Zach. The longest ten minutes of his life. "I moved to East Tennessee because I had hoped to rekindle our friendship, but she wasn't exactly happy to see me. My business exploded in a good way, so I stayed."

"You still keep tabs on her?" Peter shifted his eyes to Zach, adding a distraction enough for Zach to retrieve his gun.

"Do you blame me? She's the full package; beautiful, with an amazing personality." Adam stared at Peter; his gun still pointed at Zach.

"Kayla is … one of a kind." Peter's voice croaked as he glanced at Zach. What was that emotion about? Zach knew Peter had a crush on her years ago. Did he never get over her, either?

"Look, I might have sent her some flowers, but only once. I can take rejection." His hand quivered as he steadied the gun in his palm.

Yeah, right? He didn't look like the type that let his wounded pride go easily. If Zach gave him a profile, it would be a man that liked control and didn't take rejection well, a narcissist. Maybe got rid of Kayla because her rejection stung him every time he ran into her.

"When's the last time you saw her?" Zach slid his fingers further into his holster, inches away from the tip of his gun. *Still motions. Don't attract Fisher's attention.*

"A month ago. We ran into each other at the grocery store." A tiny smile spread across his face. "I invited her for coffee, but she declined." His smiled turned into a look that could kill. "Can you believe she rejected me? I'm Adam Fisher. Not some lousy middle school teacher. She thinks she's so much better than me. My paychecks are triple her teacher salary."

The guy looked like he could explode any minute. And his erratic behavior wasn't good, since he was pointing a gun at Zach.

Time to play good cop. Zach winked at Peter, glad that his brother could read his mind.

"Clearly, Kayla is a fool. You would make any woman a blessed partner." Peter's tone and sincerity was why he always got the top role in every school play in high school. The guy's acting talent soared beyond most professional actors.

Zach's stomach churned, threatening to empty its contents onto the newly polished hardwood floors, but he knew the consequences could be deadly.

"Drop the gun, Fisher. Let's resolve this misunderstanding peacefully. We can find a way through." Peter's calm voice reverberated in the hollow, bare room.

Adam's head dropped, tears streaming down his face, as the sound of his remorse filled the air. "I never intended to aim a gun at you. I'm sorry." With a heavy thud, he let his weapon fall to the floor. Zach swiftly drew his own gun from its holster, keeping it fixed on Adam while Peter handcuffed him and recited his rights. Retrieving the fallen gun, Zach released a sigh of relief, the tension dissipating. The situation could have taken a much darker turn.

Thank You, God. That thought shocked Zach, as peace flooded his soul. Maybe God was closer than Zach thought.

****

Day four or five, she didn't know which one, as a prisoner of her perfect nightmare. The cottage style house's decor jumped right off her vision board. Every detail was exactly how she had planned to decorate her new home. But not anymore. The familiar decor would only push her back into this nightmare. And once she escaped, she was destroying her vision board and burning the pastel pink curtains and every other decoration she bought with penny pinching her money. Extreme? Kayla didn't care. No way would she live in a house that reminded her of her imprisonment. She had really thought about moving to North Carolina and putting Tennessee and all her false dreams behind her. Zach being the biggest regret and fleeing point. What if he really had Annabelle? He'd probably fight for custody and win partial custody and visitation rights. Being away from her energy-packed three-year-old was the worst thing about being held prisoner. She couldn't imagine sharing her with Zach. If only they could work out their differences and start afresh as husband and wife. But some things never worked out.

Kayla pounded her fist on the floor, desperation creeping up her arms, trying to destroy her. As far as captors went, she never saw her abductor. Only heard his deep, chilling voice over the intercom system. He inflicted no bodily harm at all, but his words felt like sharp claws destroying her insides. She needed to see her captor. Try to take him out, but his mind game was destroying her mentally.

Retaliation would be sweet. Kayla stared at the pile of matches and lighter fluid. In a few minutes, she'd either burn to death or escape into the darkness surrounding the wooded lot. Knowing that her captor was planning something involving kidnapping her baby, she had to get away before he had the opportunity. If she had to injure or even kill the creep, she would.

God, guide my actions. Get me out of this nightmare and back home to Annabelle.

God had become her sounding board. Her still water amidst the rocky valley of life. Without His closeness, Kayla would have succored to the battle raging in her mind. A battle that she could never win.

Taking a deep breath, she slowly scooted towards the pile of fire damage, concealed discreetly beneath the couch. She had meticulously disabled the cameras days ago, but a lingering sense of paranoia still gripped her. What if the fire spread too quickly, trapping her in a blazing inferno? The thought sent chills down her spine. If her captor failed to arrive, what awaited her? The uncertainty gnawed at her, fueling her determination. She couldn't bear to die or let a psycho trap her in a twisted marriage. Nor could she let him lay a finger on her precious daughter. This was the only choice she had left.

Her trembling fingers wrapped around a solid, golden candlestick, its weight reassuring in her grasp. It was no flimsy, plastic ornament, but a weapon capable of inflicting significant damage if aimed correctly. Beads of sweat formed on her palms, making the grip slippery as she tightly clenched the bottle of lighter fluid. With a shaky resolve, she began dousing every inch of the living room with the pungent liquid. The frantic pounding of her heart drowned the sound of the fluid hitting the floor out. Taking a deep breath to steady herself, she struck the match and watched as it ignited with a flicker of flame. With precision, she tossed it into the farthest corner, away from the front door. Time was running out. She had a mere five minutes, maybe even less. In an instant, the flames roared to life, devouring the room in a furious blaze that consumed everything in its path. The acrid smell of charred wood and melted plastic filled the air, stinging her nostrils.

Doubt creeped in, whispering that this might have been a terrible mistake. But there was no turning back now. Desperation fueled her actions as she lifted the hem of her shirt, covering her face to shield herself from the suffocating smoke. Violent coughs wracked her body, each breath a struggle. Panic surged through her veins, a realization that she was truly facing death. Her mind screamed for escape, urging the door to open and grant her salvation and a fight for freedom.

The intense heat swirled around her curled-up body like a fiery tornado. Flames danced and clung to fragments of the ceiling, spreading rapidly. They slithered down the curtains, devouring the couch, leaving no piece of furniture untouched. Beads of sweat erupted from her forehead as she convulsively coughed, her parched mouth feeling as dry as sandpaper. Desperately, she reached above her head, gripping the doorknob, praying for an escape route.

Locked.

The fire toyed with the tips of her toes as it devoured the hardwood floors. Gasping for breath, she uttered desperate words through her hacking coughs, her voice tinged with fear. She kicked her shoe at the encroaching flames, only to be met with searing pain as they licked up her leg. She didn't want to die, especially not like this, not with so much unfinished business.

"God, if you can get me out of here, I'll confess everything to Zach. No more secrets," she pleaded, her fingers tightening around the candlestick. Determined to escape, she raised it high, ready to shatter the thick-paned window. Unbeknownst to her, the door swung open, and as she spun around, the candlestick collided with a body. A body much taller than hers, possibly six feet, crumpled to the burning floor. Gasping for fresh air, she kneeled down and checked for a pulse. Strong.

Glancing at the nearly consumed house, she rolled her eyes. Why did she have to be a woman of integrity? She hadn't asked to be abducted by this creep, who vowed never to let her go. He hadn't laid a finger on her yet, but the thought lingered. The least she could do was drag his unconscious form away from the inferno's reach.

With grunts and a surge of strength, she pulled the man a few feet away from the flames. Without looking back, she sprinted off into the nearby woods, knowing that any delay could allow the man to regain consciousness and foil her escape. Running through the darkness, she savored every gulp of fresh air. Leaping over tall grass and evading entangling vines and trees, she knew not where she was or how to reach safety, but at least she was no longer a prisoner.

Regret tinged her thoughts as she berated herself for not glimpsing the creep's face. If only she had, she would know who her relentless stalker was. But it was too late now. Feeling lightheaded and shaky, she dared not stop or take a moment to rest. The distant chorus of croaking frogs and the rustling of animals in the underbrush reminded her of the dangers lurking in the wilderness.

Images of slithering snakes and spiders the size of golf balls haunted her thoughts, but she shook the pictures away as she ran until her feet would move no more.

****

Zach set Annabelle's backpack on the couch, giving her one more squeeze before he tried placing her on the floor. The morning wasn't going well. Annabelle cried for her mommy inconsolably for at least two hours. Four days ago, Mrs. Smith dropped his daughter at his house, never looking back. He didn't know if Mrs. Smith had slipped into a cruise ship and was living it up, because she sure wasn't in contact with him. She had returned no texts or phone calls. The single dad thing wasn't working out for

Zach. He needed to call his mom and tell her she had a granddaughter, and he would, but not now. He could only take so much stress.

"Princess, I'll be back in a few hours." Zach kissed the top of her lopsided pigtails, prying her death grip off his neck.

"With mommy?" She shoved her thumb in her mouth, a habit he hoped was just a phase.

Kid, if I knew where your mommy was, she'd already be here. Instead, he kneeled by her tear-stained cheek. "Your mommy loves you, and can't wait to come home."

Annabelle stomped her sandaled-foot on the hardwood floor, creating a little echo in the room. "Mommy, now!"

Zach rubbed the bags under his eyes. He had camped out again on the floor next to Annabelle's bed. His six-foot body barely fit on the floor, even curled up. But he couldn't sleep with the nightmares that jerked him out of a sound sleep, threatening to attack his logical mind. Every time he closed his eyes, he saw a dark shadow whisk his daughter away, never to be seen again. He wouldn't fail her like he did Kayla.

Sensing a full-blown meltdown coming, he wrapped his obstinate three-year-old in his arms, squeezing her lightly, whereas not to squash her. "I'll find her and bring her home."

"You love mommy?" She buried her candy-scented face in his chest, causing a tsunami of emotions swirling through his body. How could she be on the verge of a tantrum one minute and sweet as pie the next? The kid was an award-winning actress.

He stared into her baby-blues, like stepping in a time machine and looking in the mirror. Of course, he loved Kayla, but the feeling was platonic. Right? No romantic feelings at all. Kayla's brown eyes flashed into his mind as she leaned closer to him, feeling her breath tickle his chin, anticipating another kiss from his beautiful wife. What he wouldn't give to hold her one more time, begging for her forgiveness and praying to God, she'd give him a second chance. The buried emotions came so fast, like a wave pulling him under the water. He couldn't breathe.

Belle stepped into the living room, dusting her floury hands on her puppy-themed apron. "You okay?"

No, he wasn't okay. And he wouldn't be until Kayla rested safely in his arms. How could he deny and almost sabotage his feelings for Kayla by messing around with her sister? As if God smacked some sense into him, a light bulb went off in his mind. His wounded pride and jealousy locked away his love for Kayla. It never went away, but he masked it in the sea of pain. He favored his father more than he cared to admit; nursing his wounded flesh, never addressing his pain or love because it hurt. Not anymore.

God, I've failed You and I've destroyed any chance of a relationship with Kayla. Forgive me for running all these years. I'll do whatever it takes to get Kayla back. Help me.

Paul stepped into the room, shoving his last piece of waffle into his mouth. "I think God finally smacked some sense into him."

Belle shot her husband a quizzical look before stepping to Annabelle's side, ushering the child into the kitchen. "We have princess-shaped waffles with syrup."

Hearing his daughter's cheerful response, he wiped his teary eyes. "Peter got called to a four-car-pile-up downtown. He won't be working on the case today."

"Good thing I'm back. A man can only take so much Disney tunes." Paul grabbed his phone off the coffee table. "Let's go find your wife."

Zach knew a long road stretched out before him before he could call Kayla his again, but he'd do whatever it took.

"Where to?" Paul jogged to the passenger side of the SUV, sliding behind the wheel.

"I need to question Susan White again. Sixth grade geography teacher and good friends with Kayla."

Twenty minutes later, they pulled into the middle school. For Saturday, cars lined the parking lot. But Zach knew teachers were preparing for students' arrival in two days.

Zach slid a mint in his mouth, noticing the cool, minty sensation contrasting with the sticky heat of the unusually humid spring day. The heat wave was lasting longer than the weatherman predicted.

"You take the lead. I'll fill in when needed." Paul's stride matched Zach's as the overwhelming scent of books and glue filled the hall.

Zach shook off more awful memories from middle school as they followed laughter down the brightly lit hallway. He had to remind himself again that he wasn't a scared eleven-year-old hiding behind rebellion. Instead, his swagger matched his confident persona of a detective with the sheriff's office. He glanced at the gray lockers, fighting the urge to lean against the rusty metal, going back in time and reassuring his eleven-year-old self that he would do great things, even if no one believed in him.

Get your head in the game. He wondered if memories of middle school attacked the teachers that traveled through the halls daily? If so, he'd hate being them. He could imagine eleven-year-old Kayla, the envy of half the student body; beautiful, smart, and athletic. She probably didn't mind reliving her middle school days every day.

"Hey, man, you holding it together?" Paul stopped abruptly, staring into his partner's eyes. "I barely survived during Belle's kidnapping. Love, hate, and every emotion fought inside my heart like a hurricane. But God brought me out of that a better man, worthy of Belle's love."

"I'm holding it together." Barely.

"It's a suffocating feeling knowing that evil-intended men are trying to destroy your woman and you're powerless to stop it." Paul fidgeted with the badge clipped on to his pants. "I've never prayed so hard in my life." Of course, it didn't help that his father was the mastermind behind the hit on Belle's life.

"I appreciate your concern, but I can handle this." Zach took a deep breath, running his fingers through his disheveled hair. With a high-maintenance daughter, he couldn't remember if he brushed it or not.

Paul grabbed Zach's arm, preventing him from entering the classroom. "Don't be a hotheaded fool. Kayla's life depends on it. Ask for help, and I'm not talking about from me. Although I am your partner, and I've got your back."

Zach bit the inside of his lip, mulling over Paul's words. He needed God's help, or he'd be a widower and single father before age twenty-five. "Thanks man. Let's go find my estranged wife, so I can make her my wife again."

With a wide, beaming smile stretching across his face, Paul graciously motioned for Zach to enter the room before him. As they crossed the threshold, their footsteps resonated against the polished floor, creating a rhythmic beat that reverberated through the air. A life-sized world map, its vibrant colors catching the eye and igniting a sense of wanderlust, adorned the wall. As they approached Ms. White, Zach's deep voice carried a commanding presence, its echoes bouncing off the walls of the mid-sized classroom, filling the space with authority and determination.

****

"A drop of water." Kayla licked her parched lips, longing for a measly drop of water to cool her rough throat. She leaned over, hands resting on her thighs, panting. She looked around at the hilly, wooded terrain, completely lost. Stumbling around the heavily rooted wilderness had gotten her roughed up with scratches and torn jeans. The only positive being daylight aided in her trek. Even though she could have wandered aimlessly in the dark. Shivers attacked her body as she remembered running in the darkened woods in a daze. The blackness provided a shield from her attacker, but that meant nothing if his familiarity trumped the blinding darkness. Every few minutes, a breaking twig or an animal's movement tricked her brain into believing her abductor was gaining on her. She had hoped he was still unconscious or had given up his evil fantasy and had let her go. But that thought would get her killed.

"Gotta keep moving." She mumbled as her foot brushed over a patch of leftover dead leaves from winter. The crunching sound jerked her out of her daze, causing her senses to stand on high alert.

What if the abductor had known where she was the whole time? And letting her think she was escaping was part of his sick game? He wouldn't have known about the fire, not with broken cameras all over the house, but he had left the matches and lighter fluid in the kitchen. Who does that?

Kayla swiped a low-lying branch out of her face, mumbling nonsense under her breath. Who would want to kill or abduct her? Kayla's mind drifted to the incident in the bathroom where she almost drowned to death. That sicko, being a woman, could not be her abductor. No. That person wanted her dead for wrecking a home she knew nothing about. She had encouraged no married men to pursue her. Honestly, she flirted with no men; married or single. Her abductor lived in a fantasy world where they were a happy couple in love. Her heart only ever beat for Zach. In some twisted, sick way, was Zach behind this? Could he be her abductor?

Maybe he regretted walking out on their marriage four years ago and the only way he thought he could have their happily ever after marriage was to steal her and condition her. A thought smacked her in the face, leaving her dizzy and disoriented. If the entire case was a sham, and Zach was the creep after her, Thomas was telling the truth. That would mean Sarah, her sister, had tried to kill her. She had claimed nothing would stop her from getting what belonged to her. If Zach had Annabelle, but was secretly plotting this deranged plan, it would destroy her little girl's heart. She formed attachments too easily.

Kayla loved Zach, always had and always would. If he was behind everything, would it really be so bad? They could be together even if a twisted scheme brought them back together. Maybe he moved to East Tennessee because Zach had been stalking her and knew she was here. Kayla tripped over an uprooted root, tumbling to the hard ground. Pain shot up her leg as she winced; holding back the tears. No, as much as she wanted to forgive Zach and start over, this was not the way. Would Zach really risk a career he loved to hatch out a psychotic plan that wouldn't end well? Maybe. Maybe not.

What if Thomas secretly had a crush on her, and was behind the creeping notes and flowers? Her rejection could have spurred a raging sicko inside of him, causing him to snap. But who would the female trying to kill her be? Any woman the handsome Thomas had led on. The woman only tried to kill her once. Maybe she ditched that attempt and moved on.

Kayla gingerly rolled up her pants leg, revealing the raw scrape on her skin. As she examined the injury, crimson droplets of blood gathered around the cut, creating a stark contrast against her pale skin. Though it was just a minor scrape, the pain shot through her leg, making her feel as if it might detach at any moment. Determined, she placed her hands on the rough, earthy root beneath her, feeling its texture against her fingertips. Using it as leverage, she slowly lifted her body off the ground, wincing at the discomfort. With each deliberate step, she could feel the strain on her wounded leg, a constant reminder of her perseverance. But she continued her trek and her wandering thoughts.

And then there was Silas. His entire personality revolted her. Had the guy never heard of soap or deodorant? His caked on greasy stench was stomach curling. He had tried to steal her, and without her jumping out of a moving vehicle, no telling where she'd be. But honestly, he lacked brain cells to pull her abduction off. Only if he had a partner; the brains of the operation.

Then names from the past popped into her mind like Adam Fisher and Wallie Hill. Kayla shook her head in frustration. This was why she was a language arts teacher and not a detective.

Kayla, drenched in sweat, hauled herself over a small, rugged hill, her muscles burning with exhaustion. Her parched throat begged for water; her vision blurred from the strain. But as she squinted ahead, a glimmer of hope emerged - a campground, perhaps? The tantalizing aroma of sizzling bacon wafted through the crisp air, intensifying the growls of her protesting stomach. Torn between desperation and caution, she hesitated, ready to flee into the dense woods. Suddenly, the door of a nearby camper swung open, revealing a face she thought she knew. Confusion flooded her mind - was it salvation or a cunning trap?

"What do we have here?" The stranger's voice, smooth as honey, sent shivers down her spine, amplifying the goosebumps that dotted her skin.

God, help!

Chapter Eleven

"So, Ms. Smith wasn't in a relationship?" Zach's monotone voice filled the silent classroom, the sound bouncing off the cold, white walls. His tired eyes locked onto Susan White, the fluorescent lights overhead casting a harsh glow on her face. Talking about his estranged wife's romantic relationships was as unpleasant as a root canal. He clenched his jaw, determined to maintain a professional demeanor, no matter what he discovered about her.

"Look, Detective Rivers," Susan replied, her voice soft yet tinged with a hint of nervousness. She reached up to tuck a loose strand of her shoulder-length brown hair behind her ear. The scent of her floral perfume lingered in the air, mixing with the faint aroma of chalk and old textbooks. "Kayla attracted a lot of attention from the male species, but she always brushed it off with a laugh. I'm surprised she never married."

Zach's leg shifted uncomfortably on the cold, tiled floor, the sensation jolting him back to reality. He needed to regain his composure. Why had Kayla kept their marriage a secret from her best friend? The memory of how their relationship had ended weighed heavily on him, and he couldn't blame her for wanting to distance herself.

Paul, his partner, cleared his throat, breaking through the cobwebs of Zach's thoughts. The sound echoed in the stillness, accompanied by the ticking of the clock on the wall. "Did she casually talk to any male teachers? Any that were married?"

Susan tapped the end of a pencil on her desk, the rhythmic thumping creating a steady beat. Her pale skin flushed with a mix of embarrassment and discomfort at the question. "There were a few men who broke through the fortress around her heart. Thomas, being one of them."

Zach recalled the last time he had spoken to Susan and had noticed her friendly interactions with Mr. Holmes. The memory brought a sense of unease. Leaning in closer, he locked his gaze with Susan's icy green eyes. "I saw how friendly you and Mr. Holmes were. Did you feel jealous of the attention he showered Kayla with?"

Susan's face reddened further; her discomfort clear. She stumbled over her words, searching for a response. "I-I…"

Zach's curiosity piqued at her reaction. "Were you jealous of the attention he showered her with?" he pressed, his voice steady and unwavering.

"I did nothing!" Susan blurted out, her voice filled with a mix of frustration and defensiveness.

The tension in the room thickened. The pieces of the puzzle were slowly coming together, revealing a complex web of relationships and emotions. It was certainly interesting.

"Did you feel you had to get rid of the competition?" Zach's piercing gaze locked onto hers, causing her to squirm uncomfortably in the cold metal chair behind the desk. An eerie silence filled the room, broken only by the faint humming of the air conditioner.

"You wanted Thomas. He couldn't stop flirting with Ms. Smith," Zach stated, his arms crossed over his chest, a smug smirk playing on his lips. He was a seasoned interrogator, but he couldn't help but question if she could truly attempt to kill Kayla.

"Him and I are soul mates. We're supposed to be together!" Her frustration boiled over as she slammed the palm of her hands on the desk, causing her chair to jolt. The metallic sound echoed in the room, intensifying the tension.

"That's a powerful motive for murder," Zach leaned forward, trying to match her gaze with his own, his eyes locked onto her green eyes that shifted like a mood ring. "Where is she?"

"Hold on a minute!" Trembling hands ran through her hair, causing strands to fall out of place. "You can't pin this on me."

"You just said you envied her relationship with Mr. Holmes," Zach pointed out, his voice unyielding.

"True, but Kayla was like a sister to me. I'd never stab her in the back." Ms. White's voice rose an octave as she leaped out of her chair, pacing in front of the chalkboard. The screeching sound of her shoes against the floor added to the escalating tension in the room.

"How about water? Would you ever try to drown her?" Zach probed, knowing that most people cracked under pressure. He needed to understand what made her tick. "Where were you last Friday night around seven pm?"

"Thomas and I were on our way to dinner," she responded, her voice quivering slightly.

"Restaurant?" Zach pressed for more details; his tone unwavering.

"Um … We were going on a picnic," she stammered, her voice trembling. She reached for her phone, the faint clicks of her nails against the screen breaking the stillness. She scrolled through social media, her eyes darting anxiously across the device.

Zach, his arms crossed, took a step back, his words tinged with skepticism. "Ms. White, anyone with a knowledge of photo editing can manipulate the time stamp. Not a very convincing alibi." The weight of his doubts seemed to hang in the air, adding to the already suffocating atmosphere.

Her lip trembled as she nervously chewed on it, tears threatening to spill. "Do I need to call my lawyer?" Her voice quivered, the desperation in her eyes mirroring her fear. Zach, though relentless, couldn't help but feel a pang of sympathy.

"You tell me." He responded; his voice laced with determination. The room fell silent once again, the tension thickening with every passing second.

Just as the air grew heavy with uncertainty, Paul stepped forward. The sound of his badge hitting the side of his holstered gun echoed through the room. It was time for him to play the good cop, to offer a glimmer of hope in the darkness. "Okay, I've heard enough," he declared, his voice calm yet commanding.

"I'm sure there's been a misunderstanding. Ms. White, as a Southern, Christian woman, would never abduct or attempt to murder anyone." Paul's words hung in the air, offering a faint sense of relief in an otherwise grim situation. The room seemed to relax ever so slightly, as if his words lifted a heavy weight.

Zach, never one to miss an opportunity, rolled his eyes and scoffed. "Jealousy is an undoing of many Christian values," he retorted, his voice dripping with sarcasm. He reveled in playing the bad cop, relishing in the discomfort he could provoke.

"Yeah, I go to church weekly. I even attend prayer meetings," she replied, her voice filled with a mix of defiance and desperation. The room seemed to hold its breath, waiting for the next move.

Paul, a master at interrogation, skillfully twisted her words to expose her guilt. "That's dedication. And a dedicated person would not willfully sin against God," he stated, his voice unwavering.

"Not premeditated, but attempted murder is still punishable by the law, no matter how the suspect concocted the plan," Zach chimed in, his tone firm.

"Detective Rivers, look at her. Can you truly believe that this petite, shorter-than-average woman can murder Kayla Smith?"

"Hey, never judge someone's capabilities based on their physical appearance. I matched Kayla's..." Her eyes widened, realization dawning on her. She covered her mouth with shaky hands, the weight of her own words sinking in. She had unknowingly argued against herself, her defense crumbling before her very eyes.

"Continue your statement, Ms. White," Zach urged, his doubt beginning to waver. He didn't truly believe she was involved, but he couldn't ignore the possibility. After all, he had been mistaken before.

Standing to her feet, she squared her shoulders with a defiant look. "No, we're done here. Direct any further questions to my lawyer."

"Very well." Zach sighed, stalking out of the room.

****

Kayla stood frozen in motion as the burly male with pops of gray sprinkled through his brown hair approached her in two steps. He reminded her of a daddy-long-legs; all legs, not much upper body besides his bulging muscles.

219

She couldn't remember where she knew him from. Kayla scrolled through the pages of her memory, only to come up short.

"You don't remember me?" His rumbled laughter sent chills through her body. Was this guy her stalker? She glanced around the clearing. If she backed up slowly, she might could outrun him, but he could also put a bullet in her back. "Come closer. I want to see how good time has been for you."

No way was she getting close enough for him to force her inside his camper. Been there, done that, don't want to be a prisoner again. At least outside, she felt a surge of freedom.

"Have it your way." He kicked at a plastic water bottle on top of the grass. "I see you haven't lost your obstinate ways."

And he knew this how?

"I'm hurt." He grabbed his chest, pretending to fall over. "I thought we had a connection."

That was the worse pickup line ever. Kayla folded her scratched up arms over her chest. Her eyes gazing at the bottle of water. Suddenly, her parched throat resurfaced, making it difficult to even swallow.

With a smile that bordered on creepy, he pointed to a cup of water on a small table next to the camper. "Want a bottle?"

Yes. "No." She couldn't afford to let her guard down. He could easily lace the sides of her bottle with something, and the next thing she knew, he had locked her back in a prison. Only this time, she'd never escape.

"Suit yourself." He popped the lid off, guzzling the liquid down his throat. She now knew what Esau felt like when he sold his birthright for a bowl of lentils.

Annabelle's smiley face dashed before her eyes. Kayla would not sell her soul for a bottle of water. No matter what.

"Want to get comfortable inside my camper? It's a muggy day." He took a step closer to Kayla. His biceps were bigger than the muscles in her entire body.

Like a deer in headlights, she just stood there staring, unable to process what the guy was talking about. Her mind couldn't get off the water bottle feet away.

"I see you have some trust issues." He took another gulp of water and wiped the stray droplets from his chin with the hem of his shirt.

Kayla's eyes darted past his toned abs to the teardrop tattoo under his ribcage. Years of memories came flashing back as she dazed at the man in front of her.

"What do you say? Let's get out of here and go have a good time." *The enticing smile spread across his tan face as he wrapped his arm over Kayla's shoulder.*

"I'm married." *She stepped out of his arms, glaring at him.*

"I've heard the rumors. It hasn't stopped you from having a good time with Adam." *He leaned closer to her ear, his breath tickling the side of her neck.* *"I'm way better than Adam."*

Bile threatened to spew out of her mouth any minute. *"Leave me alone."*

"Baby, we belong together." *He raised his shirt, revealing a little teardrop tattoo under his ribcage.* *"I got that for you. Every time I see you with Zach or Adam, it pierces my soul like the needle did when I got this tattoo."*

Kayla opened her mouth, but nothing came out. What do you say to a deranged individual?

"Remember this: the universe destined us together. One day, I'll get you back."

No way this was the same guy from college. She hadn't seen him since her sophomore year at NC State when he dropped out, but man, his psyche completely changed. Kayla shook her head as she stared at the man in front of her.

"I take it you remember who I am." He bowed slightly, extending his hand in her direction. "Donnie Davis at your service."

Like she'd actually shake his hand. "What happened to you?"

"I hear a hint of admiration in your tone." A tight smile tugged on the corner of his lips. He was handsome in an I-take-enhancing-drugs kind of way. "I aspired to be like the men you gravitated towards; muscular and toned. I've never been happier until I saw you a few minutes ago. The universe is bringing us together again."

Kayla leaned over, gagging. Why were so many basket cases after her? He had to be her stalker. "Are you … stalking me?"

"Baby, when I shower you with attention, it won't be in secret." He flexed his arms, revealing his muscles. "I've been working on my psyche, bidding my time. I didn't want to run into you until you could appreciate my transformation. The universe had other plans."

Gag. As if. The putrid smell of Donnie's cologne mixed with the stench of sweat made Kayla's stomach churn. No way she would fall for his slimy charm and the sight of his overly toned body. She took a cautious step back, her heart pounding in her chest, wondering which would be worse - dealing with her unknown stalker or this arrogant muscle head? The sound of her own rapid breathing filled her ears as she weighed her options. If she went backwards, her stalker might catch her. If she stayed here, Donnie might decide to take matters into his own hands, claiming the universe lined up everything for their reunion.

"Where are you going? The party is in my camper," he sneered, taking a threatening step toward her, his fingers reaching out, ready to grab her arm.

"No!" Kayla's voice trembled, desperation lacing her words as she fought to ward off Donnie. She scanned the area. The dim lights of the two other campers in the clearing were barely visible. The occupants were probably off fishing or hiking, leaving her alone with this monster.

"Baby, stop. You belong to me," he growled possessively, his massive hands encircling her skinny arms, squeezing tightly, causing a searing pain to shoot through her body.

She did not escape the clutches of a deranged stalker to fall victim to a guy like Donnie. Determination surged within her as she thought of her self-defense classes last summer. Her mama didn't raise a coward, and she would fight tooth and nail to protect herself. Even if she was a little rusty with the techniques, she hoped muscle memory would kick in, just enough to ward off this menacing man.

"Let go of me!" Kayla's voice held a mixture of fear and defiance as she jerked her arm away from Donnie, his grip tightening, leaving a painful pink mark on her skin.

"Stop playing hard-to-get," he snarled, his arm snaking around her shoulder, his grip possessive, leading her towards his camper. Kayla's senses heightened, her heart pounding in her ears, as she desperately searched for an escape.

Feeling a surge of adrenaline, Kayla jabbed her fingers into Donnie's side, the sound of his startled grunt breaking the silence of the empty campground. She side-swiped his leg, the impact connecting with his knee, causing him to stumble and curse under his breath. Taking advantage of the moment, Kayla sprinted towards the nearest camper, her feet pounding against the hard ground, the sound of her labored breath filling the air.

"You'll pay for that!" Donnie's enraged voice echoed behind her as he chased after her. His face, flushed and contorted with anger, was a sight she desperately wanted to escape.

"Help!" Kayla's voice filled with desperation as she reached the two steps leading to the camper's door. She pounded her open palm on the screen, the sound reverberating through the silent day, while kicking her foot at Donnie as he lunged towards her, desperately trying to pull her away. In the chaos, she lost her footing, her body tumbling to the unforgiving ground.

God, protect me!

As the camper door swung open, a man and woman emerged, taking in the fresh outdoor air. With a shotgun perched on his shoulder, the man exuded an air of confidence.

"What in the world is going on?" she asked, her eyes scanning the chaotic scene before her.

"My wife and I got into an argument. She's a little dramatic. I'll take her home now." Donnie wrapped his arm around Kayla's waist, half carrying her off the tiny porch.

"Kayla?"

Her head jerked, her heart pounding in her chest, and she thanked God for sending deliverance. The forest surrounding her was a blur of vibrant green leaves and dappled sunlight.

"Josh? Help me," she pleaded, her voice trembling. "He's trying to get me into his camper."

Josh Rivers, Zach's older brother, lifted the shotgun, his hands steady as he aimed it at the man. The metallic glint of the gun caught the sunlight, casting a glimmer in the air. "You have one minute to let the lady go, or I'll start shooting."

Donnie's eyes widened, fear flickering across his face as he stared at Josh. He refused to release his grip on Kayla's waist.

Josh, determined, trained his eyes on the towering trees ahead. Without hesitation, he pulled the trigger, the deafening sound of the gunshot reverberating through the woods. The echo hung in the air, a warning of the consequences that awaited. "Next time, I'll aim it at you."

Donnie rolled his eyes, finally releasing his hold on Kayla. "You're too much trouble, anyway," he sneered before turning and sprinting towards his camper.

Relieved, Kayla ran into the waiting arms of her best friend, Britney. She could feel the warmth of Britney's embrace, a comforting refuge amidst the chaos. She glanced up at Josh, his features resembling a more refined version of Zach. "Thank you," she whispered.

"Oh, sweetie. I'm so glad you're safe," Britney said, her voice filled with relief. Her eyes narrowed, casting a glare towards Donnie's camper. "God protected you. We were about to leave for a hike."

"But not anymore," Josh said, setting his shotgun down. He gently guided his wife and Kayla into the camper, the scent of pine and adventure lingering in the air. "Let's call Zach and get you home where you belong."

"I hear you have a little girl very impatient for you to get home. And your husband is waiting," Britney said, guiding Kayla to the couch. As they sat down, Kayla noticed the comforting scent of vanilla. Britney grabbed a cookie off the end table, crumbs dropping onto her protruding belly.

"Husband? Brit, that didn't work years ago. Nothing has changed now," Kayla said, her voice tinged with a mix of hope and uncertainty. She longed for Zach, for a chance to start anew.

"Don't be so quick to assume the worst. God gets the final say," Britney reassured her, patting Kayla's arm. She handed her a cellphone. "Call Zach. He's waiting for you."

Could it really be that simple? After all these years, could they truly mend their broken marriage and start afresh? Kayla's heart swelled with love for Zach, knowing that there would never be another man for her. But did he feel the same way? What about her sister, Sarah? Did Zach love her too? Only time would tell.

Taking a deep breath, Kayla dialed his number. After three rings, his voice, filled with warmth and love, resonated through the phone.

"Hey Britney," he said, his voice a lifeline amidst her tears. With a stalker still lurking, she knew she wasn't completely safe. But in that moment, talking to Zach, she felt secure.

"Zach," she choked out the words, tears of relief cascading down her face.

****

"Mommy will be here soon?" Annabelle glanced out the window for the hundredth time. "Where is she?"

Zach plopped on the couch next to his daughter, staring at the setting sun. "Uncle Josh and Aunt Britney are bringing your mommy home."

"They must drive really slow." She fell onto the couch, her bottom lip poked out in a pout. "No bedtime until mommy gets home."

"Wouldn't dream of it." A smile tugged on his lips.

Would Kayla come back and demand to take their daughter to her home with little visitation rights? Was this the start of an ugly custody battle? Somewhere along the almost five days of Kayla's disappearance, God had tugged on his heart, reminding him of the vows he had taken for Kayla, and how He could repair any marriage. Maybe it was a crazy dream, but he didn't want Kayla leaving tonight, or any night. For Annabelle's sake, they needed to work through their differences. Okay, not just for Annabelle's sake. He was madly in love with his wife, and if she'd have him, he'd like to start over. Would she? He couldn't blame Kayla if she wanted no part of their marriage. He foolishly let pride and insecurities rip the best person out of his life. They had four years of heartache to deal with. Five if you count the first year of their marriage where they actually tried having a successful marriage.

"Look!" Annabelle's high-pitched squeal pierced through Zach's thoughts, jolting him back to reality. "Mommy!" Her excitement propelled her off the couch, her little feet pounding against the floor as she dashed towards the door, her tiny fingers desperately reaching for the cold metal of the deadbolt. Zach's brawny arms encircled his daughter's waist, gently pulling her back as he turned the doorknob. A rush of warm air surged towards him, nearly knocking him off balance. The relentless heatwave showed no signs of relenting. His gaze fixated on Kayla as she

227

gingerly stepped out of the truck, her movements hindered by a slight limp. With each step, the scratches on her skin became more pronounced, fueling an intense anger within Zach. The mere thought of the perpetrator ignited a fiery rage in his heart, but he knew he had to maintain self-control. Kayla glanced at him sheepishly, her bottom lip caught between her teeth. Ignoring his impulsive instincts, Zach gathered her into his embrace, burying his face in her earthly-scented hair as tears welled in his eyes. Leaning down, he pressed a tender, lingering kiss on the crown of her head, her hair adorned with delicate leaves.

She pushed away from him, staring into his watery eyes. Her eyes held a mixture of longing and confusion. Zach wanted to kiss away the confusion until she felt the depths of his love, but now wasn't the time.

"Mommy!" Annabelle jumped into her mommy's arms, wrapping her hands around Kayla's neck. "You came back!"

"Oh sweetie, nothing could keep me from you." Kayla stepped past Zach, falling onto the couch. Clearly, fatigue was taking over her body.

Zach stood at the door, staring at his brother, Josh. "Y'all coming inside?"

A smile played on Josh's lips. "No. Britney is craving Mexican food, and if I want to live another day, I better get her some tacos."

Another thing Zach had missed by leaving his pregnant wife. Would he have left if he had known they were having a baby? As immature and foolish as Zach was, he probably would have. He envied his brother for marrying his high school sweetheart and building a life together. Noticing his brother waiting for a response, Zach shook the thoughts out of his mind. "Thanks, bro, for rescuing her."

"I don't know the details, but I figured you'd take her statement. Get enough evidence and I'll prosecute this guy to the fullest."

They had to identify him first. "Thanks"

Zach watched as Josh pulled out of the driveway and a patrol car pulled into the driveway. Peter.

"Is she here?" Peter stepped toward the house, a smile filling his face. "I knew God would bring her back." He slid past Zach, wrapping his arms around Kayla in a brotherly hug.

"Nice to see you, too." Zach closed the door, joining Kayla and Peter on the couch. A sting of jealousy shot through him as he stared at his brother holding Kayla.

With a wink, Peter slid off the couch, motioning for Zach to take his place. "Did you get a look at your abductor? Any identifying marks? Something about his voice that stood out?"

Kayla adjusted Annabelle on her lap, running her fingers through her daughter's wavy hair. "I'm sorry, Peter. But I never saw the guy or heard his real voice."

"It's okay. When Zach takes your statement, I'd like to be present."

"Of course." She leaned her head on the back of the couch, closing her eyes.

"Hey squirt, why don't we go watch cartoons and eat a giant bowl of ice cream while the adults talk?" Peter grabbed Annabelle's hand, tugging her gently out of her mom's grip.

"Do I have to?" Annabelle's bottom lip poked out again.

"You can have extra sprinkles on top." Zach wasn't against bribing his daughter to get her to listen to him.

229

"Yay!" She jumped out of her mommy's arms, running toward Peter, grabbing his arm, and following him into the kitchen.

"Zach," Kayla whispered, her voice trembling as tears glistened in her eyes. She wrapped her arms tightly around her chest, aching with vulnerability.

He shifted closer on the couch, the soft fabric brushing against his skin. He reached out, pulling Kayla into his embrace, feeling the warmth radiating from her body. The comforting touch brought solace, as if it were a gift from above. "Shh, we don't have to talk right now. I just need to hold you," he murmured.

Tears streamed down Kayla's cheeks, dampening his shirt as she buried her face in his chest. His heartbeat quickened, the rhythm matching the intensity of his emotions. "I promised myself I would tell you everything, holding nothing back. Please, before I lose my courage," she pleaded.

"Okay, but I have lots to say, too." Kayla's finger gently brushed against his lips, the featherlight touch soothing his soul.

"Zach, let me," she whispered, her voice barely audible. Leaning in, she pressed her lips against his in a tender kiss, igniting a longing for healing and restoration.

In a haze of love, he gazed at her, taking in the delicate beauty of her scratched face. Kayla was a fighter, and he needed to declare his love before his heart burst with emotion. But first, he had to listen to her.

"Four years ago, I was driving back to campus after a routine prenatal checkup. A pickup truck crossed the yellow lines, colliding head-on with my car. The impact trapped me in the totaled car. The firefighters had to cut me out, and when I regained consciousness in the ER, our baby was gone," she revealed, her voice heavy with grief.

Shock washed over him. Kayla appeared flawless, with no visible signs of the lingering effects of an accident. But four years could heal so much. "What?" he stammered, disbelief coloring his words. "Annabelle is in the other room. Are you saying she's not our daughter?"

Kayla trembled, tears streaming down her face like a torrential downpour. "Zach, we had twins," she confessed, her voice breaking.

The revelation hit him like a tidal wave, threatening to consume him. He closed his eyes, seeking solace in prayer, begging for God's peace to wash over him. The weight of four years' worth of secrets felt insurmountable, a vast chasm between them. Yet, despite the pain, he couldn't deny the longing in his heart. She shattered his trust, but could love prevail?

****

Kayla glanced at Zach's ashen face, her heart sinking as she took in the shock etched on his features. An eerie silence filled the dimly lit room, broken only by the faint hum of the air conditioner. The scent of stale coffee lingered in the air, a stark reminder of their strained reunion.

She felt a lump forming in her throat as Zach slowly released his hold on her, his movements measured and distant. As he scooted inches away, Kayla could sense an invisible wall building up between them, suffocating any hope of a rekindled relationship. The pain in her chest intensified, a sharp stab at her heart as she felt the weight of his rejection.

Memories of their troubled past flooded her mind. Four years ago, he had walked away when their marriage hit a rough patch, leaving her shattered and alone. She had hoped that Zach had grown and matured during their time apart, maybe even regretting the way they had ended things. But now, history repeated itself as he withdrew from her once again. It was only a matter of time before he shut her out completely.

But this time, it was different. This time, she had her daughter's fragile heart to consider.

Desperate to break the tense silence, Kayla mustered the courage to speak. Her voice trembled slightly as she addressed Zach, her words slicing through the air like a knife. "Don't you want to know what happened?"

Zach's gaze turned cold, his eyes piercing hers with an icy glare. It was a mistake to come here, to hope for a different outcome. She could feel her cheeks burning with embarrassment, a mix of frustration and disappointment.

Unable to bear the pain any longer, Kayla rose abruptly from her seat, her hand hastily wiping away a fallen tear. Her voice cracked with anguish as she spoke, the words laced with a tinge of bitterness.

"This was a mistake. Why did I ever think you had changed?"

Zach crossed his arms over his chest, a frown etching deeper lines on his face. "Now hold on a minute. You can't drop a tremendous revelation like that and expect it not to affect me."

His words hung heavy in the air, as if daring her to challenge his reaction.

Kayla's tongue brushed over the bottom of her lip, feeling the roughness of her chapped skin. She fought back tears, her voice filled with a mixture of pain and frustration.

"No, I expected you to hold me, to comfort me. Something you didn't do four years ago," she said, her voice barely above a whisper. "You weren't the one who plunged into darkness after the news of our babies; one dead and the other fighting for her life in the NICU. Not only that, but I had to heal from a car accident that almost took my life."

"Kayla … you should have told me."

"Don't waltz in here all self-righteous," she continued, her voice tinged with anger. "How could I have told you? Zach, you disappeared, and I had no one." She dabbed her nose with the back of her hand, the scent of tears filling the air. "If not for my mom, I wouldn't have survived," she whispered, her voice muffled by the sobs. "My heart still aches for Izzy."

Zach stared at her like he was a statue, his face devoid of any emotion. Silence enveloped the room, broken only by the sound of Kayla's deep sobs. Each sob seemed to echo off the walls, amplifying the pain she felt within.

Kayla's arms trembled uncontrollably as the pain wracked her body. She sank into the chair on the other side of the room, the fabric cool against her skin. In that moment, all she longed for was her husband's love and care, the warmth of his embrace to provide solace.

God, I thought You were bringing us together, she prayed, her voice filled with a mix of desperation and disappointment. *But now I see that was just a dead dream.*

Zach reluctantly climbed off the couch; his footsteps barely audible. He approached Kayla, his presence a silent reassurance. Taking her weeping, trembling body into his arms, he whispered soothing words, a balm for her pain. The sound of her sobs subsided, replaced by the gentle rhythm of their breathing.

"Shh, I'm sorry," he murmured, his voice filled with remorse. "I'm an idiot. I didn't know." Zach rested his chin on top of her hair.

"I can't be vulnerable with you and open up my heart if you're just gonna leave again," Kayla's voice trembled with a mixture of fear and disappointment. She pushed off of his body, her gaze fixed on his soaked shirt, a visual reminder of her breakdown.

Zach pointed to the back room. The faint scent of ice cream lingered in the air. His eyes reddened with a hint of tears, glistening under the flickering overhead light. "I never want to leave her again. I'm not going anywhere," he whispered, his voice choked with emotion.

That's what she feared. She didn't really want to share her daughter with anyone, but she pushed the selfish thought out of her mind. Zach had every right to be in Annabelle's life. "I'm glad to hear that, but what about us?" she asked, her words barely audible over the distant sound of her daughter's laughter.

A painful look crossed Zach's tired face. His fingers went stiff around her waist, the fabric of her shirt bunching in his grip. "I-I..." he stammered, his voice trembling.

"That's what I thought. I'll get my lawyer to deliver the divorce papers and a custody agreement," she said, her voice tinged with disappointment. She should have known Zach didn't love her. Women like her sister thrilled him, and she was nothing like Sarah.

"I'm taking Annabelle to my place for the night. I'll see you in the morning," she declared, determination lacing her words. She lifted her body off the worn oversized chair, her muscles aching from the tension, before Zach's gentle touch pulled her back into his arms. The warmth of his embrace enveloped her, providing a momentary sense of solace amidst the chaos.

Kayla locked her gaze with Zach, captivated by the depth in his sky-blue eyes. She felt her heart skip a beat as she looked into his eyes, filled with longing and love. The distant sound of rain tapping against the windowpane created a soothing rhythm, contrasting with the storm brewing in her chest.

"I'm blotching this whole thing. Please, let me explain. Then, if you want to leave, I won't stop you," Zach pleaded, his voice laced with vulnerability. The confident detective, always so sure of himself, rubbed the side of the chair with nervous energy, the sound of his fingers grazing against the wood echoing in the silence.

Kayla inched away from him, determined to shield her heart and avoid the humiliation of stumbling into his waiting embrace. She couldn't fall for his charm until she knew he would commit to her forever this time. Uncertainty hung heavy in the air, suffocating her with its presence.

"Four years ago, I ran away. It sounds foolish now, but I let my pride and arrogance convince me I was sharing you with the football team. If you get my drift. Memories of high school and everyone's silent mocking flashed into my mind. I didn't want to be that weak kid anymore."

"Zach..." Her voice trembled with frustration. She had heard the rumors, false tales of her infidelity with Adam and Donnie. Just two guys trying to tear apart their marriage, and sadly, they succeeded.

"I now know you weren't unfaithful to me," Zach started, his voice laden with regret. "But the overwhelming desire to escape consumed me. I couldn't stay."

He reached out for her hand, a feeble attempt to bridge the gap between them. But hesitated and slid it under his thigh, the tension between them palpable.

"We had our problems, I admit. But I had devoted all of my days to you until you left me. Where did you go?" Her eyes searched his, longing for an explanation.

"I finished my criminal justice degree and ended up working in West Virginia with my father. He's the police chief in a town slightly larger than ours."

"You never looked back?" The words hung heavy in the air. She had thought of him every day, but it seemed the feeling wasn't mutual.

"Kayla, my father convinced me you were the problem, not me. He abandoned my mom and us boys, never once looking back. I never wanted to be like him, but somehow, I turned out just like him."

She couldn't argue with that, so she looked at him, waiting for him to continue.

"Every time your face invaded my thoughts, I pushed it aside. I threw myself into my career, fueled by my father's admiration. I became a detective within a year on the force."

"Why did you move to Tennessee? Did you know I lived here?" Her fingers nervously picked at the skin on her finger, avoiding eye contact.

"I honestly didn't know you were here." Zach took a deep breath, running his fingers through his hair. "I watched a man shoot and ultimately kill my partner during a routine welfare check. I needed to get away, so my father pulled some strings and got me transferred to the MCPD. But last year, Paul and I both moved to the sheriff's office. The other detectives retired, and I love Peter, but I didn't want to work with him."

She had hoped that he moved here for her. But clearly, that wasn't the case.

"Why my sister? In a town full of single women, why did you have to choose her?" The bitterness in her voice booming into the room.

Zach shifted on the worn-out chair, the scratchy fabric sticking to his skin uncomfortably. The dim light from the lamp cast a faint glow on his face, highlighting the worry lines etched on his forehead.

"We started talking and hanging out," he said, his voice filled with a hint of regret. "I never knew you lived here until the incident at the school. I never expected it to turn from friendship to a relationship so fast. She intrigued me, and didn't care that we were still legally married."

A lump formed in Kayla's throat as she listened, her heart pounding in her chest. The room seemed to close in on her, the air heavy with tension. This wasn't how she envisioned their reunion.

"I'd say I'm happy for you, but I'd be lying," she replied, her voice barely above a whisper. Nausea churned in her stomach, twisting her insides.

Zach's face contorted into a tight smile, his eyes filled with a mix of remorse and longing. "But I broke off whatever we had. I never should have laid eyes on her," he admitted, his voice tinged with regret. "What I'm trying to say is…"

Suddenly, a shrill ring cut through the room, jolting them both. Zach swiftly grabbed his cellphone, the sound piercing through the quietness of the room. "Rivers," he answered, his tone urgent. "Yes, she is here. Okay." He tossed the phone onto the end table, the sound of it landing with a hollow thud. "Your parents found out about your escape. They want to meet us at church in the morning. And since you don't have your phone, they called me."

The weight of the situation settled heavily on Kayla's shoulders, exhaustion seeping into her bones. She stood up, her legs feeling weak. "It's getting late. I'm exhausted," she murmured, her voice trembling.

Zach rose from the couch, his fingers intertwining with hers. "Stay here in the guest bedroom. You can bunk with Annabelle," he suggested, his touch offering a sense of comfort amidst the chaos. "We can finish our conversation later." Leaning down, he pressed a tender kiss on top of her head. "I'm so thankful you're home."

With a slight nod, Kayla stumbled down the hallway, the dim light casting eerie shadows on the walls. Confusion clouded her mind, her thoughts swirling in a disarray. Zach's words made no sense. Neither did his kiss on her head. Did he want her as his wife or not? A shiver ran down her spine as she recalled the sensation of their lips meeting.

"God, I can't play these games with Zach," she silently prayed, her voice a desperate whisper. "Restore our marriage or help me walk away."

Chapter Twelve

"It doesn't hurt that bad, Mom." Kayla glanced at the red scratches on her arm, pulling out of her mother's embrace.

"Considering you could have died, still can, I'll take a few scratches over the alternative." Mrs. Smith adjusted Annabelle in her arms as they walked toward a pew in the back of the church.

"Save Daddy a seat." Annabelle jumped out of her grandma's arms, landing on the cushioned pew.

Mrs. Smith's eyes lit up at the mention of her estranged son-in-law. "How is my gorgeous son-in-law doing?"

What had her mom been reading? "Gorgeous son-in-law? Mom, why are you playing matchmaker?" Kayla released a deep breath of air. Zach definitely deserved to be on a cover of a magazine, but he didn't need any extra female attention.

"Is it so bad that I'm praying for my oldest daughter's family to be restored? Annabelle needs both parents, and I saw the way your eyes beamed at the mention of his name." Mrs. Smith set her Bible on the pew, propping her foot on a pillow.

"Mom, don't get your hopes up. Life's not one big fairytale. God can't save all marriages." Kayla sounded so cynical, but after the way they ended their conversation last night, all hope deflated from her.

Kayla begged God all night through her fitful sleeping to open Zach's heart and eyes toward her, but it didn't work. He barely looked at her this morning, and when he did, it made her regret running into his arms yesterday. His icy stares made her want to lose whatever cereal she got down. He treated her like she was a suspect in one of his cases, not the victim. Surely, he didn't think she had made everything up just to get back with him. That train of thought would be completely ridiculous.

Peter welcomed her with open arms. Why couldn't Zach be more like his brothers? That was one reason she drove to meet her parents and to church separately. Peter, with the help of his brother Josh, found her car parked at her new house. She wouldn't have to depend on Zach anymore. That thought pierced her heart. She didn't want to go back to separate lives, only occasionally running into Zach in town. Kayla wanted to spend every day of the rest of her life in Zach's arms as his wife. She wiped her cheek as a tear fell onto her black, knee-length skirt. If she didn't pull it together, her mom would give her one of her famous looks, and Kayla might have a breakdown in front of the whole church. Her life was beyond the point of no return.

School started back tomorrow, but how could she focus on twenty sixth graders and the parts of a sentence when a stalker still had her in his grips? Her marriage was truly over, but she didn't want to let go. And she felt like she was being suffocated and one breath stood between her and death.

"Breathe." Gentle arms grazed along the back of her shoulder as Zach whispered into her ear. Kayla's heart dropped at his nearness. His earthly cologne teased her nose, sending shock waves shooting through her body. Why couldn't they get past the secret pain and mistrust of

four years apart? She'd do anything, even beg, to repair
what they once shared.

Zach moved around the pew, grabbing Annabelle and
sitting thigh to thigh with Kayla. She couldn't breathe for
entirely different reasons. How could she concentrate on
the service when her heart pounded like a schoolgirl with
her first crush?

"Breathe." He flashed her one of his charming smiles,
running his thumb across her cheek.

Kayla's heart exploded, and heat traveled up her cheek
from his touch. She leaned into his side. "Zach…"

"Shh. Not here." The depths of his eyes shone with love
and a mysterious emotion she couldn't identify. What had
happened to him on the drive to church? Whatever it was, it
was the answer she had begged God for. Hope.

Clearly amused by her reaction, Zach handed her a
songbook as the congregation stood to sing. "Think your
mom can watch Annabelle, so we can have lunch
together?" His whisper tickled the inside of her ear.

Kayla couldn't speak. She nodded her head, trying to
focus her attention on the service, not the ruggedly
handsome man next to her.

The service breezed by as the pastor preached on
forgiveness out of Matthew chapter six. Before she knew it,
the service had ended, and she was sitting next to Zach,
going to lunch together for the first time in four years.

"So, I see I still have that effect on you." He jumped out
of his SUV, opening her door and offering her his hand.

She didn't have to ask what he was talking about. She
knew. Her heart once burned with contempt and anger
toward him. Now she longed for his closeness. Kayla
wasn't sure when God had changed her heart, but
somewhere along her captivity, she fell in love with Zach

Rivers. Not the man that was her estranged husband, the one whose memory haunted her with disappointment. No, she had fallen in love with the man that let God direct his steps and showed forth His grace and love. The boy that walked away four years ago was not the same man standing before her. That thrilled and terrified her simultaneously.

Zach leaned over, his lips grazing her cheek, causing a warm blush to spread across her face. "Your blushing is quite endearing," he remarked with a smile.

Overwhelmed by the fear of embarrassment, she remained silent, trailing behind him to a secluded table in the dimly lit Mexican restaurant. The air was filled with the tantalizing scent of salsa and tacos, teasing her senses. The soft melodies of Spanish music enveloped her, creating a soothing ambiance. Leaning forward, she slid into the booth across from Zach, her eyes fixated on him. Surprisingly, the Sunday morning crowd seemed nonexistent, granting them the luxury of privacy. Kayla couldn't help but watch intently as Zach delicately dipped a tortilla chip into the fiery salsa.

Wiping his chin with a napkin, he held her gaze, laughing. "Do I have salsa on my chin?"

"Sorry. I was staring." She bit her bottom lip, trying to stop the butterflies flying around her stomach. Why was she so nervous about eating with Zach? This was the guy she rescued from the throngs of high school. The guy she shared her first kiss with, and the guy she promised to love all the days of her life. He was no stranger, but everything felt so new. Yet, if she breathed the wrong way, it'd disappear, replaced with her nightmares of yesterday.

His deep laughter filled the air around their small booth. "Kayla, I never thought you'd want to look at me like you are now. So, by all means, stare away. I might just return the favor." He reached across the table, snagging her hand in his. "I messed up four years ago, and every day since by walking away and never trying to make amends. I convinced myself that I was better off without you. But my heart will stop beating without you. I can't knowingly live in the same town as you and keep my distance."

She squeezed his hand, basking in the warmth of his touch. "Are you moving?"

He let go of one of her hands, popping a chip into his mouth. "Actually, I am."

"What?" Surely, he wasn't stringing her along again, and planning on leaving. Maybe he was trying to charm her enough to split custody.

A twinkle danced in his blue eyes. "I want you and Annabelle with me."

"What are you saying?" Kayla's body trembled as the confusion of their conversation wrapped around her.

Zach leaped out of the booth, his knees hitting the cold, dark-tiled floor. With a sense of anticipation, he reached into his pocket and produced a small black box. He then tenderly held onto Kayla's hand, cherishing the connection between them. "I love you so much," he whispered, his voice filled with a desperate longing, "and the thought of living another day without you is unbearable." His voice cracked with emotion. "Will you marry me again?"

Kayla ran her tongue along the bottom of her lip, holding back tears. "Really? I did not see that coming."

"Let's just say God took me to the woodshed last night, and now I see things clearly." As he slid the diamond ring onto her finger, it glimmered in the soft light, casting a radiant reflection. "What do you say?"

"Yes!" Kayla's excitement bubbled over as she jumped up from the booth, eagerly wrapping her arms around his neck and showering him with kisses, releasing all the pent-up love she had buried for four long years.

"Let's get married this time, with both of our parents and family present. And then we can house hunt or move into your new home. I don't care where we are. All that matters is you and Annabelle."

Peace flooded her heart. This was God's redemptive restoration. He took a broken, bitter marriage and turned it around, replacing hurt with love and anticipation. Only God could do that.

"Can you solve the case first?" Kayla didn't want to start a fresh life with a fear of a stalker watching her every move.

"My beautiful wife, I will catch the stalker and we'll live happily ever-after." Zach smiled, pulling her closer to his body.

She gave him a stern look, trying not to laugh.

"Okay, we won't live happily ever after, but we will live in God's redemption, and when life intensifies, I won't walk away this time. I'll never leave you again." Zach placed a kiss on her forehead, smiling.

Tears streamed down her face. That's all she dreamed of hearing from him for four years. God not only healed both of their hearts, but He turned their hearts toward each other. Now, if He would just let Zach catch the bad guy.

****

Kayla adjusted the ponytail on the back of her head as she pointed to the chalkboard. Her students were anything but thrilled to continue identifying the parts of speech and dissecting sentences. She, being the language arts teacher, could not skip the parts of the sentence. Her students would just have to get over it. Kayla laughed to herself at the image of her students' shocked expressions if she told them to get over it. Life was more important than adjectives and gerunds. But she had to do her job or face unemployment.

"Can anyone tell me what the preposition is in the first sentence?" She pointed her finger at the chalkboard, glancing at the faces of her sleepy looking students. She couldn't blame them for zoning out. Third period language was right before lunch, and most students spaced out in a tantalizing hunger strike.

A chubby hand shot up, and she dreaded Bobby White's smart aleck answer. "Why do we even have to learn the parts of a sentence? It's not like we will stop talking mid-sentence and identify what part of speech the word we just said was. It's quite pointless. If you ask me."

No one asked you Bobby White. Kayla grounded her teeth together, trying to hide her frown. "An understandable reaction. But, if you want to pass the sixth grade, you need to learn the parts of a sentence."

"Fine, have it your way, but when I become an award-winning actor, I won't thank you for torturing me with appositives, direct objects, and all the other parts of speech that gave me nightmares." Bobby White shook his head, causing his too long brown hair to whip across his face. All the girls swooned over his taller-than-average frame and charming but annoying personality.

Kayla stared at the clock, hoping and waiting for the bell to ring. Anything to save her sanity. She probably should have taken an indefinite time off of school until the police found the creep after her. But she'd go stir crazy doing nothing besides entertaining her three-year-old daughter.

The loud shrill of the bell echoed in the room as students stuffed their books into their backpacks and shuffled out of the room. Kayla wanted to shout praises to God for lunchtime and a break from her uninterested students.

The secretary pushed her way into the room, dodging students and backpacks. Marybeth Asher adjusted her bifocals as she set a vase of white roses on Kayla's desk. "You have a lot of admirers. What's your secret?" The fifty-year-olds laughter sounded forced. "Well, I better go." She saluted as she inched out of the room, her heels echoing down the hall.

Not again. With shaky hands, Kayla reached into the vase, pulling out a pink envelope. Her breath caught in her throat as her eyes scanned the heart-shaped note.

Care Bear, I'm disappointed in you. You belong to me, not Zach Rivers. He will never have you. I'm not beyond getting rid of all your family to shape you into submission; Annabelle first. My patience is running thin with you. Next time I catch you kissing Zach Rivers, that might be your last kiss. Don't worry. We'll meet again real soon.

She dropped the card on the floor, running to the window, looking around. What if her stalker lurked in the shadows, waiting for her to come outside alone? Could he be an employee here? Could the perp had bugged her classroom? No, what purpose would that serve? Learning the parts of speech? Doubtful. Kayla slid to her desk, retrieving her phone from inside her desk. Another hour until she had students. Should she call Zach? Or wait until after school? The flowers were just a verbal threat, and she didn't want to ruin her students' first day back at school.

Feeling goosebumps shoot up her skin, Kayla dropped her phone into her skirt pocket, walking to lock the door.

No students meant she could secure herself inside the classroom, at least for an hour. The wooden door had a square peak hole the size of her hand. Peering out, she shivered at the deserted hallway. The students and staff on her floor were at lunch. Right on cue, her stomach rumbled like a bolt of thunder. She had to eat and sustain her energy to teach a class full of sixth graders. Kayla grabbed her purse, unlocked the door, and peered down the empty hall. Nothing unusual besides the eerie silence of a public middle school.

Kayla sauntered down the hall, clinging to her purse like it could protect her from whatever lurked in the school, waiting and watching to abduct her again.

Her ring caught on the side of her knit-topped blouse, pulling a piece of the thread. Her thoughts traveled to Zach as a full smile covered her face. Since his proposal, they had spent the evening snuggling together, watching Annabelle chatter nonstop.

They decided she and Annabelle would stay in Zach's guest room until Zach and Paul caught her stalker. Then they'd have a simple wedding ceremony and move into Kayla's new house as a family. They were already married, but they needed to renew their vows and commitment as two believers who fully relied on God to guide them every day to build their marriage and home for His glory.

Butterflies danced in her stomach at the thought of marrying Zach again and displaying to the entire world the work God was doing in their lives. And she no longer had to hide Annabelle from her family. The shame of a broken marriage and the guilt from going through pregnancy and single parenthood urged her to seal off that part of her life, keeping that secret from everyone, even Stephen.

Kayla crossed her arms tightly over her chest, feeling the gnawing hunger pains intensify. The old building lacked a staff elevator, and she couldn't help but wonder why. The thought of walking down two flights of stairs in her heels seemed utterly unappealing. Especially if it meant subjecting herself to the lunch ladies' mysterious meal options. On such days, Kayla settled for an apple and a bag of chips, hoping it would suffice.

As she made her way down the dimly lit staircase, a sudden door slam and the subsequent sound of approaching footsteps jolted her senses. Teachers strictly forbid students from wandering the staircases during class hours, especially after the incident last year that led to the suspension of two seventh graders. Feeling a surge of unease, Kayla hastened her pace, her heart pounding in her chest. Who could be behind her?

Fear paralyzed her as she reached for her phone, desperate to find Zach's number. Just then, a searing pain shot through her back, and she felt a sharp prick on her neck. Arms, tight and suffocating, wrapped around her. Kayla's survival instinct kicked in, and she dug her fingernails into the assailant's arm, causing him to loosen his grip momentarily. It was her chance to escape, but her legs felt like lead, refusing to move. Panic surged through her, urging her to run, but a dizzying sensation overwhelmed her. He must have drugged her.

Struggling to turn her head, she looked into the eyes of someone all too familiar, blinking back tears. "You! Why?"

This couldn't be happening. Her vision blurred, and the face of evil before her took on a crooked smile. Before he could utter a word, she stumbled and crashed into a stair, her head throbbing with pain. She fought against the darkness that threatened to engulf her. *Must keep fighting.*

No! Kayla's mind screamed as her muscles lost all feeling, plunging her into an abyss of unconsciousness.

****

"Kayla!" Zach grabbed his keys off his desk, motioning for Paul to follow. "He's got her."

Zach bolted out of the stuffy sheriff's office, the scorching heat of the late afternoon smacking him in the face like a fiery punch. Beads of sweat erupted from his forehead, streaming down his face as he sprinted towards his unmarked SUV. With little time to spare, he barely allowed Paul a moment to slide into the passenger seat before he veered onto a desolate road, avoiding the dreaded lunch hour traffic jam on the primary route.

His grip on the steering wheel tightened, his knuckles turning bone-white as he punched a number on his phone. The device trembled in his hand, as if mirroring his anxiety. "Peter?" he exclaimed; his voice laced with urgency.

"What's up, bro?" Peter's voice crackled through the line, the sound of hurriedly gulped bites of lunch barely allowing him time to breathe.

"Since you're closer to the school. Can you please check on Kayla?" Zach's heart pounded in his chest, his foot pressing harder on the accelerator, pushing the speedometer fifteen miles beyond the limit.

"What's happening?" Peter's voice held a tinge of concern, mirroring Zach's own unease.

"Not sure. I heard a commotion, and then Kayla's voice cried out before the line went dead." Zach berated himself for not sticking to Kayla like glue. But she had insisted on not wanting his presence to intimidate her students. Safety first, he reminded himself, his mind filling with desperate thoughts. There had to be a next time. Shaking his head to clear the negative thoughts, he reaffirmed his determination. Kayla was alive, and he would find her. The only problem was that he had failed to locate her the last time the perp abducted her.

"I'm on my way." Zach heard wrappers rustling before the line went dead.

"Come on. Did you really have to pull out in front of me going ten under the speed limit? I should pull you over for reckless driving." Frustration consumed him as he pounded his fist on the steering wheel. The loud, echoing bangs reverberated through the vehicle.

Paul glanced at Zach, gripping his seatbelt. "Check your speedometer. They're probably going the speed limit. If you get us killed, we can't help Kayla."

"I got this. Almost there." Zach sighed a deep breath of air when the middle school came into view. *God, don't take her away from me.*

"Peter's getting out." Paul swung his door open, grazing his gun with his fingers.

"Not even gonna ask how you got here at the same time as me." Peter wiped a crumb off his police uniform, stepping next to his brother.

"Don't. You might have to ticket him." Paul's dry voice cracked.

Like his brother would give him a speeding ticket. "No wasting time. Let's go." Zach slid his gun out, gripping it out of view. All he needed was for a group of kids to see an armed man walk through the hall.

"What's the plan?"

"Peter, go around back and cover the exit points. Paul, you take the side entrance and I'll go through the front. She called from the staircase." Not waiting for a reply, he ran toward the building, expecting the worst, but hoping for the best.

The aroma of lunch overwhelmed him as he hurried down the empty halls. Faded laughter seeping from the cafeteria was the only signs of life in the populated building. His stomach churned at the repulsive smell and the memory of Monday lunch specials. No wonder he spent his lunch break shooting hoops in the gym.

Approaching the dimly lit staircase, he cautiously scanned the surroundings, desperately searching for any sign of Kayla; a clue to her whereabouts. The flickering overhead light cast eerie shadows on the walls, heightening his anxiety. As he reached the stairs, his heart plummeted at the sight of Kayla's crumpled, unconscious form sprawled out on the cold, hard steps.

Leaning over her motionless body, he felt a rush of relief as he detected a steady pulse beneath his fingertips. The pungent metallic scent of blood filled the air as he dabbed the back of her head, his fingers becoming sticky with the crimson fluid.

Panicking, he swiftly dialed the emergency services, his voice trembling as he requested an ambulance.

"How is she?" Paul's voice crackled behind him with concern.

"She's alive," he replied, his voice laced with both relief and worry. Knowing he shouldn't disturb her, but unable to stand idly by, he retrieved a handkerchief from his pocket, pressing it firmly against her head wound. "Looks like she had a scuffle with the perpetrator, and something spooked him, causing him to flee."

Footsteps echoed on the stairs, causing Zach to tense up. Sitting on a step, he cradled Kayla's fragile body in his arms, shielding her from any potential danger. Paul swiftly raised his gun, ready to confront the intruder.

"It's just me," Peter called out, his hands raised in surrender. "I found nothing left behind. How is she?"

"Nothing seems broken. Apart from the head injury, she appears to be okay," Zach replied, his fingers gently caressing the sides of her face as he whispered soothing prayers into her ears.

Slowly, Kayla stirred in his lap, attempting to sit up. Confusion filled her eyes as she looked at Zach. "Zach, what are you doing here?"

Zach's frown deepened; worry etched on his face. She had suffered from amnesia before, and another head injury so soon was concerning. "Do you remember anything?"

Pain twisted Kayla's expression as she winced. "No. Oh wait, I remember white roses and feeling like someone was after me."

"Did you see his face?" Peter inquired; his voice filled with urgency.

"Just a blurry shadow in my mind," Kayla replied, her arms wrapping around Zach's waist as she sought comfort. "You saved me."

Zach lowered his face, brushing his lips gently against hers. "Consider me your shadow until we catch the person after you."

A slight grimace crossed Kayla's face as she ran her fingers over her hair. "Ouch."

"Take it easy. You have a gash on your head," Paul interjected, his voice filled with concern.

"Alright, lovebirds. The paramedics have arrived," Peter announced, stepping aside to allow two male paramedics to pass.

Dismissing their help with a wave of her hand, Kayla insisted, "I'm fine." However, as she attempted to stand, her legs wobbled beneath her, causing her to stumble into Zach's waiting arms. Embarrassment flushed her cheeks. "I guess my mind is stronger than my body."

****

Zach pulled into the driveway, glancing at the bandage wrapped around Kayla's head. Five hours in the ER, thanks to Stephen Smith. Otherwise, they'd still be waiting in the tiny, overpopulated waiting room. Kayla didn't have amnesia, but she still couldn't remember who attacked her; the face of her stalker.

Zach nudged Kayla's arm as he took his keys out of the ignition. He'd carry her into the house, but Annabelle snored in the backseat. If she woke up at this hour, nearing eight o'clock, she'd stay up all night. Zach was not in the mood for a princess movie marathon with a plastic tiara and all. His daughter liked to party in style, thus making him dress up as a prince. He didn't mind. Zach had almost four years of absence to make up, and it was exhausting.

"Honey, we're home." He leaned over, brushing his lips over Kayla's cheek, never getting over the feeling of her skin next to his.

"Why did you let me doze off?" She batted her eyes, trying to wake up. "Was I snoring?"

"Let's just say I know where Annabelle gets it from." He jumped out of his SUV, unbuckling Annabelle and placing her in his arms.

A patrol car pulled on the side of the road as Peter swung his key chain in the air. "I noticed nothing out of the ordinary, following you."

"Thanks for always having my back." Zach smiled at his brother. What would he do without his younger brother that could pass for his twin?

"Someone has to keep you out of trouble." Peter's smirk played on his handsome face. He lifted the sunglasses off his face, sticking it in his pocket.

"Mind carrying Annabelle? I want to make sure Kayla makes it inside, okay?" Zach handed his brother Annabelle, who could sleep through anything.

As Kayla stumbled towards the door, her legs were heavy and unsteady, Zach hurriedly followed behind her. The atmosphere was heavy with an eerie silence, causing a knot to tighten in Zach's stomach. Glancing across the street, he squinted, trying to discern any signs of danger. There was no one in sight, but a sense of being watched sent shivers down his spine. With a swift motion, he drew his gun from its holster, his fingers trembling slightly as he scanned the surroundings. They couldn't afford to let their guard down, not when they were so close to apprehending the culprit.

"Sweetie, let me handle the door," Zach said, taking just two cautious steps forward. And then, without warning, chaos erupted. A thunderous explosion ripped through the tranquil evening air, engulfing their home in a blazing inferno. The force of the blast lifted Kayla's body, propelling her feet away from him. Panic surged through Zach's veins as he rushed to her side, his heart pounding in his chest. Blood streamed down Kayla's forehead, the metallic scent mingling with the acrid odor of smoke. Desperation consumed him as he yelled out to God. "God, why is this happening?" Clenching his fists tightly, he made a vow to exact vengeance on the person responsible for this unfathomable tragedy. Annabelle. He totally forgot about his daughter.

Peter, reading his mind, shouted. "Annabelle is sleeping in the back of the patrol car. She's unharmed."

Zach's eyes widened as he stared at his unmarked SUV, the flames dancing and crackling on the hood. The acrid scent of smoke filled the air, a sharp reminder of the danger that had befallen his vehicle. Grateful that his personal car was secure at the sheriff's office, he muttered, "Good thing we don't have any neighbors—country living."

His gaze swept the area, searching for any signs of the perpetrator. A hooded figure suddenly sprinted down the deserted rural road, prompting Zach to spring into action. "Stop! Police!" he shouted, his voice echoing through the stillness. He couldn't allow the suspect to escape, even if it meant tearing himself away from cradling Kayla's unconscious body until the ambulance arrived.

Peter offered to move Kayla to his own car. "Go," he said, determination in his voice. "I'll even try to beat the ambulance to the ER." With gentle care, Peter scooped Kayla into his arms, disappearing into the safety of his patrol car.

Zach's heart pounded as he pushed his legs harder, refusing to let the perp slip away. Amidst the chaos, he sent a quick text to request backup, knowing his partner would arrive soon. He focused on the task at hand, rounding a curve in the road and bending over, panting heavily. The lack of time for his usual three-mile daily run had taken a toll on his body, but he couldn't let it hinder him now.

As he scanned the countryside, the setting sun peeked out from behind a distant mountain, casting a breathtaking display of pink and purple hues across the evening sky. The rural surroundings enveloped him, devoid of the usual sounds of traffic or bustling town life. The only audible noise came from the chorus of crickets chirping in the nearby field, creating a symphony of nature's serenade. In this isolated no-man's-land, he strained his ears for any sign of movement, his senses heightened.

Zach's eyes caught a flicker of movement, and he cautiously approached a nearby wooded area, his grip firm on his gun. He whispered a silent plea, "God, help me catch this guy." The hooded figure crouched low to the ground; face hidden from view. Without hesitation, Zach seized the person's arms, swiftly placing handcuffs on their wrists. "You're under arrest," he declared, his voice steady as he recited the Miranda Rights. As he pulled the hood down, his heart skipped a beat, icy, red-rimmed eyes locking onto his, piercing his soul.

"Let go of me."

A woman? Why would a woman be stalking Kayla? Recognition darted across his mind. "Susan White?"

"Don't act all surprised." She tried jerking her hands free, to no avail.

"Why?" Kayla would be heartbroken when she found out a friend had tried to kill her.

"Please, I couldn't let Kayla steal my man." Hatred spewed from her over-sized lips. "But I finally got rid of her."

This woman was not the same one he had interviewed days before. "Thomas Holmes?"

"That cheater? Not on your life." Am eerie, heart wrenching laugh popped out of her mouth. "Before you ask, I'm not her stalker. I figured she sent herself white roses to make the female staff jealous. I've only tried to kill her three times; drowning, a gunshot, and the bomb."

"The woman's wild eyes and erratic behavior confirmed his suspicions; insanity consumed her. But he had just extracted a confession from her." Zach swiftly pulled Ms. White out of harm's way, the screeching of tires filling the air as Paul steered his SUV to the side of the road. Stepping out, Paul quickly opened the back door, guiding Ms. White into the comfortable seat.

As Zach's heart raced with worry, he realized that if Ms. White wasn't the stalker; it meant that Kayla's life was still in danger. His eyes fixed on the road ahead, he watched as smoke billowed into the sky, mingling with the vibrant hues of the pink and purple setting sun.

"Take her inside. I need to go check on Kayla," Zach urged, his voice laced with urgency.

"Get in the SUV. She's not at your house. The fire crew is already there, working to extinguish the flames," Paul said, fastening his seatbelt before accelerating the vehicle once Zach had scrambled into the passenger seat.

Thoughts raced through Zach's mind. What had happened to Kayla and Annabelle? Was the bomb a ploy to isolate Kayla? No, Peter had taken her to the emergency room. Zach would join them after he had finished interrogating the suspect. Desperately, he reached into his pocket, retrieving his phone and dialing his brother's number.

"Hey, bro."

"How's Kayla?" The urgency of his words echoed through the line.

"She's conscious, but dazed. Waiting in the ER now." Zach breathed a sigh of relief. Kayla would be fine, and he'd put a stop to the perp after her once and for all. Until then, he needed to figure out what Ms. White knew, and which guy secretly had a crush on Kayla. When he figured that out, he'd uncover the stalker's identity.

Chapter Thirteen

"You okay, man? Want me to take the lead?" Paul handed a paper cup to Zach, sloshing some of the water on his fingers.

"I appreciate that, but Ms. White is mine." Zach rolled his shoulders, trying to ease away some of his tense muscles. He'd rather be waiting in the ER with Kayla, but he trusted Peter and Stephen to protect her until he got there. Then what would they do or where would they go? The explosion destroyed his house. His buddy, the fire chief, confirmed his suspicions moments ago. Zach thanked God that Kayla was outside the house when the bomb went off. If she would have been inside, Kayla would have died on the scene. A deep shiver ran through his body at the thought of her sprawled out on the concrete, blood spewing from her head. *Kayla is alive. The explosion did not kill her.* Of course, he didn't know how bad her injuries were. Maybe he should have handed the suspect over to Paul. He was more than capable of interrogating Susan White. What kind of man left his unconscious wife to finish a job? This case messed up his priorities. When Zach made lifelong vows to Kayla this time, he needed to adjust his life to keep them. Zach would not abandon her again. But he needed to oversee this case until the end.

"I'll hang back. If you need me, give me the signal." Paul nodded his head, stepping into a room next to the interrogation room.

Zach took a slow, steadying breath as he entered the dimly lit interrogation room. The sterile scent of disinfectant permeated the air, mingling with a faint hint of tension. Susan White sat rigidly upright in her chair, her hands clenched tightly on the table, the pressure turning her knuckles pale. The soft click of the door closing echoed in the room as Zach approached, placing a glass of water before Ms. White. Her gaze, cold and piercing, bore into him. Despite her petite stature, there was an undeniable fierceness about her that caught him off guard.

"When do I get my phone call?" She ran her fingers along the edge of the cup, not making eye contact.

"Do you want your lawyer present?"

"Nope. I just need someone to check on my dog, Shredder." She fixed her eyes on a spot on the table, not making eye contact like her life depended on it.

Might want to give the dog away, since you'll be in prison for attempted murder. "You'll get your phone call when I'm done."

"Fine." She crossed her arms over her chest, pouting like he'd seen Annabelle do on multiple occasions.

Zach straddled the back of the chair, his glare enough to make an innocent man squirm. "Tell me about your relationship with Kayla Smith."

"Detective, you already know this."

"Humor me." Zach peeked at his watch, knowing this interrogation would take a while.

"Whatever. Kayla and I met during teacher orientation two years ago. Our personalities clicked, and we started hanging out outside of school." She drummed her fingers on the table, chewing on her bottom lip. "We both even sang in the church choir."

"Church name?" Zach scribbled a note on his notepad.

"Fellowship Community," she added dryly.

The church his brothers attended. Man, he needed to go to church more. He didn't remember ever seeing Kayla or Ms. White at Fellowship.

"When did Kayla and your relationship change from friendship to animosity?" Or did it ever? Maybe a stab in the back was better than an enemy posing as a best friend.

"When I noticed all the male attention she received." Susan White gripped the edge of the table, her fingers discoloring. "I'm just as pretty as Kayla, but no one showed me attention besides the player, Thomas. His charm isn't deep enough to erase his player ways."

"So, I'm guessing you're not swooning over Mr. Holmes." Susan White's oddly shaped face, skinny nose, thick lips, were unique, maybe even a defining beauty mark that set her apart. But her fiery personality would turn any man away.

A thunderous laugh flew out of her bright red lips. "He wished."

"So, who is this secret man?"

"I won't reveal that yet." Zach wanted to shake some sense into her. This wasn't a game. Kayla's life was at stake.

Pounding his open palm on the table, Zach pushed the chair back, pacing the tiny space. "Why try to kill Ms. Smith? And how does a geography teacher know about making explosives?"

As a dark shield fell over her face, her features became obscured, creating an eerie and sinister presence. "She stood in my way. My man won't keep his eyes off of her. He watches her during the church service more than the pastor of the church."

"So, you plotted this scheme while in church?" Zach had heard it all.

"Don't act all righteous. I never see you at church." The words tumbled out of her mouth, hitting its target.

Yeah, right? Because an attempted murderer was right in the sight of God, but an officer of the law, who worked most Sundays, was not? Susan White's thought process made no sense.

"It's Kayla's fault. She should have died when I tried to drown her. She has too much fight for her own good."

"What other attempts did you make on her life?" His stomach felt queasy. He'd be dead emotionally if Ms. White's confession didn't make him want to throw up. They were talking about the woman he loved.

"Let's see. I shot at her a few times, but she just wouldn't die." Susan White jumped out of her chair, knocking it to the ground with a thud. "I blame you." She reached across the table, trying to grab Zach's shirt.

The door flew open as Paul stepped into the room, handcuffs dangling in his hands. He grabbed Ms. White's arm, slapping the cuffs on her wrist.

"Don't you want to know who her stalker is?" Ms. White blurted out a name, causing Zach's head to spin.

No way. She was insane.

"Don't believe me? His handwriting is on the cards, and Kayla's picture fell out of his Bible once." With a satisfied smirk, Paul led her out of the interrogation room.

Zach fell into the plastic chair, yanking his phone out of his pocket. He needed to hear Kayla's voice. He dialed Peter's number, getting agitated after each ring. "Come on, bro, pick up the phone."

Zach pounded his fist on top of the table, pain shooting up his arm. He dialed another number, holding his breath.

"Zach, what do you need? I'm heading into my patient's room as we speak."

"How's Kayla?"

"How am I supposed to know? You're her husband." Stephen's voice held a hard edge to it. He never really trusted Zach, which hurt.

"Peter brought her to the ER a couple of hours ago." An unease settled into his stomach. What if Ms. White's accusations were true? If so, he was the biggest fool in Tennessee.

"Impossible. I checked the logs a minute ago, and surprisingly, the ER is empty." Stephen spoke to someone in the background. "Find my cousin, or I'll find her myself."

Zach stared at the dropped call. *God, what am I supposed to do? Enlighten my eyes and show me where Kayla and Annabelle are.*

****

Kayla winced as she touched her head, sticky blood staining her fingers. What in the world had happened to her body? She tried moving in the seat, but pain shot through her body like electricity. Leaning her head on the seat, she basked in the coolness from the air blowing out of the air vent. Zach's hums floated through the small compound of the vehicle. A smile spread across her face, thinking about the man next to her. As long as they were together, she was safe. Kayla glanced at the driver's seat, arrows shooting through her neck. What was he doing here?

"Peter. I thought you were Zach." Kayla's heart pounded in her chest. Where was Zach, and why was she driving with Peter? She stared out the window, trying to figure out where they were going. "Where are we at?"

A tight smile traveled up Peter's tan face. He looked so much like Zach, they could pass as twins, besides Peter's skin being a tad darker than Zach's. Both were handsome men.

"We are on I-75." His clipped response sent chills through her body. Peter glanced out the side mirror. He seemed distracted and on edge. A side of Peter she had never seen before.

"Why? Where are we going?" Kayla ran her finger through her hair, but stopped as pain pulsed through her head. Whatever had happened, she hadn't gotten medical help. Her pain level was a seven at best.

"To a safe house." Peter adjusted the air vent, talking in a monotone, acid tone.

"Why? Where's Zach?" Kayla noticed Peter's death grip on the steering wheel at the mention of Zach. Something was definitely going on.

"He's meeting up with us." Peter glanced into the mirror for the hundredth time. "Zach thought it was best if I get you and Annabelle to safety. Especially since the explosion could have killed you."

Explosion. Memories ran through Kayla's mind— screams, fire, and being thrown to the ground. How could she have forgotten about the bomb that went off? Was Zach okay?

"Can I use your phone to call Zach?" Kayla had an uneasy feeling crawling through her stomach. Of course, Zach trusted Peter. Nothing nefarious was going on.

"I can't let you do that." He grabbed the phone in the middle console, stuffing it in his shirt pocket. Peter glared at her with icy eyes.

Kayla took a deep breath, feeling the rush of air fill her lungs as she tried to calm her jumbled nerves. This guy wouldn't hurt anyone. She needed to relax. "Why?"

"No service." His eyes focused on the road stretched before them. For a Monday or Tuesday, she didn't know which, the interstate felt empty.

"Can I at least try?" How could he refuse her offer? If Peter was a good guy, it wouldn't be a hard request.

"Care Bear." Peter's chilly, hard words slipped from his mouth. What did he just call her? Peter was her stalker? How could that be?

As if on cue, a vivid scene flooded her mind. She could see herself running frantically through the dimly lit staircase at school, the sound of her hurried footsteps echoing off the cold concrete walls. Suddenly, a man appeared behind her, his firm grip restraining her arms, and the sharp sting of a needle piercing her skin sent a wave of fear coursing through her body. The acrid smell of burned coffee filled the air as the creep's face came into view. It was Peter, the sight of him making Kayla's stomach churn, threatening to make her vomit on the floorboard. "You!" she exclaimed, her voice trembling with a mix of anger and fear.

A faint smile tugged at the corner of Peter's lips; his eyes gleaming with a twisted sense of satisfaction. "I see you, remember," he taunted. "No matter, it's time to start our new lives together as a family. You won't get away this time." Kayla's hand tightened around the doorknob, her mind racing with the thought of jumping out of the moving car.

But Peter's calm and controlled voice stopped her in her tracks. "If you want to see your daughter again, I wouldn't do that if I were you," he warned. Kayla's heart sank, and she turned in her seat, relief flooding through her as she caught sight of her precious daughter, Annabelle, soundly sleeping.

As Peter turned down a secluded country road, veering off the bustling interstate, the world outside seemed to fade away. Kayla couldn't help but notice the absence of a car seat, a sharp pang of worry shooting through her. "No car seat? Do you know how dangerous that is?" she exclaimed, her protective instincts kicking in. The tension in the car intensified, as Kayla mumbled that if Peter dared to harm Annabelle, she would unleash her fury upon him.

Chuckling deeply, Peter dismissed her concerns. "Care Bear, I couldn't think of everything. I had to take advantage of the situation. Besides, she's not waking up for a while," he said, his laughter sending a chill down Kayla's spine.

Fear and anger surged within her, and Kayla's palm connected with Peter's hand, causing the car to jerk. "What did you do to her?" she demanded; her voice filled with desperation. The intensity of their gaze locked, and she could see the pure malice emanating from his eyes. How had she been so blind to Peter's twisted infatuation with her? His deceptive acting skills had masked his true nature.

"The same thing I'll do to you, if you try that again."

Her hands trembled in her lap as she voiced her deepest fear. "What's going to happen to us?" The car slowed down, navigating a curvy country road, and the sense of isolation grew stronger.

"That depends on you," Peter replied, his voice dripping with menace. "If you willingly go with me, I'll spare your life. If you give me any problems, I'll kill Annabelle. Then I'll torture Zach until you submit to me."

Sighing a deep, frustrating sigh, Kayla begged God to deliver her and bring Zach to rescue her. "Why are you doing this? Zach is your brother."

"He's a fool. And so are you for choosing the wrong brother." Peter reached across the middle console, taking her hand in his. Her hand went limp at his touch. "Since high school, you've always been the girl of my dreams. But Zach messed that up. Remember the note you slipped to me? That was all the proof I needed."

What note? Kayla never led him on or even spoke to him much in high school.

"I see you're confused. I'll enlighten you." He stroked his thumb against the backside of her hand. "You sent a secret admirer, heart-shaped note to me, but instead of me getting it, Zach found it and claimed it as his. Then he started pursuing you. That note was mine. You were mine!" Something flipped a switch in Peter's brain. Outrage and desperation controlled his movement.

"I don't remember that. But high school was years ago." Who held onto anything that was done in high school?

"Don't think I never noticed the secret smiles you sent my way. When you left for college, I knew we'd see each other again."

"Did you follow me and track me down?" Peter stalked her for years before the roses and cards.

"Your secret marriage really surprised me. But I used that to my advantage. You deserve better than Zach. Still do." Peter ran over a pothole going way over the speed limit.

Speechless, Kayla opened her mouth in surprise. How could she answer an obsessed stalker?

"I look so much like Zach. Kayla never has to know I'm not Zach." Peter lifted his hand away from hers, turning and staring at Annabelle with predatory eyes. "My daughter."

Kayla gaged back the bile rising in her throat. "Peter, this is not right. I won't sit by and pretend you're Zach."

As the rain poured down, Peter recklessly sped through a massive puddle, causing mud to splatter all over the patrol car. The sound of the sloshing mud filled the air, making Kayla's heart race with fear. Surrounded by dense trees and the calls of wildlife, dread engulfed her as she desperately searched for an escape. Finally, Peter pulled the stolen car behind a worn-out cabin. Kayla's pulse quickened as he retrieved a pair of handcuffs from his pocket, forcefully fastening them around her trembling wrist. "Once I know you won't bolt, I'll take them off."

God, where are You? I can't get out of this situation without You.

"Care Bear, let's go check out our new home. It's nothing like our last one, but you burned it down." A crooked smile filled his face. "Don't worry, we have a lifetime together to build a new house." He opened the back door, cradled Annabelle in his arms, and jerked Kayla's body forward. "Smile. This is the first day of forever with me."

****

"What do you mean she's missing and so is your brother?" Stephen pointed his finger at Zach's chest, getting into his personal space. "If anything happens to her, I'm holding you responsible."

"Cool it off, big brother." Paul stepped between Zach and Stephen. "He's not to blame."

"My position still stands; you never deserved her. If you would have stuck around four years ago, this wouldn't have happened." Stephen forcefully pushed past his buddy, Paul, shooting Zach a menacing glare that sent shivers down his spine.

"That's enough. Don't make me arrest you for assaulting a police officer." Paul crossed his arms over his chest, looking unfaded by Stephen's attitude. "You're my best bud, and your sister will have my hide if I arrest you, but you won't intimidate my partner."

"Uniform or no uniform, if you don't find her safe, you'll wish you had." Stephen threw his arms in the air, walking away.

"Is that a threat?" Zach stepped around Paul, not caring that Stephen had an inch on him. He knew he could take the doctor down if needed. And he didn't need a military dad on his side.

"Take it how you want to." Stephen walked to the door, glancing out the window. "Warning, my uncle's here, and he's as fierce as my dad."

Great. Just what I need, a Smith family reunion right in the sheriff's office. He needed to be searching for Kayla, not extinguishing fires.

"Son, is it true your brother is involved in this case?" Mr. Howard Smith folded his arms over his broad chest. He did not look like the same man he met days ago.

He wanted to say, detective, not son. But Zach didn't think that would go well. Besides being Kayla's dad, technically, he was Zach's father-in-law.

"Sir, it's speculation at this point. No evidence to back up my brother's involvement." How Zach wanted to believe those words, more than anything. How could his flesh and blood betray him like this, and abduct his wife and daughter? It wasn't possible. Zach knew his brother. There had to be a logical explanation.

"Are you too close to the case? Maybe you should step back and let Paul take the lead." Mr. Smith furrowed his thick eyebrows, staring at Zach.

"Of course, he's too close to the case. It's his wife and daughter." Mrs. Smith slapped her husband on the arm, frowning.

"Martha, stay out of it." Her husband's stern voice caused her to buck back, sighing before she stomped off in the opposite direction.

"Smooth, Uncle Howard." Paul's low chuckle seemed out of place as he followed his aunt to the other side of the building.

"Sir, I promise you that my closeness to this case will not hinder my ability to see justice prevail."

"Let me ask you this. If it came down to Kayla's life or your brothers, could you pull the trigger?" Mr. Howard adjusted the glasses on his face. Never taking his eyes off of Zach.

Could he wound or kill Peter? The boy that he played cops and robbers with, the same guy he watched transform into an honorable man. But, if he was behind Kayla's stalking, he was not honorable. And he deceived his whole family and his fellow officers. Zach's mind traveled to Kayla's gentle smile. The way she peered into the depths of his heart, seeing the part of him he hid from everyone else. The love she offered him when he didn't deserve it. He loved her with a yearning that would never go away. Watching her die would be like sucking the life out of him.

She would come first. Besides, if his brother committed this heinous crime against her, he deserved punishment.

"Mr. Smith, I will do whatever it takes to protect my wife." Zach's eyes watered at the implications of those words. He meant them, but it wouldn't be easy.

"Son, we have a lot to talk about once Kayla is safely back at home. It's her choice to forgive you after abandoning her. But it doesn't mean I'll just forget it. I'm her father. And you haven't earned my blessing yet."

Talk about awkward. He had completely forgotten to make amends with her parents. Not only Kayla's parent's but Stephen, too. There was an open hostility toward him from her cousin. Sometimes, it pounded on him more than other times.

"I understand, sir." Zach glanced at Paul, holding the phone to his ear, deep in conversation. "If you will excuse me, I need a word with my partner."

"Don't keep me out of the loop. I'd hate going rogue and find my daughter myself." Mr. Smith stalked off, mumbling under his breath.

Zach slid behind Paul, staring at the map on the wall. They had marked off certain areas of interest with pins.

Paul dropped his phone in his pocket. A hard look on his face. "Peter's captain says he AWOL. His patrol car is missing, and he didn't show up for work this morning."

Zach felt like someone had punched him in the gut. Dizziness tried knocking him over, rendering useless.

"You need a moment?" Paul gripped the top of Zach's shoulder. "I got a warrant to search Peter's belongings. I can go alone."

"No. I need to find my wife. The explosion destroyed our house. I think we should check his locker at the precinct." They were roommates, but he never went into

Peter's room or looked through his stuff. Now, the explosion destroyed any evidence he might have had. He hoped Peter left any clues in his locker.

Minutes later, they pulled Zach's unmarked SUV into the police station. Patrol cars lined the side of the brick building. Zach and Paul stepped into the police captain's office, handing him the warrant to search Peter's locker. The scent of stall coffee wafted through the department, reminding Zach he had missed his caffeinated cup this morning. He stayed with Josh and Britney, leaving Annabelle in their care. And he barely had time to eat a bite of burned toast before he dashed out of the house. The last twelve hours had flown by in a blur. How could his brother, his own flesh and blood, abduct his wife?

"Detectives, I hope you're mistaken about my officer. But if not, we'll cooperate fully."

Zach and Paul, familiar with the police captain from their brief tenure at the department, exchanged a subtle nod before stepping out of his office. With their familiarity with the surroundings, they easily found their way to Peter's locker room in a matter of minutes. As Zach twisted the lock, a rush of anticipation filled the air, mingling with the faint scent of sweat and freshly brewed coffee. The sight that greeted him inside was a chaotic jumble of clutter, evidence of his brother's neglect in cleaning out his locker. The combination of the overpowering stench and Zach's already frayed nerves threatened to overwhelm him, but he fought back the urge to retch. Determinedly, he sifted through a stack of crumpled receipts, searching for any clue that could shed light on the situation. *Bingo.*

"I found receipts from a local florist. White roses ordered on the days Kayla received them." While Zach handed the receipts to Paul, he multitasked by sifting through a stack of photos. As Zach stood there, a sense of impending doom seemed to swirl around him, making it hard to breathe.

"I need a moment." He sat on the worn wooden bench, its surface rough beneath his fingertips, next to the metallic lockers. The faint sound of chattering officers filled the air as he handed the stack of glossy photos to his partner. In the middle of the stack, a photo of Kayla, her vibrant smile frozen in time, stood out. Peter had manipulated the pictures with some kind of software, creating a false reality; Peter and Kayla in an embrace. The caption beneath the photo read: "My Care Bear, soon, we'll be a family, forever."

Paul, his partner, collected the evidence and settled down beside him, his fingers tracing the grooves of the bench's wooden top. Concern etched his face as he asked, "You okay?"

Zach tilted his head back, staring up at the ceiling, as darkness threatened to engulf his thoughts. "I doubt I'll ever be okay again."

"I thought the same thing, but time slowly heals," Paul reassured him, empathy clear in his voice. He understood Zach's pain all too well. Paul's own parents had conspired to kill Belle, and had even hired a hitman, nearly ending Paul's life, too. The betrayal had cut deep, almost destroying him, but he had found solace in God's loving mercies. And that's what Zach needed now.

"I'm in shock, but I'll process my emotions later," Zach replied, his voice hollow. "Right now, we need to find Kayla and Annabelle before it's too late. I don't know what state of mind my brother is in."

273

Paul nodded in understanding, rising to his feet. "Can you think of any property Peter might have that's off the grid?"

Zach racked his brain, searching for any hidden location. They used to go fishing at a cabin, but the owners had torn it down years ago. He needed to think, to remember. And then, as if a divine clarity washed over him, a place came to mind. "He bought a hunting cabin about two hours from here. I've only been there once, but it's in no-man's-land. It's in Campbell County."

"I'll call the sheriff and request backup." Paul pulled out his phone and stepped to the side to call the sheriff.

"You ready. It's time to rescue my family." Zach glanced at Paul as he stuffed his phone inside his pocket.

"Let's roll."

Zach followed Paul out of the police station, praying as his mind jumped in millions of directions. *God, use me to rescue my family, and whatever happens, keep Kayla and Annabelle safe.*

****

Kayla yanked at the cuffs on her hand, looking around the small living room. Rustic was an understatement. Electricity surprised her, as well as running water. Of course, Peter had bound her to an old pipe in the living room, leaving her in the dark for the entire night. Annabelle had slept the night away, not even waking once. She ran through different scenarios on escaping, but with both hands bound and numb, chances were low. If Peter loved her so much, why was he treating her like a hostage?

The door creeped open as sunlight poured in the front door, momentarily blinding her. Who stepped foot into the cabin? Peter? Or maybe Zach had found her and safety would soon engulf her.

"I see my sleeping beauty has finally awoken." Peter leaned over, rubbing the side of her cheek with his thumb. Shivers pulsed through her body. What was wrong with him?

"Not in a talkative mood? It's okay. I'll learn all your quirks and what sets you off." Peter's eyes twinkled as he pulled out a donut from a paper bag. "In the meantime, eat, my love. You need your strength."

Yeah, to fight you off. Kayla jerked her head to the side as Peter tried shoving a glazed donut into her mouth. She spit the donut out of her mouth, landing on the floor.

"Playing hard-to-get?" He leaned over, stuffing the donut back in the bag. "I like a sassy woman."

Kayla opened her mouth to respond, but the front door swung open. She watched as a man out of her nightmares strode inside, a giant smirk playing on his lips.

"You remember Silas. He's my partner in crime. I couldn't be in two places at once, and since he is obsessed with you, our partnership worked." Peter took a swig of his coffee before setting it on the coffee table.

"Hey, beautiful. Maybe we'll get to finish what we started days ago." He stared at her with predatory eyes, like she belonged to him.

Not happening. One maniac was enough, two was beyond her worst nightmare.

Peter stepped to Silas' side, slapping him on the back with too much force. "Back off. Not part of our deal."

"Bro, you don't determine what cut of her I get. If I have to turn you in to the law, I will. But you won't stop me from pursuing her."

Peter, not liking to be challenged, got up in Silas' face. "The deal is off. Kayla's my wife now."

A wicked laugh erupted from Silas' mouth. "You acting all righteous now? You planned this entire scheme to get her away from Zach, and get what you deserved since high school. Well, you know what, I was there in high school too, and I think she belongs to me."

Whoa, she did not remember Silas from high school, but even if she had, he was definitely not her type.

"You can keep the kid. I have no use for her." He stuck his hands in his pocket, playing with the contents inside.

"Why me?" As if the two men remembered she was present in the room. They both glared her way.

"We both had a crush on you in high school. It became a friendly wager who would win your heart." Peter slid his hand inside his lightweight jacket, staring at Silas. "Over the years, we've added a hefty reward to the wager."

If she could turn them against each other, maybe she could escape. Curious about how much money they sold their souls for, she spoke in a quivering voice. "How much am I worth?"

"Baby, you're priceless," Silas said.

"Smooth." Peter rolled his eyes, frowning. "One hundred grand."

"Why wait all these years to pursue me?" Kayla's voice trembled with a mixture of fear and frustration, echoing through the dimly lit cabin. The scent of stale cigarette smoke hung in the air, mingling with the tense atmosphere. If they both truly wanted to be with her, she thought, they wouldn't resort to hurting her or Annabelle.

Peter, exhausted and on edge, collapsed onto the worn-out couch, his new sneakers propped unceremoniously on the coffee table. The creak of the old furniture filled the silence as he leaned back, placing his hands over his head.

Silas, clutching an envelope bulging with hundred-dollar bills, revealed the truth. "I borrowed the money from a buddy," he confessed, his voice laced with desperation. "I didn't want Peter to outshine me. But I never knew my buddy was a shark, ready to collect his debt with double interest or eliminate me altogether. I have a week, tops, to come up with the money or my life is over. I need Peter's share or I'm dead."

Kayla's heart sank at the realization that a deadly web entangled both men. They had nothing to lose.

"I love you," Peter pleaded, his eyes filled with a mix of desperation and regret. "But I need the money to disappear with you and Annabelle before the police arrive. I don't trust my brother. We need to leave together."

A sense of unease settled over Kayla as she contemplated her options. She didn't want to go with either man, hoping they would eliminate each other and she could escape with Annabelle. But the thought of her daughter waking up and getting caught in the crossfire sent shivers down her spine.

The tension in the room reached its peak as both men drew their guns, the metallic click of the triggers filling the small space. The air grew heavy with the weight of impending violence. "I guess it's whoever has the quickest finger," Peter declared, his voice icy and determined.

In an instant, chaos erupted. The sharp cracks of gunshots reverberated through the cramped cabin, drowning out Kayla's piercing scream. One of the men's bodies tumbled to the cracked hardwood floor, blood pooling around him. The echoes of the shots faded as a soft pitter-patter sound resonated down the hallway.

"Mama?" Annabelle's groggy voice cut through the chaos, filled with urgency and confusion.

Kayla's heart sank even further. It was not a good time for her daughter to wake up. "Go back into the room, baby," she pleaded, her voice quivering with fear. "Everything will be okay." But deep down, she knew she couldn't protect her daughter while Peter left her hands cuffs, rendering her defenseless.

Peter, his gun hastily returned to its hiding place, stared at the lifeless body on the floor. With a mixture of relief and greed, he snatched the blood-splattered envelope from Silas' limp fingers. Running his fingers through the bills, a sly smile creeped across his face. "First thing in the morning, we disappear forever," he whispered. "How about a tropical paradise?"

"One question. Was Thomas involved?" Kayla didn't really want to know, but Thomas was his stepbrother.

"That pansy? He knew nothing about this."

Relief flooded her heart. At least Thomas wasn't a phony. But one thing still nagged at her heart. "Peter, I thought you were a Christian. It's not too late to ask for God's forgiveness." Kayla pleaded.

"I'm a master actor, and fooled everyone. I don't need God or his rules. This man couldn't care less about God." Peter nodded his head in the air like he was hot stuff.

"What if I refuse to go with you?"

Peter stepped to her side, running his fingers through her knotty blond hair. "Care Bear, if you refuse, I'll kill you and steal Annabelle. I'm sure I can make some money off of her down the road."

The room remained silent, the weight of his words hanging heavily in the air. Kayla couldn't catch her breath.

Zach had to come in time, or she'd never see her family again.

****

"The sheriff scattered local deputies throughout the woods surrounding the cabin." Zach dropped his phone in the middle console and glanced out the window. "Peter parked his patrol car behind the cabin, but so far, no movement detected."

"ETA is roughly ten minutes." Paul maneuvered the SUV over a pothole in the gravel country road. "We'll get there in time."

Zach needed to believe that, but he had to prepare himself for the possibility that they were too late. If Peter felt pressured or threatened, he'd shoot first, contemplate his actions later. As an impulsive man, logic definitely didn't guide him. Zach didn't know what was driving his brother at the moment. Never in a million years would he suspect his brother of kidnapping and whatever other crimes he didn't know about. Fire burned deep inside Zach's heart at the thought of Peter putting his filthy hands on his wife and daughter. If he hurt them, it'd take an act of God to hold him back from acting out on his rage. Zach took a calming deep breath. He was better than that. God was molding him into a better man than he used to be. He couldn't act out on his emotions.

"Can you handle this?" Paul glanced at Zach, adjusting his head to the right.

Zach knew Paul wasn't questioning his professional abilities, but the emotional whirlwind that would soon try to suck him up. "I have no choice. Paul, I won't let him hurt my two girls."

279

"Leave revenge up to God and the justice system. Your job is to apprehend the suspect and protect the victims. Don't let him egg you on to doing anything unlawful. Your wife doesn't need her husband behind bars because he allowed rage to consume him."

"I've prayed the whole two hours. God's not gonna let me fail or turn into my biggest enemy." Zach slid his fingers over his gun, taking comfort in the metallic feel of protection. "We'll stop here and hike the rest of the way. Cabin should be just over that hill."

Paul slowed the SUV down, parking it behind a canopy of shrubs. "You ready?"

Zach ducked his head under a low-lying tree branch. Sweat dripping down his forehead. The low eighties temperature had nothing to do with the sweats covering his body. A light breeze swirled around Zach, doing nothing to stop his nervous energy. They had two hours before darkness set in the surrounding wilderness. Being unfamiliar with the woods, it seemed best to make the situation end as quickly as possible. Unless it turned into a hostage situation. Paul was a skilled negotiator, but that was the worst-case scenario. Best-case would-be Peter surrendering with no injuries or casualties.

Zach listened to the serene sounds of crickets and frogs chirping and croaking like chaos wasn't about to disrupt the calmness of the wilderness. A gunshot burst through the air as Zach honed in on all of his disciplined training, not to dash off to the cabin with guns blazing. His heart pounded in his chest, echoing the loudness of the gunshot. What if Kayla or Annabelle died while he slowly trekked through the woods? He'd never forgive himself. His one job right now was to get them to safety. If he couldn't save his own family, he was a lousy detective and would turn in his badge.

Zach motioned for Paul to stop. His phone buzzed as he lifted it to his ear. "Suspect spotted by the window. A clear shot to take him out." Zach shook his head as he relayed the message to Paul.

"Negative. We're going in. No snipers unless absolutely necessary." They rounded the corner, passing by a tiny window. Peering inside, Zach's breath caught as he saw Kayla handcuffed to a rusted pipe, her eyes filled with fear. *She's alive.* "I'm going through the back door. See if you can find an unlocked window or another way inside."

"Be careful." Paul lifted his gun, disappearing into the side of the cabin.

God rescue Kayla and Annabelle. Zach jerked his gun out of the holster, tapping the back door with his booted foot. The door opened with a squeak. Great, he didn't want to advertise his presence. Moving stealthily, he rounded the corner, having Peter in his sight line. A body laid sprawled out on the floor.

"I see you made it to the party." A scornful line etched across Peter's forehead, his voice sending chills through Zach's body. Who was this man? Not the same boy he grew up with.

"Let Kayla and Annabelle go." Zach steadied his gun in front of him, taking a quick peek at Kayla. She seemed unharmed besides the paleness of her skin.

"No can do, bro. They're my family now. I'll never let them go." A whimper escaped Kayla's lips.

Peter stepped to her side, yanking on a handful of her hair, causing her to wince in pain. "You'd rather go with him?"

Kayla bit her bottom lip, trying to hold back her tears.

281

"You tramp! Everything I've done for you and you pick my flight-risked brother." With a forceful swing, his palm collided with her cheek, propelling her backwards into the wall.

"Leave her alone." Zach eased closer to Peter, pointing the gun at his chest.

"Or what? You'll shoot me?" Peter's sinister laugh wrapped around Zach's heart. "You don't have it in you."

Zach could easily take his brother out. But he wanted him to rot in jail and pay for the crimes committed against his wife and daughter. "Don't make this harder than it already is."

"I'll tell you what's hard," Peter's voice trembled, the words laced with bitterness, "always being compared to you." A hard look fell on Peter's face, his handsome features now etched with frustration. "Everywhere I went, people boasted of your greatest. Even at the police precinct. I couldn't get away from you and your reputation. You have everything I've ever wanted; the job, woman, and kid."

Envy was a huge motive for many crimes committed. But Peter never once acted like he envied Zach. Nothing made sense.

"Why? I trusted you. You are my brother," Zach's voice cracked, tears welling in his eyes. He fought to hold himself together. Now was not the time to fall apart.

"Blood only means so much," Peter's voice turned bitter, his hands slipping into his pockets. A metallic click echoed through the room as he pulled out a small handgun. "You're a fool if you think our bond means more to me than success and everything I deserve in life." A smirk danced on Peter's lips as he aimed the gun at Zach.

282

"You won't get away with this," Zach's voice trembled with defiance.

"Oh, but I will," Peter taunted, waving Zach's identification papers in the air. "We look so much alike. I'm planting my wallet on you. Peter died, and I'll become Zach Rivers. We even share the same blood type."

"Backup is close by." Zach's eyes darted around, searching for his partner.

"I'll kill anyone that stands in my way," Peter's eyes glazed over, a dangerous glint in his gaze.

"Where's Annabelle?" Zach's voice pleaded, a desperate prayer in his heart.

"The whine bag made me put her to sleep again," Peter sneered. "She'll be okay after a few hours." The cold metal of the gun shifted in Peter's outstretched hand.

"You drugged my daughter," anger surged through Zach's veins, a burning fire in his chest. His finger trembled on the trigger; the gun pointed at his brother.

"Pull the trigger. I dare you," Peter taunted, his voice filled with arrogance. "You don't have it in you."

"No, I'll let the legal system deal with you." Zach nodded to his partner as he stepped into the living room, aiming his gun at Peter.

"The jig is up. The police have surrounded the cabin." Paul stared Peter down as Zach slowly stepped toward Kayla, shielding her body from Peter's insanity.

"I will not go to jail." In a moment of despair, Peter aimed the gun at his chest, his finger tightening around the trigger. Kayla's high-pitched scream pierced the air, blending with the thunderous sound of the gunshot as Peter's lifeless body hit the ground.

Paul kneeled over, checking for a pulse. He shook his head, opening the door to the deputies stationed outside.

Disappointment and anguish flooded Zach's heart as he glanced at his brother's limp body. Tears freely fell from his face. This wasn't the way life was supposed to go. Kayla cleared her throat, reminding Zach that the cuffs still bound her to the pipe.

"Sorry, sweetie." He twisted a key in the cuffs, pulling her into his arms. "I love you so much." He placed a kiss on her tear-stained lips, vowing to never leave her side again.

"I love you too. I knew you'd rescue us."

"Daddy!" Annabelle ran down the hall, fumbling some from the effect of the drug Peter injected into her body. She jumped into Zach's arms, clinging to her dad and her mom. "Can we go home now?"

Whispered laughter floated through the crime scene. Zach took one last look at his brother before leading his wife and daughter away from their biggest nightmare.

THE END

Epilogue

Three months later

"I need to apologize for how I've been acting toward you." Stephen extended his hand out for Zach to shake. "I've never seen my cousin happier."

"I agree." Mr. Smith pulled his glasses off of his face, wiping the lenses on the end of his shirt. "Since the abduction, my daughter has glowed and my granddaughter has blossomed. It's because of you."

"Thank you both. I feel so unworthy that God would grant me a second chance at life." Zach stared behind him at his newly declared wife. Hours ago, they tied the knot in front of family and close friends. Two family members' absence tried putting a damper on the ceremony, but Zach made peace with God over his brother's crime and death, and Kayla clung to the hope that her sister Sarah would find her way back to God and their family. Noting that God could do the impossible.

"If you'll excuse me, I'd like to steal my wife away." Zach stepped past his father-in-law with a hope in his step and a yearning to be the man God intended him to be. He glanced at his beautiful wife, blushing as his eyes glanced over her. At that moment, no one else was present, just the two of them and the love that had developed over five years of running from each other. Only to have God bring them back together.

He draped his arms around her waist, pulling her body close to his. Whispering in her ear, he leaned over, smiling, "Mrs. Kayla Rivers, how about we ditch this party and take a walk?"

Her eyes twinkled at his closeness. "I thought you'd never ask."

They walked hand-in-hand down the long, curvy country road. Neither speaking, just basking in the love and warmth they shared. Dust blew off the dirt path when they walked across the road.

Kayla stopped on the side of the road, clasping her hand in his. "I wanted to give you something that signified our past and represented our bright beginning."

"Okay." He leaned over, running his lips over hers. He'd never tire of embracing his wife and feeling her closeness.

She pulled out a white envelope, placing it in his hand. Zach looked inside as tears formed in his eyes. "Is this what I think it is?"

She swiped at the corner of her eyes. "It's the only picture I have of our girls together. The nurses took this picture in NICU before Izzy passed away. I thought you might like a copy."

"I don't know what to say." He wrapped his arms over her shoulders, brushing a piece of her hair off her shoulders. "This will remind me of what happens when I walk away from God and step away from the blessings He has given me to protect."

"You're not that man anymore. And I am not the same selfish woman I was years ago." She placed his hand over her chest. "Now, I give you my heart. That heartbeat you feel, it's my devotion to you. Every beat God gives me, I'll live it by loving you forever."

"Oh, my sweet Kayla, I'm so thankful that God took our anger and distrust, molding our lives into a beautiful picture of his redemption and grace. I'll stick beside you. All the days of my life."

A breeze twirled around them as Zach wrapped his arms around his wife, vowing to never let go again.

Poisonous Cuisine
An East Tennessee Mystery Series
Book four

Preview:

"Make sure you sanitize all the food prep surfaces, check the inventory list, and secure all perishable food in the proper refrigerator." Sarah tucked a fallen strand of her red hair behind her bandanna. She slid her phone into her chef's coat pocket and stepped to the counter.

"Head chef, Sarah, everything is taken care of. Relax." George Baker, Sarah's sous chef, saluted her in a mock manner, hiding back his smile. "You are the most precise chef I know."

Sarah let out a steam of hot air. Everything had to be perfect. After getting fired from her last job in New York City, no other restaurant would hire her. It wasn't her fault the owner forged a complete lie that not only ruined her reputation professionally, but put a stamp on her back as a loose home wrecker. That might have been true two years ago, but since then, Sarah gave her life to Jesus. Moving back to East Tennessee replayed in her nightmare, but she needed a job, and Mr. and Mrs. Beecher happily offered her the head chef position for their ritzy, over-priced brasserie. Being younger than the sous chef and most of the kitchen staff meant she had a lot to prove. And her career rested on this job. Working as a chef was a cutthroat industry, but she couldn't fail. Wouldn't fail. She hadn't put herself through culinary school for nothing.

She glanced around the industrial-sized kitchen. The stainless-steel appliances glistening in the low light of the kitchen, and from the recent clean George had applied. George unsnapped his apron, balling the lightweight material between his fingers. Sarah wondered how his skin remained so tan when he stayed holed up in the kitchen as much as she did; no social life at all. Of course, his tall, dark, and handsome qualities could mark up his calendar with dates, but he hid away in the kitchen, never given interested females a second look. Sarah didn't know his story. She didn't care. Not because curiosity didn't eat at her, but because some secrets should stay buried, like her past.

George's eyes met hers as a slow blush creeped up her pale skin. Busted. "Don't you have anything better to do than to gawk at my good looks?" He removed his hat, running his fingers through his black, wavy locks.

"I was just … um… how about I…" Sarah dropped her gaze to the Metropolitan ceramic tile, rubbing her white sneakers against the gray tile.

A tight smile played across George's thick lips. "I'm flattered, really, but if we don't hurry, I'll miss the Vols football game. I recorded it with my DVR, but I'll be too exhausted to watch it. The guys are coming over in an hour."

Right. He actually had a life unlike her. Sarah moved into her sister Rachel's condo, just until she could find her own place. Rachel, as an aviation missionary, currently on furlough, welcomed Sarah in as the wayward prodigal sister. The rift between Sarah and the rest of her family was deeper than the Grand Canyon. They didn't know she had moved back to Tennessee, and she liked it that way. Rachel tried dropping tidbits of information about her sister Kayla and her husband Zach. But embarrassment kept Sarah from really listening. What sister throws herself at the other's man, desperately trying to break up their relationship? Her past sickened her.

"So, what's left on your checklist?" George stepped closer to Sarah, his spicy cologne mixing with the smell of bistro and steak.

Sarah smiled at his flippant attitude about her list. She needed multiple lists to stay on target. He just couldn't see the beauty in her organization. "Why don't you head home, and I'll lock up? I just need to take the trash out."

"My momma didn't raise a fool." He swiped the trash bag off the floor, swishing around the pungent odor. "I got this."

"George, if I were a male, would you be lingering around, insulting me with your chauvinist implications?" Sarah glanced at the wall clock, grimacing at going in the back alley at ten O'clock on a Friday. She just couldn't let George see her weakness. Sarah couldn't run the kitchen if the men viewed her as weak.

"The Redstone bar is around the corner. Unsavory folk hang out there." He dropped the trash bag with a thud. "But you're right, women can protect themselves. I'll let you lock up." George jerked his keys out of his pocket, jingling them in his hand. "See ya tomorrow, Sarah."

"Don't stay up too late watching football." She face-palmed at that remark. What? Was she his mother? His personal life was of no concern to her as long as he gave one hundred and ten% on the job, which he did.

Sarah slid her purse over her shoulder and hauled the black trash bag in her fingers, stepping into the back alley. She twisted the lock and slid the door shut. No need to go back inside when she cleared her list. Late September air whirled around her, making her wish she had grabbed a jacket. Ten steps and she would have completed her task. Maybe she'd go home, unwinding with a romance novel while relaxing in a steamy bubble bath. But first she needed to walk to the dumpster. Mr. Beecher really needed to fix the flickering light next to the building. It cast an eerie group of shadows on the brick exterior. She shook off the goosebumps attacking her bare skin.

"East Tennessee not New York City." She mumbled under her breath, trying to reassure her senses.

She hurriedly made her way to the dumpster, the loud clacking of her shoes reverberating on the cold cement. With a swift motion, Sarah tossed the bag into the dumpster, her eyes scanning the dimly lit night. The darkness enveloped her, but an inexplicable unease sent shivers creeping up her neck.

As she stood frozen, the sound of footsteps reverberated through the alley, their echoes bouncing off the cemented walls. Fear gripped her, causing her instinctively to hide behind the dumpster, crouching low. A pungent stench assaulted her senses, assaulting her nostrils. She silently prayed for whoever was out there not to discover her. The absurdity of the situation threatened to break through her lips, almost triggering a burst of nervous laughter. If it turned out to be George, she knew she would never hear the end.

Muffled and heated voices intertwined, their words weaving through the alley. Tension hung in the air, and Sarah cautiously peered over the edge of the dumpster, careful not to expose her hiding place. The cold metal sent a chill seeping through her trembling fingers.

"I told you to take care of my problem!" A male voice bellowed, his attempt at whispering failing miserably.

"I quit," a familiar male voice retorted defiantly.

"No one quits and talks about it."

Sarah's heart pounded in her chest as she watched the first man retrieve a gun. He grabbed the other man by his shirt collar, pulling the trigger and dragging his limp body towards the dumpster. Panic surged within her. If he spotted her, he would surely end her life as well. With no other options, Sarah swallowed hard, feeling bile rise in her throat. She inched towards the edge of the dumpster, then propelled herself into a full sprint. Why had she locked the restaurant door? Now she had to circle around the building to reach her car. Glancing behind her, she saw the man closing in, his menacing figure growing larger.

"Stop!" A deafening noise pierced the night air as a bullet whizzed past her head.

Letting out a blood-curdling scream, she collided with something solid, arms wrapping tightly around her waist.

Sarah knew she couldn't die without seeking her family's forgiveness. Desperation fueled her as she dug her nails into the assailant's face, desperately trying to break free from his grasp. After a few muttered words, his hands released her, allowing her to dart towards her car parked in the front lot. Fumbling with her keys, she screamed in terror as arms yanked her away from her only means of escape.

No, God. Help me.

Made in the USA
Middletown, DE
03 September 2024

60271056R00166